ALE'S FAIR IN LOVE AND WAR

AN ENEMIES-TO-LOVERS ROMANCE

LOVE ON TAP
BOOK 1

SYLVIE STEWART

ROLLING HEARTS PRESS

Ale's Fair in Love and War Copyright © 2023 by Sylvie Stewart

ISBN: 978-1-947853-51-5

ALSO BY SYLVIE STEWART

Smooth Hoperator (*Love on Tap*, Book 2 - Coming Summer 2023)

The Fix (*Carolina Connections*, Book 1)
The Spark (*Carolina Connections*, Book 2)
The Lucky One (*Carolina Connections*, Book 3)
The Game (*Carolina Connections*, Book 4)
The Way You Are (*Carolina Connections*, Book 5)
The Runaround (*Carolina Connections*, Book 6)

The Nerd Next Door (*Carolina Kisses*, Book 1)
New Jerk in Town (*Carolina Kisses*, Book 2)
The Last Good Liar (*Carolina Kisses*, Book 3)

Between a Rock and a Royal (*Kings of Carolina*, #1)
Blue Bloods and Backroads (*Kings of Carolina*, #2)
Stealing Kisses With a King (*Kings of Carolina*, #3)
Kings of Carolina Box Set

To Donna Stoll, our lovely neighbor and one of my very first fans. I hope heaven is one giant library of dirty books with a sunny deck where you can enjoy them.

ABOUT THIS BOOK

Hollis Hayes is the worst neighbor in the entire history of neighbors.

She's also the hottest.

F.M.L.

I don't have time to fight with the dog groomer next door. There's a brewery to run, siblings to rein in, and a mom to look after. So if Hollis thinks I'll roll over and let her drive me out of business, she's not nearly as smart as she thinks she is.

Sure, I enjoy the little pranks we play on each other, and I don't hate watching her prance around in those tight leggings. But she's gone too far this time, even if she pretends to know nothing about it.

I'll do whatever it takes to save my business from going under, and if that means playing dirty with the girl I love to hate, game on.

CHAPTER
ONE
VIRGIN SAYS WHAT?

CASH

"BLUE BIGFOOT BEER," I bark into the phone, tucking the receiver between my shoulder and ear. The customer across from me holds out his hand as I count his change from the drawer.

A breathy voice on the other end of the line has my hand freezing in midair.

"Is this Cash?" she purrs.

Hmm. Seems like my day might be about to turn around.

I drop the change into the customer's palm and toss him a chin lift.

"That's me. What can I do for you?" I have a few ideas if the voice matches the body.

She lets out a little giggle that has my dick twitching in my jeans. "I'm calling about your virginity."

My hearing must be going because it sounded like she just said I'm a virgin.

Turning away from the prying eyes of my brother a few

feet down the bar, I take the receiver in hand and press it firmly to my ear this time. "Sorry, come again?"

"Your virginity," she repeats, her voice still filled with sex but carrying a tinge of amusement now. "I'm interested in relieving you of it."

I squint at my reflection in the mirror of the back bar, wondering if I always look this tired and trying to figure out which of my three brothers is fucking with me. I settle on Denver because that asshole has been way too jolly since he talked his girlfriend into moving in with him.

"Very funny, Rosie. Tell Denny I'm gonna kick his ass next time I see him." The phone drops back in its cradle with a heavy *clang*. I don't have time for jokes today. There's a brewery to run, a taproom to serve, a newbie to train, and a pale ale release tomorrow that I haven't promoted nearly enough.

I glance down the bar just in time to see Miller, my youngest brother, slosh water all over the floor mats as he drops a bus tub in the sink. The towel I throw hits him square in the face. "You *trying* to create a hazard, or does it just come naturally?"

He sends a glare over his shoulder, a new eyebrow piercing glinting at me as I brush past him to serve another customer. It's a regular named Smitty, so there's no need to ask for his order. I press a pint glass onto the glass rinser, then pull back the tap on *Squatch This*, a golden wheat with a crisp finish. It's one of our most popular beers.

The phone rings again, and I'm somewhat encouraged to see Miller answer it without any prompting while I get a card to start Smitty's tab.

"It's for you." My little brother thrusts the phone in my direction.

I gesture for him to make the rounds of the taproom as

I grab the receiver. If I've got to work with him, I'm at least gonna train him right. Family can be a real pain in the ass sometimes.

"This is Cash."

"Oh, uh, hey." The masculine voice on the other end stumbles. I'd half expected it to be Denny cackling at his own stupid joke, but this voice doesn't belong to anyone I know. I wait another second for him to speak, but time is money.

"Who is this?" I demand, knowing I'm taking my busy day out on a stranger and hearing my mama's voice in my head urging me to be patient. It's never been my strong suit.

"Tom."

I rack my brain looking for any trace of a Tom but can't recall a soul apart from the guy who runs the smoke shop a couple spaces down. This is not that Tom, and I know this because that Tom is always high as an eagle's nuts and only refers to me as "Cool Money."

"Do I know you?" I glance out into the taproom to see Miller parked on his ass at a four-top of attractive brunettes. That little…

"Uh, no," Tom mutters.

Jesus, get to the point. "What can I do for you, Tom?" I repeat, impatience bleeding through.

"I was, uh, hoping *I* could do something for *you*."

For the love of Larry.

My eyelids drop closed as I brace a hip against the back bar. "Oh yeah? What exactly can you do for me, *Tom*?"

"Pop your cherry?"

When the receiver hits the phone's base this time, the clattering echoes through the entire taproom.

Someone is definitely fucking with me.

And I'm pretty sure I know who.

Recognizing the look on my face and the mood it signifies, Miller hauls ass back behind the bar, hiking his jeans up his hips as he goes. My little brother's contempt for belts is one of life's greater mysteries.

I take my agitation out on Larry, the Bigfoot statue that stands beside my register and watches over the patrons, scrubbing at some beer residue on its base with my towel. The ring of the phone has my molars gnashing, and I leave the receiver right where it is.

"Aren't you gonna get that?" Miller asks.

"Don't touch it!" I throw the towel onto my shoulder and stalk down the hall to the office.

If she wants to start something, I'll only bite back harder. My eyes narrow to slits as I attempt to bore a hole through the wall separating my brewery from the neighboring pet groomer.

Happy Tails Salon. The name is just as sickly sweet as her fake-ass smiles and fluttering eyelashes behind those misleadingly innocent glasses.

Miller's disembodied voice breaks through the speaker of the desk phone. "It's Mama, jackass. Line two."

Well, shit.

"Hey, Mama." I do my best to brush off my irritation. She doesn't need to know about any of my frustrations.

"Hello, darlin'. How are you?" Her concerned tone has me instantly wary. My eyes dart around the office, but I haven't one damn clue what I'm expecting to find.

"I'm great. How are you? Did you find Mango?" Mango is the love of her life, and everyone knows it.

She clucks her tongue. "You know, he showed up in the kitchen a few minutes after you left. I don't know what he got himself into, but he's here now, safe and sound. *Aren't you, my little sweetheart?*" she coos at the mongrel, and I realize I'm just being paranoid.

"That's good to hear." I glance at my watch. "Hey, aren't you late for work?" It's already halfway through the afternoon and I haven't gotten shit done.

"I'm leaving in a few. We're doing pizza and movie night," she replies. She works at the senior center coordinating activities and generally causing trouble. "I just wanted to call about your problem."

My butt drops into the desk chair, and I smile into the phone. "I wouldn't say he's *my* problem. I like to think of Miller as *all of our* problem."

"Oh hush, you. I'm not talkin' about your brother— although I am so glad you took my suggestion and hired him."

Took her suggestion? More like folded to her edict. Hiring Miller was not my idea at all, but the asshat crashed his bike and got fired from yet another job, so my hands were tied. Blue Bigfoot Beer is a family venture in many ways, but my oldest brother, Carter, and I are the only ones left holding the bag at the end of the day.

"Yeah, well." There wasn't much more to say than that. Mama always did teach us if you don't have something nice to say, don't say anything at all. "So, what problem are you talking about?"

"Your virginity, darlin'."

Fuck. My. Life.

Twenty minutes later, I'm staring at a Craigslist ad on my laptop that has both my name and Blue Bigfoot's phone number on it.

"Looking for someone gentle to break my guymen. I just haven't

met the right person, and it's become a burden. Please be kind because I'm hideously ugly."

"Dude, there are easier ways."

Miller's voice sends me jumping. The bastard is leaning over my shoulder reading the screen and breathing his nicotine dragon breath in my face. I give him a good shove.

"Fuck off. I didn't post this," I grunt. "And who's manning the bar?"

Hitching his jeans up again, he snickers, enjoying this way more than I'd like. "Relax. Oscar's got it covered."

I only glare in response. There's no way I'm telling him that Mama just offered the services of her buddy Regina to help me out with my so-called problem. The same Regina who runs an escort service catering to Asheville's elite and hard-up.

Of which I'm neither, thank you very much.

"Any idea who did it?" Miller flicks his tongue ring against his teeth, sending my already raw nerve endings buzzing.

There's only one person on this earth who can get this far under my skin and make me take my eye off the ball like this.

I grit my teeth around my growl of an answer. *"Hollis."*

CHAPTER TWO

A VIGILANTE'S WORK IS NEVER DONE

HOLLIS

"HAVE A WONDERFUL DAY!" I call after Mr. Burgess and his adorable corgi named Iggy as they depart the shop.

It is, indeed, a wonderful day—for more reasons than one.

I've had my most profitable month yet at Happy Tails Salon. The mild spring temperatures have been luring the town's residents from their winter hibernation, and naturally, they're bringing their dogs with them.

Frolicking four-legged friends equals dirty coats in need of grooming, which is where *I* come in. Happy Tails has only been open for four months, so it's not like I'm swimming in profits, but I'm proud nonetheless.

And then there's that extra little something I've done today to put the cherry on my sundae.

I smile at my unintentional pun, envisioning the red-hot creep of fury climbing Cash Brooks's neck right about now.

I can't take *all* the credit, of course. My friend Rylee helped with the wording since she's a writer at the local paper and has a real flair for language.

The bell rings over the door again, and my eyes flash to the brawny figure darkening my doorway.

Speak of the devil—literally.

His scruffy jaw is locked tight, the tension in his shoulders telling the story of his less-than-ideal day. As those piercing blue eyes drill into mine, it occurs to me, not for the first time, what a crying shame it is that such beautiful eyes are wasted on a troll like him.

"Well, hello, neighbor." I paste on my brightest smile. "What brings you to my door today? Need a cold shower?" My tone is drenched in so much syrup I might give myself an actual cavity.

Cash stalks toward my counter, worn work boots scuffing the tile as he approaches. I purposely ignore the way his thigh muscles strain the denim of his jeans.

When he stops just across from me, chest heaving and lips curled into an angry snarl, I respond by wrinkling my nose and waving a hand in front of it. "I'd say so. You smell like a brewery."

This is simply too easy.

A growl spills from Cash's curled lips, indicating that I've done such an excellent job I've rendered him incapable of speaking in human. Just as well, considering what a giant bull-headed caveman he is.

It wasn't always like this, you know. Before I found out he's such an egomaniac, I almost liked him.

When I moved into the spot next to his at the warehouse shops here in the River Arts District, Blue Bigfoot Beer had been in business for quite a while already. Like any good neighbor, I popped over to introduce myself and hand out business cards in case anyone needed a groomer. The older brother, Carter, was polite but distracted, with the same strong jaw and straight nose as Cash. But that's where the similarities ended.

Cash's piercing gaze followed me as I chatted with their customers, introduced myself to a couple employees, and drummed up a little innocent business. Every situation can be a marketing opportunity if you make it one.

His stare was so intense, I'll admit it had my belly fluttering with hummingbird wings. The thought that my new hottie neighbor might find me attractive sent adrenaline coursing through my veins. Before I knew it, I was inching closer and closer to his end of the bar as I summoned my most welcoming and flirty smile.

But his brooding expression didn't budge, and I quickly excused myself in embarrassment, feeling like a colossal idiot. The next day, I told myself I was being ridiculous and to brush it off—pretend it never happened.

But then came the dumpster incident.

Since our two units share a dumpster which always appears to be full to the brim, I politely asked Cash to leave a little room for my refuse going forward. My office was piling up with boxes, and I'd had to beg the guy at the vape store to let me use his dumpster that first week.

Instead of behaving like a normal human being, Cash proceeded to mansplain that a large brewery produced more trash than my "little yappy dog place" ever could. Using the same condescending tone, he stated that he'd always had the dumpster to himself and I should take it up with the property manager if I needed my own.

Had it ended there, I could have remained polite and only stuck my tongue out at him when his back was turned. But it didn't.

His unit being much larger than mine, I'm allotted fewer parking spaces—which is fine. However, the brute seems to think he can dictate who and what parks in *my* spaces, declaring my grooming van an eyesore to his customers.

Please. His customers are drunk most of the time; they wouldn't care if they were staring at the backside of a rhinoceros with a hemorrhoid outbreak. And, besides, the van is good advertising, even though it's not equipped yet. People see it when they drive by, and who isn't looking for a convenient grooming service for their furry friends?

Incapable of holding my tongue any longer, I told him where he could shove his parking opinion, and we've been at each other's throats since then. We've fought over the blaring music from his patio area, the late-night food wrappers his customers scatter on the sidewalk, and his preposterous expectation that my customers' dogs don't pee within fifty yards of his property. With no resolution existing in the realm of possibility, things inevitably escalated from there.

My intention hadn't been to start a war with Blue Bigfoot, but as they say, shit happens.

A crimson flush licks at the skin just under Cash's stubbled chin. "You put up a fucking Craigslist ad?!"

My brows draw together as I fix a pout to my lips. "Oh, did nobody take you up on the offer?" I reach over the shiny pink counter separating us and pat his shoulder, ignoring its muscular firmness. "Don't be embarrassed. Virginity is just a social construct anyway."

He shakes my hand off with a jerk of his arm, and I cover my pout with a contemplative finger. "Although maybe I shouldn't have said anything about your looks." I lean closer to whisper, "I just didn't want anyone to be surprised when they met you."

He jabs the air in front of my nose with his finger. "You'd better prepare yourself, lady."

I slap his hand away without missing a beat. "Lady? Oh, you are cruel, aren't you?" I coo at him, causing his jaw to do that clicking thing I so enjoy.

"You ain't seen nothin' yet," Cash grinds out through clenched teeth.

With that, he whips around and stalks back to my front door, giving me a prime view of his inconveniently nice ass.

"I *haven't* seen *anything* yet," I correct him but don't get the pleasure of his responding expression. "Have a wonderful day!" I shout.

His growl is just barely audible as he disappears out of sight.

Ah, it is, indeed, a most wonderful day.

AROUND SUNSET, though, I begin to fear that karma has been keeping score because my day takes a decidedly southward turn.

"Breathe, Hadley," I urge into my phone for the third time as I sift through the box of adorable dog bandanas that arrived right before closing. "Just breathe and tell me what's wrong."

Sobs escaping between her words, my sister finally cobbles a response together. "I thought he loved me, but all he wanted was my hot body." As she dissolves into tears once more, I try not to let her word choice affect my level of sympathy. This unflinching self-confidence, even in the throes of heartbreak, is so very Hadley. But this must be serious because she called instead of texting, and I've been informed that calling someone is the height of cringe.

"Who?" I ask. Hadley talks incessantly about her boyfriends, sharing way more than I ever care to know about my teenage sister's sex life. But I didn't even know she was dating anyone recently.

She hiccups and releases a tortured sigh. "You don't know him."

This is unsurprising, given that Hadley is ten years younger than me, and we don't exactly mingle in one another's social circles.

We share a biological mother, and my stepdad—Hadley's father—is the only dad I've ever known. Harrison Hayes—Harry to those who know him best—married our mom when I was in fifth grade, plucking Mom and me out of our one-bedroom roach trap of an apartment in Bingham Heights and installing us in his mega-mansion down in Biltmore Forest. I used to think my mom knew she'd end up with him because she gave me a name starting with H.

A millisecond later, Hadley came along. With her wide cornflower eyes and golden hair, she was instantly the princess we all adored. A fact she understood from an early age and still uses to her advantage. And while I usually feel more like her parent than her sister, I'll always be on her side, even when it takes more patience than I might have.

"Those high school boys aren't worth your time, Hads." I abandon the bandanas to give her my full focus. "Besides, you don't want a boyfriend when you're headed off to college next year. You're going to meet so many new people there—people from different backgrounds and experiences. *People who don't know Mom and Harry.*" I give the last sentence a teasing tone, but it doesn't break her mood like I hoped.

Instead, she emits a pained whimper. "He *is* different. And he doesn't even go to my school. He doesn't even go to school *at all!*"

My ears perk at that, and I sink into the fuzzy black chair behind my counter. "Then how did you meet him?" While it would benefit her to make friends outside of her tiny social bubble of prep-school teens, I'm not especially excited about the prospect of her dating a high school dropout.

"Out," is all she says.

"Out?"

"Yeah, out." This time, I can hear the eye roll accompanying her response.

"How long were you seeing this boy?"

"He's not a boy. He's a *man*."

I draw in a lungful of air through my nose and adjust my glasses. "Sorry. How long were you seeing this *man*?"

"A while."

Dear God, please give me patience not to lose my ever-loving mind.

"Well, the same logic applies. You're leaving town next year where you can start fresh, date other bo—*men*. Or not! There's so much to explore that has *nothing* to do with men or these same fifty kids you've known since you were little."

Hadley has only ever attended exclusive private schools and academies catering to the elite, leaving her with what could be considered a skewed view of the world. *Cough.*

"I know, I know," she drones. "The world is a magical place, blah, blah, blah. You talk like I've never even been to Europe."

Deep breaths, Hollis.

Maybe I do lecture her too much—not like it's made much of a dent. But besides growing from the new people and places she'll find when she leaves the nest, Hadley needs to learn that she can't flirt or pay her way out of every situation. She's not yet had to deal with the consequences of her actions in any meaningful way.

Still, she's my baby sister, and she's wounded. "I'm sorry he hurt you. You deserve better."

"I know," she responds before sighing. "The Logans offered to beat him up, but I haven't decided yet."

"Um, let's maybe not," I respond.

The Logans are Hadley's two best friends, both of whom share the same first name as well as an unconditional loyalty to my sister. They also share an allergy to cardio or exerting effort of any kind, as far as I can tell. Which doesn't bode well for taking on a fight with the type of guy that usually attracts Hadley's attention.

"I want him to hurt like *I'm* hurting."

"The best revenge is moving on." God, I sound like a self-help book from the clearance bin.

This time she pauses to think before speaking. "Yeah, I guess you're right. I should date someone more my caliber." My brows draw together at that, but she continues, "He's sort of lazy and always seems to be short on cash. You'd think he'd have his act together at his age."

This has my spine tingling in a way I do not like. I fix my eyes on the display of colorful pet sweaters on the opposite wall and ask, "At *what* age?" *Please say eighteen, please say eighteen.*

"He's only twenty-one."

My eyeballs threaten to pop out of their sockets and ricochet off my glasses.

"Hadley," I begin, unsure how to navigate this new territory. My eighteen-year-old, sheltered sister has been sleeping with a twenty-one-year-old deadbeat with no job and evidently no conscience at all! He might even be lying about his age. The guy could be thirty for all she knows!

Before I can formulate more of a response, Hadley melts into tears once more. "I love him so much!"

There's nothing to do now but fill her ear with soothing words. Well, that and plot the demise of this swamp-dwelling pervert who's sunk his claws into my baby sister.

It looks like I'll have to take a break from torturing my neighbor; I have a new villain in my sights.

CHAPTER
THREE

PAYBACK'S A... GERMAN
SHEPHERD?

CASH

"YOU MAY ACTUALLY BE GOING to hell this time."

I glance up from my project to see my older brother and business partner, Carter, looking down at me.

"Worth it." My grin is appropriately evil.

Blue Bigfoot closed up an hour ago, but I'm staying as late as it takes to execute my revenge. It's become a point of pride to outdo Hollis each time she attacks.

At the warehouse shops, it's April Fool's Day every day.

I don't know who started hating who first, but the feeling is mutual. Which is just as well because the very first day her heart-shaped ass waltzed through my door—bringing with it a head of silky blond hair and a smile so heart-stopping it could make a man forget his own damn name—I vowed not to let her lure me in or distract me in any way. A vow I immediately broke by watching her fine ass traipse around my taproom for the next thirty minutes, casting some magical spell on my customers and staff that had them smiling like a bunch of lovesick morons.

So, yeah, I'll admit I was on edge at the start, but I remained perfectly polite. Well, mostly.

I might have taken out some misplaced frustration on her that first week, but the warehouse's new management had just instituted a bunch of bullshit cuts. They took out half the dumpsters, started charging tenants for salting and snow-clearing, and began shutting the outside lights off before midnight, making my employees feel unsafe.

When my new neighbor demanded half our dumpster space, I simply explained how things work. I might have been a little short. But that didn't warrant her going off on me when I politely asked her to stop blocking our brewery's sign with her giant van. Drunk Larry deserves the utmost respect—he's the two-dimensional version of the Larry statue that guards the taproom, except this Larry lumbers majestically across our logo with a frothy beer in hand. Hollis clearly doesn't get it.

We've been going back and forth ever since. The woman is manipulative and way too entitled—not surprising seeing as she comes from a filthy rich family even the Biltmores would envy. Yeah, I did some digging.

She's also a bit of an evil genius, though I'd never admit it to her face.

In the past four months, she's sent her tiny rat dogs over to pee on all my outdoor table legs, piped that Baby Shark song—loud and set on repeat—into my taproom through the overhead ducts, invited a group of religious zealots to read the Bible to my patrons, and subscribed me to a series of fetish catalogs that have the mail carrier snickering at me every time I look her in the face. And that's just a sample.

In retaliation, I've put out signs offering free grooming at her shop for anyone who brings in a farm animal, hired a bagpiper to play in her salon for two hours straight, gotten one of Miller's sketchy friends to hotwire her van and move it to a different parking spot every few nights, and kidnapped the oversized chihuahua statue that stands just inside her door. I even mailed her ransom notes and a chunk of rock that bore a striking resemblance to a chihuahua ear.

That one was probably my favorite, especially when she pretended not to care but worried that full lower lip with her teeth when she thought I wasn't looking.

But with this current stunt, I might have outdone myself.

The Craigslist ad was gone by opening time Friday afternoon, but I've intentionally given my shrew of a neighbor a few days to stop looking over her shoulder and settle in nice and comfortable again.

Now it's time to strike.

"Where did you find that thing, anyway?" Carter's wearing a frown and his favorite flannel shirt, black hair spiked all over like he just spent the day getting laid instead of tending the brewhouse on the other half of our space. In the past few months, Carter has all but taken over the brewing process, leaving me to run the taproom, make the day-to-day decisions, and manage our handful of employees. It works for us.

"The same place you find women," I answer, standing up to survey my masterpiece. "Oh, my bad. I ordered it from Amazon, not PornHub."

Carter ignores me, turning for the hallway.

"Hey, you gonna help me hang this thing or what?"

I watch as his shoulders visibly slump. "Do I have a choice?"

This has me chuckling.

Thirty minutes later, a lifelike stuffed animal head of a German Shepherd hangs mounted on a plaque just above the door of Happy Tails Salon.

Cart and I take a few steps back and admire our work. Well, I do at least. Carter is more resigned than proud as he squints up at it.

"It looks way too real—even more so in this light."

I rub my hands together in evil delight. "Yup. It sure does."

Now I just need to get to work early enough in the morning to enjoy the screams coming from next door.

You mess with the bull, you get the horns—or, in this case, the severed head of a stuffed animal.

TO MY DISAPPOINTMENT, things are eerily quiet at the warehouse shops the next morning. I spend the time answering emails and paying bills while I keep an ear out. Kelsie, one of our employees, offers to grab me lunch since she's going for a food run, but I'm only hungry for revenge.

By the time noon quietly rolls around and we open our doors, I venture out to the sidewalk to check things out.

The dog head is right where I left it, its vacant eyes staring into the distance, but the inside of Happy Tails Salon is dark. I survey the lot, but there's no sign of Hollis's Volkswagen.

Dammit. I chose the one day the woman calls in sick to play my best card yet.

But just as I'm walking back through Blue Bigfoot's doors, I catch a glimpse of Hollis's car tearing into the parking lot. Looks like someone overslept.

It's impossible to wipe the smile from my face as I hide just inside Blue Bigfoot's glass doors, keeping one eye on my nasty neighbor as she executes the messiest parking job I've ever witnessed.

She's obviously spotted my gift.

Her door slams and she instantly locks eyes with me, so I step from my hiding place. I ain't afraid of this woman, a message I hope my shit-eating-grin telegraphs loud and clear. Rage simmers in her eyes as she stalks my way, low-heeled boots slapping the pavement with each angry step.

She stops about two feet in front of me, chest heaving and cheeks pink with temper, and I have the craziest urge to drag her into me and kiss the hell out of her. It's like my body just got a wild hair and is trying to block my brain's number. It's going rogue.

Thankfully, the urge takes a back burner when the angry line of Hollis's mouth parts to speak, each word coming out sharp and pissed-the-hell off. "*Where. Is. Your. Brother?*"

Say what?

I take a half step back before it dawns on me that she thinks one of my brothers did this.

My grin returns. "Somethin' bothering you, Ms. Hayes?"

But she doesn't play along, instead shoving me aside and stomping into the taproom. Her eyes scan the empty place before landing back on me. "*Where is he?*"

Maybe she's drunk. It could explain both her confusion

and her shitty parking job. "I'm right here." I bring a palm to my chest.

She huffs and stomps her foot like a bull preparing to charge. "Not you. *Miller*." She says my brother's name like even the sound of it on her tongue might make her gag.

"You think Miller could have pulled off that thing of beauty? That was all me, baby." If she's gonna aim those fiery eyes of fury at anyone, it's gonna be me. Something about that thought doesn't sit right, but it needs to wait while I enjoy this moment.

Hollis narrows her eyes and steps closer again. This time I can make out the light spray of freckles on her nose and a hint of something unfamiliar in her expression. I can't quite put my finger on it until she opens her mouth.

"What are you talking about?"

It's wariness I'm seeing—and hearing. I'm way more used to haughty annoyance.

"What are *you* talkin' about?"

"I asked you fir—never mind," she cuts herself off with a scoff. "I'm talking about your sleazebag of a brother seducing my sister and then ditching her."

"Whoa, whoa, whoa." I step back, both hands up. "So this isn't about…" I stop because I realize Hollis somehow hasn't even seen the dog, and there's no way I'm spoiling the surprise.

The bit about Miller is, let's just say… unsurprising. While I don't necessarily approve of the way he whores around, his reputation *always* precedes him. We're all adults here, last I checked.

Hollis is only getting her panties in a wad because of Miller's last name. Hell, she's never even met him, as far as I know.

"Seems to me like this is a private situation between your sister and my brother. I suggest she come over and speak to him if she's got a bone to pick—not send a representative."

"She can't." Hollis's brown eyes glint with renewed anger.

I cross my arms, kinda pissed that the morning's prank has been waylaid by our respective siblings screwin' each other. Who knew? "And why's that?"

"Because Hadley is currently *grounded*. Which is what parents sometimes do to *high school juniors* who sneak out to see *grown men*."

My arms drop almost as fast as my brother's name does from my tongue. "Miller! Get your ass out here! Pronto!" He's even more of a dipshit than I thought.

I lead Hollis to the end of the bar by Larry in case a customer comes in, holding loosely to her upper arm out of instinct. She doesn't even appear to notice, she's so focused on murdering my brother, but it takes more effort than I like to keep my expression neutral. The second my fingertips feel the warmth from under her thin sweater, they light on fire—like in one of those sci-fi movies where you can see the flames racing through the character's fingers and on up through their arm to their whole body.

I let go almost immediately, feeling like I need to shake my hand out, but I've got other things requiring my attention.

"Yeah, boss." Miller saunters in from the back hall, pressing his luck with that kiss-ass greeting.

"You wanna tell me why our neighbor says you slept with—" I pause, turning back to Hollis and her pink cheeks. "How old did you say your sister is?"

Her glare is fixed on Miller with an intensity that might actually leave a mark. "Eighteen. *Barely*."

Thank heavens for small favors, not that it makes it much better, but at least Miller won't end up in jail. Again.

"Right." My eyes dart back to my idiot brother. "You wanna tell me why our neighbor says you slept with her barely eighteen-year-old sister and then dumped her on her ass?"

Oscar coughs from down the bar, telling me he's on john duty tonight for damn sure.

But Miller's palms shoot up. "I didn't sleep with anyone's sister." I send him a glare that I hope expresses how utterly stupid I know him to be. "Well, you know what I mean. I don't know who she's talkin' about."

But Hollis is right on top of it, her fury lighting the air between them on fire. "Does *Hadley Hayes* ring a bell? You just dumped her a couple days ago!"

"Oh, her? Wait, she's your sister?" Miller relaxes against the bar, crossing his arms like a man without a single care in the world.

I wince into my chest. *Not the move I would have made, little brother.*

Hollis seethes. "*Yeah, her.* You are unbelievable." She pokes Miller in the chest, but he has the wherewithal to give her another foot of space and keep his cool as he explains.

"Look, I don't know what she told you, but I never slept with that girl—Hadley. She and some of her friends have been hanging out the past few weeks with a couple guys I know. She kept tryin' to get me to buy alcohol for her."

"And?" Hollis crosses her arms, and it has what I'm sure is the unintentional effect of serving her tits up on a platter. My fingers flex at my sides.

"And nothin'. She knew our family had a brewery and

she thought it would be no big deal. I flirted with her and stuff, kissed her a couple times, but the second I found out she was jailbait, I told her to get lost."

Always the sensitive soul, my brother.

"Well, there you go," I say, gesturing to Miller. For once, my brother acted with the head above his shoulders instead of the one down below.

Hollis's teeth snag her lower lip as her eyes dart back and forth between us brothers. "That's not what Hadley said." Her voice has lost its edge; it's now hesitant, confused. And maybe even a little hurt.

Dammit. I want the other Hollis back. The one who's so damn sure of herself—a dozen snarky comments ready at hand for when we might run into each other. The Machiavelli in a pink sweater and sexy librarian glasses. This one is no fun. This one is… vulnerable. *Fuck.*

Miller, oblivious to the change in mood, opens his big mouth. "Not to be rude, but your sister seems to make a lot of shit up—not just this story. I mean, I assume your dad isn't actually friends with the president?"

"Um, no. Not that I'm aware of." Hollis's tone is distracted and she keeps worrying that lip.

I can see the wheels moving in her head, and a new frown turns her lips down as she studies the wood of the bar. I gesture for Miller to get lost and leave us alone.

"What can you do? Family sucks sometimes." I shrug and make my tone light, hoping to snap her back out of her funk. So what? Her sister lied to her. If I had a nickel for every time one of my jackass siblings lied to my face, I'd own this whole damn warehouse.

She glances up, and I can see the instant she mentally shakes herself off because her lips do that thing where they curl at the corners in a way that reminds me of an evil queen. Ah, there's the Hollis I know and hate.

"I'm sure your family says the same thing about you."

Oddly enough, the burn makes me smile, as does her ass when she turns on a heel to walk on out of my bar. But nothing can compare to the joy I get five seconds later when Hollis's scream echoes through the parking lot.

Life can be downright beautiful, can't it?

CHAPTER
FOUR
IF WE WERE DOGS

HOLLIS

"KNOCK KNOCK." The bell and my mother's voice ring out simultaneously as she sweeps into my salon.

I'm behind the half-wall separating the grooming section from the rest of my space. The mini Goldendoodle on my table barks at her. "Shush, Penelope." I frown at the little sassafras, and she licks my hand. "Hey, Mom." My voice is wary because this is only the second time she's been here since I signed the lease.

Wrapped in a trim bell-sleeve dress, she rounds the partition to drop a kiss on my cheek while her eyes scan the interior. Happy Tails is half grooming salon and half shop with adorable temptations for every dog owner. The color theme is pink—since it's my favorite—with black and gold accents.

"You've really done a lot with this place," my mom says. When her gaze lands on the floor beneath my feet covered in dog hair, her sculpted eyebrows draw together and she carefully adjusts the swath of long blond fringe across her forehead. She and Hadley could be twins. "You should let Marjorie do some decorating."

"I'll, um, keep that in mind," I reply as I clip Penelope's overgrown mustache. Marjorie is my cousin on Harry's side and has never been known for her taste in, well, anything really. But that doesn't stop my mother from pimping out her decorating services.

Now, if I could only get her to pimp my business out half as vigorously. Still, this is the most enthusiastic she's been about my new venture, and she *did* drive all the way over here to see me, which I take as progress in the right direction.

When I graduated college with a very practical degree in business, I gave the corporate route a try, much to my parents' delight. Harry was probably born wearing a tie, so any other decision would have sounded ludicrous to him. But it never felt right. I'd found myself rushing to my car at the earliest possible moment to get to the animal shelter where I volunteered or home to whichever dog I was fostering that month. Animals give love back tenfold —well, apart from a few here and there—and spending time caring for them filled my soul in a way my day job didn't.

I was up for a promotion last year, which would have meant longer hours and no time for foster pups or shelter animals, so I shocked everyone by putting in my two weeks' notice. Mom and Harry were distraught, to say the least. Harry tried coaxing me to join his corporate real estate firm, even offering to let me create my own position, which is insane.

Instead, I downgraded apartments and cars, took a job at a grooming salon, and practiced my craft on all the dogs at the shelter until I got my license and found a space I could afford. Unfortunately for me, I hadn't known at the time that I'd be forced to share oxygen with a beer-guzzling Neanderthal.

I still can't get the sound of his smug laughter out of my head in response to my horrified screaming yesterday. But I couldn't help it; the man went too far this time. I swear it took me a good minute to realize that dog head wasn't real, and another twenty to get the disgusting thing off my property and into the dumpster. I shudder to think how many people saw it and mistook *me* for the deranged lunatic.

But revenge is a dish best served cold, and I have plenty of plans in the deep freeze.

I narrow my eyes at the thought, and Penelope whines at my expression. Now Cash is making me scare my poor clients!

"You shouldn't scowl, honey. It'll give you premature wrinkles," my mom advises, reaching into her clutch and pulling out a small white box with a glittery pink bow. "Here, I got you a little something."

"Mom." I set my shears down and wipe my hands on my canvas grooming apron before reaching out to accept the gift. She frowns as she hands it over, carefully avoiding contact with my canine-contaminated fingers and likely regretting her choice of setting in which to forfeit whatever designer doodad awaits inside.

All of my childhood was spent pining for a dog of my own. My mom always said we couldn't afford one, and then it was Harry's allergies preventing it. But last fall, when I adopted Marco and Polo, my inseparable mixed-breed little dynamos, it became clear that my parents are just not dog people. Their loss.

I must have inherited the animal-loving gene from my

biological father—the only decent thing he ever did for me, it seems.

I carefully untie the bow before setting it aside to save.

"Wow," I say when I lift the lid. Inside lies a pair of earrings that could conceivably pay my rent for an entire month.

"Pink topaz and diamonds," my mother shares.

Make that two months.

I glance up to see her eyes sparkling almost as brightly as the gemstones. "Mom, you shouldn't have." I pull her into a hug, which she grudgingly accepts but doesn't return.

"Hollis, you're covered in dog hair!" she scolds.

"I know." I pull back and choose my next words carefully. "What's the occasion?" It's in my parents' nature to throw their money around, but things between us have been strained since my career change and my insistence that I don't want their financial help. I've been quite clear, and I suspect this is my mother's way of skirting around my rules.

"It's for dealing with that… *monster* next door." Her tone turns sharp. "I still think we should call the police."

Ah, that explains it. When I stopped by the house yesterday morning to borrow a drill, Hadley let her "beloved's" name slip out over breakfast. Thank God Harry wasn't home, or Miller Brooks would be in traction by now. I pulled my mom aside and told her I'd deal with Miller, and believe me, I designed quite a few strategies for his demise.

My stomach gurgles as I recall my confrontation with Cash and Miller yesterday. While I hate that Cash saw me off my game, I hate even more that my own sister was responsible. At least now I know why the little fibber had been keeping Miller's identity a secret. She had to know I'd go next door and find out the truth. I'm waiting until I calm down before reading Hadley the riot act, which only gives her time to squirm.

My mom clicks her purse shut and frowns at the wall separating my salon from Blue Bigfoot Beer.

"We went through this last night, Mom," I remind her. I explained it all over the phone, but it sounds like it didn't sink in—and who knows what other stories Hadley might have made up in the meantime. Of course, I didn't call Hadley a liar outright, but maybe I should have from the way my mom is staring daggers at the wall.

Penelope whines from her spot beside me, and I turn to give her a scratch. "I know, girl." She's been more than patient. "Let me finish your haircut and you can help me sweep the floor."

When I glance up again, my mom's attention is back on me, but her expression has soured in a new way. I do my best to keep my eyes from rolling.

I'll have to figure out later what to do about the earrings, but now is not the time to argue with my mom—especially since it's her first time here since I opened my doors, and I can see she's trying.

Or not.

"I should have known Hadley would get into trouble visiting you in this part of—" She cuts herself off. "Never mind." Sometimes I marvel at her ability to forget we used to live in a part of town way worse than this one.

I bite my tongue, knowing I'll only frustrate myself if we go down this road again. Mom and Harry will change their minds one of these days about my choices. And if they don't? Well, I'll do what I've always done: straighten my spine and be my own cheering squad.

In the meantime… "Mom, about that boy," I begin, trying to figure out how to call Hadley a bald-faced liar without using those exact words.

But she interjects, "Your father is livid. Lord knows what he might do."

Crap on a cracker! "You told Harry?!" I specifically told her not to mention a word of it to him! He's not one to take anything lying down—doubly so when it comes to his baby girl.

I hold not one speck of loyalty to any of the Brooks family members, but I genuinely believe Miller's version of events, and there's no reason for retaliation where he's concerned. I'm saving all my ire for his brother, and I don't need my family's help to deal with Cash.

I set down the earring box and watch my mother closely. Her eyes dart around the room, giving her away, even as she radiates poise and self-assuredness in the rest of her manner. She's forever regal—the former teenage beauty queen from Southern Pines, but she's far from cold. And she shares Hadley's inability to keep a secret as well as her fondness for drama.

"Mom?"

She doesn't look at me.

"Hadley is eighteen, and this won't be the last time her heart gets broken," I remind her. "Besides, I told you she was being melodramatic. She and Miller were never even—"

"Oh, you know me and your dad," she interrupts again, pursing her lips. "We don't have secrets."

This is no surprise, but we both know Harry Hayes being deployed with only half of a story will not end well.

"So you also told him Hadley exaggerated and nothing in fact happened, right?"

She shifts to one hip. "How can you possibly know that for sure?"

Uh, because the way Miller characterized Hadley's behavior sounded one hundred percent like her? And because she purposely kept his identity a secret from me?

"He has reason to lie, Hollis." My mother gives her head a dismissive shake and does one of her customary hair flips. "Your dad just wants a little justice—and to make sure this young man gets the message to leave innocent little girls alone once and for all."

Are they insane? Given that Harrison Hayes's idea of "justice" means something altogether different than it does to a normal, rational person, this spells shitshow loud and clear. "Hadley is an adult. Exactly what is he planning? A beheading in the town square?"

She exhales and glances down at her dress with a casual shrug before wrinkling her nose at the fresh dusting of dog hair from my hug.

I reach to the cart beside me and hand her one of the dozen lint rollers I keep around the shop. "Here."

She swipes at the fabric with the roller and sighs. "I'm just thinking out loud. You know me."

Yeah, I do know her. And I know Harry. He doesn't take any perceived insults or affronts well, and that includes those dealt to his family members. The last time he sought "justice," Mom received a hand-delivered apology—complete with a bouquet of contrition lilies—from the head of the museum trust for seating her at a table in the back of the room at some fundraiser.

"Don't let him do anything, okay?" I don't blink until she raises her eyes to meet mine. "Nothing illegal happened, and there's more to the story than Hadley's claiming. Miller says they didn't do anything more than kiss a couple times." I imbue my words with every speck of earnestness I possess, but she doesn't answer me.

Instead, she asks, "And you believe him over your own sister?"

"Yes." The word is out before I can cushion the blow, but it's the truth.

I can't read her expression now, and I feel a little nauseated.

She hands the lint roller back to me, and then whatever she was thinking is masked by what I like to call her "society smile." The one she uses to glide through the world, giving everyone the impression that her life is nothing but a fairy tale come true. "Well, I should head out. I have so much to get done before we leave for vacation. They said not to worry about mosquitos, but I'm preparing for anything," she says.

She turns to go, ever graceful in her heels, but she stops to face me again from the other side of the partition. "I hope you know how much I love you girls."

"I do." My throat threatens to close, and I swallow hard. "I love you too."

With a soft nod, she turns and click-clacks her way across the shop floor, the ringing of the bell punctuating her departure and setting my stomach churning again.

Penelope licks my arm, and I turn to face her again. "Thank you, sweetheart."

Life would be so much simpler if we were all dogs.

CHAPTER
FIVE
JUST YOUR EVERYDAY
EXISTENTIAL CRISIS

HOLLIS

"HOLLIS, I NEED A WORD WITH YOU?" There's no need to turn to confirm the identity of the man breathing down my neck.

I ignore my neighbor and smile extra brightly at my customer. "So, if Beau is pulling when you walk him, you'll want a harness with a ring on the front like this one. That way, when he pulls, it'll turn him sideways, see?"

"Right," Mrs. Michaelson responds as she takes the blue polka dot harness from me, her tone distracted and her eyes volleying back and forth between me and the dill-hole at my back.

I continue pretending he doesn't exist. "Don't mind him, Mrs. Michaelson." I lean forward with a pretend whisper, "He's a little obsessed with me, poor thing."

Her eyes widen and flash back to Cash, and I swear the woman undresses him with her eyes as she takes her sweet time looking him over. The way her cheeks are lit up, he might truly be standing there stark raving naked for all I know. I can sense a flush start on my chest at the thought, and I truly hate myself for it.

When Cash doesn't respond, I take it as permission to add more detail. "Unfortunately, he still lives with his mommy, and he's got a little personal hygiene issue." I wrinkle my nose. "A girl's got to have standards, right?"

Mrs. Michaelson nods absently, so I usher her to my pretty pink counter and ring up the harness while I train my eyes on anything but my neighbor. It's not like him to let my shenanigans go like this, so I'm on high alert.

Before Mrs. Michaelson reaches the door, a young couple and my two o'clock appointment enter, offering more distraction. I chance a tiny glance Cash's way. His nose is buried in his phone and he's muttering to himself, the usual surly frown firmly in place.

He somehow senses my attention before I can avert my gaze and strides my way. Dammit. How does he do that?

I scurry around the counter to place my two o'clock and his pug between Cash and me.

"Hollis, I need to talk to you. Now." There's an unfamiliar edge to his voice.

"I'm a little busy, as you can see." My eyes stay on the balding man and his little dog. My smile tortured, I'm sure. "I'll take good care of Raymond, I promise." I take the pug from him, and he leans over to kiss the dog's head, getting way too close to my boobs for my comfort. I falter back a step, banging an elbow on the counter and almost dropping the dog. "I'll text you when he's ready to be picked up." My plastic smile hides the sting as best I can.

"Hey." Cash steps forward. "Did that guy just—shit." He spears frustrated fingers through his dark hair. "We need to talk right the hell now."

"I'm sorry, but that doesn't work with my schedule." I

lift Raymond up between us to reinforce my statement, and the little angel pees on Cash's shirt—a perfect arc from his tiny little weenie. I could not have planned this better if I'd tried.

Cash jumps back, uttering some choice expletives and plucking the gray "Drink Local" T-shirt away from his chest. I swear to God, if that man takes his shirt off in my shop, I'm going to have a true existential crisis on my hands.

"Would you lower your voice? I have customers," I hiss at him as I cradle my new favorite dog in the world.

Cash glances at the couple, his brow furrowed so hard I'm giving new thought to my mom's advice about premature wrinkles. His index finger stabs the air, but he does lower his voice this time. "You come see me the minute you're alone," he demands, his eyes crackling with fire so intense I feel it in my clitoris. Damn the man.

"Fine. Just go," I whisper impatiently.

I don't know why I agree, except that I need him out of my store before I lose my mind and let my ovaries start doing the thinking. And that, we cannot have.

He keeps his finger pointed at me, those dark slashes of eyebrows pulling together until he's satisfied I'm not lying. Only then does he turn to stalk back to the sidewalk.

I'm seriously starting to think I may need to either move, kill him, or bang the man to get any peace. And right now, I don't like the option that's winning.

TWO HOURS and one very strongly worded lecture to myself later, I have my wits about me again as I saunter into Blue Bigfoot. I'm determined to get whatever this is over with as quickly as possible so I can get on with what has otherwise been a great day. Josh, the high school junior who helps me out a few days a week, is arriving any minute now, so I'll be able to groom my next client uninterrupted. And Hadley even called this morning with a mumbled apology for "stretching the truth *a little*," so my stomach is no longer threatening to expel its contents.

Carter, the oldest of the Brooks brothers, points me toward an office in the back and gifts me with a hint of a smile. See, it's not that difficult to be a decent human! I even get one of those subtle hip waves from Miller, and I'd been nearly ready to assault him yesterday. Personal growth—that's what Cash needs.

Unfortunately, that seems to be the only thing he's lacking. Because I'm now standing in the office doorway in front of a man who looks like an ad for *Lumbersexual Monthly* in a fresh flannel shirt rolled up at the sleeves and the top three buttons undone to reveal a smattering of chest hair I don't find terribly unattractive.

He hasn't noticed me yet, his attention caught on the stack of mail he's opening at his desk.

"So, tell me. What is so terribly important that I had to put up my 'back soon' sign and enter your lair?"

Without batting an eye or looking up at me, he responds, "Call off your dogs."

"What did Marco and Polo ever do to you?" I cross my arms and lean a shoulder into the door jamb.

"I'm serious." Cash finally looks up, and I notice dark circles I missed earlier lurking under his eyes. "You're fucking with my livelihood now."

"I'm sorry. What is it I'm supposedly doing again?" He obviously didn't sleep last night, which might explain the hallucinations.

"The health inspector. I don't know who you had to screw to get them in here like that, but you've gone way too far this time." He all but tears a letter in half as he opens the envelope.

"I have absolutely no idea what you're talking about, but I must say hiring someone to impersonate a health inspector does sound like something I would undoubtedly do." In fact, I'm kind of mad I didn't think of it myself.

"But you just had to take it that extra step, didn't you?" His eyes narrow, seemingly searching for something in mine. But, for once, I've got nothing to hide. "I clocked your stooge the minute he walked in this morning and introduced himself. We already had our inspection three weeks ago—passed with flying colors. In fact, I was looking forward to shoving your failed prank in your face." He snatches up a padded envelope without breaking eye contact. "But then I find out two hours ago that the guy you sent is one hundred percent legit, as you well know, and now he's threatening to shut us down with some bullshit violations."

I push off the doorway and straighten. "Wait, what?"

"So, like I said, call off your dogs. If you need me to wave a white flag, consider it waved." He shakes his head. "I knew you were nuts, but I didn't know you'd go this far just to prove a point." He drops the package onto the desk and throws his palms up. "I'm out."

Something about the finality of his statement hits me in a heavy way I don't fully understand. But he's accusing me of something I didn't do. "It wasn't me." My voice has a pleading tone I despise but can't seem to help.

"Nice try." His eyes are cold, and they somehow make it feel like the temperature of the entire room has dropped.

I step toward the desk. "It wasn't me, I swear! I may

think you're an ass, but I would never do something to endanger your business like that." How can he think that of me? Oh, wait, that's right—he's a reactionary caveman with a wicked temper and maybe a dozen brain cells to work with.

"You sure about that?" The mouth breather sneers as he blindly works on unsealing the package. "I'm guessing you'd be happy as a fucking clam to see me out of your life forever."

"Well…" I can't help it. "Sorry." I take another step, and his motions become almost frantic as he takes out his frustration on the padded envelope. "You have to believe me, Cash. It wasn't me," I insist.

Just as he opens his mouth to respond, the seal on the package finally gives way. A massive burst of pink and purple glitter explodes from the inside, coating his shirt and hair and fluttering to the desk and floor. I jump back, narrowly avoiding the glitter geyser. But Cash, his flannel, his chest hair, his eyebrows, his desk, everything—fully glitterfied in a fluorescent blizzard.

I bite my finger and wince, willing myself not to open my mouth, but it has a mind of its own.

"Now, *that*," I say, "Was *me*."

Cash shakes his head like a dog, clearing enough glitter for me to make out both the fury in his eyes and the sharp line of his tight lips. When he stands, an avalanche of pink and purple sparkles spill from his hair and shirt onto the desk, and I'm having trouble tamping my smile down.

But any urge to smile vanishes when he stalks toward me, closing the distance so fast I hardly have time to draw in a single breath before his mouth crashes onto mine.

CHAPTER
SIX

THIS CHANGES NOTHING

CASH

EVERY OUNCE of pent-up frustration from my shitty day—hell, the last four months—fuels my mouth's assault on Hollis's silky-smooth lips. There's no finesse, no care, just a soul-deep need for contact with this infuriating woman.

Her surprised yelp tries penetrating my brain, telling me to stop, but it's only a second later when Hollis grips my hair with both hands and spears her tongue past my lips to tangle with mine. The frame of her glasses bites into my eye socket, but I don't give a single fuck. The kiss is wet, violent, frantic. Her tits press into my chest, and I groan into her mouth while slanting my head to devour her. I want to eat her alive until there's nothing left—so she can't drive me so fucking crazy anymore. And then I want to do it all over again.

She pulls my hair hard, and I respond by digging my fingers into the flesh of her ass cheeks and hauling her hips into my growing erection. Her scent of fruit and vanilla—a delicate combination contradicting her callous nature—fills my nostrils as I inhale deeply and bite her plump lower lip. I can feel the stiff plastic of glitter dotting our lips and raking our tongues, but it only adds to the riot of sensations.

She growls, biting me back—harder than mine, I might add—and a chuckle escapes my throat, only to be swallowed by Hollis as she slides her tongue back into my mouth and digs her nails into my scalp this time.

Fuck, is she hot. My dick is rock hard against the fly of my jeans where I press into her. But I need to be closer, so I skim my hands from her round ass to her thighs, and I don't have to ask her twice. She does a little hop and wraps her legs around my hips like a python, rocking her pussy into me and making my head go light.

But there's no way I'm passing out and missing a second of this.

She rips her mouth from mine, sucking in quick breaths. I can't see her eyes because she's too close, but I feel them burn into me as specks of glitter on her skin reflect the overhead lights.

"This changes nothing," she hisses against my lips. "I still hate your guts."

"Right back atcha, princess."

This has her yanking my hair harder and grinding her pussy into me. Its heat radiates past the denim of my jeans and the cotton of her leggings—the same leggings that cling to her every curve and make me want to pin her against the nearest wall every time she wears them.

"Don't call me princess, assho—" I don't let her finish, taking her mouth again and diving into the sweet taste of her. How can someone so sour taste so sweet?

Echoing my thought from before, I stagger forward

until Hollis's back hits the wall. It's not gentle, but she doesn't protest. I readjust my grip on her thighs to hike her up a fraction so I can grind the head of my rock-hard dick closer to her hot center. With the wall's support, I now have one hand free to explore more territory.

"Fuck," I groan into her mouth as my thumb brushes a hard nipple pressing against my chest. Hollis's breasts are full and tight, and I can't stop my mind from imagining what color her nipples are. Pink? Brown? Peach? Any which way, I need them on my tongue.

Hollis comes up for air again and I can hear her head *thunk* into the wall behind her. "This is a terrible idea. We should stop."

"The worst," I echo, rubbing circles over her tight nipple and rocking my hips forward.

"Oh, god," she moans, and my dick grows impossibly harder.

I glance up to see her eyes closed, glasses crooked, cheeks flushed, and her wet lips parted in pleasure. A dusting of pink and purple glitter on her skin gives her an otherworldly glow, and I swear I wouldn't be surprised if she morphed into some kind of enchanted goddess right here against my office wall.

It's time to get naked. Right fucking now.

"Jesus! Fuck!" comes a loud voice from the general direction of the doorway. Hollis and I both jerk our heads toward it to see Miller standing there, mouth agape and a box in his hands.

Without consciously intending to, I drop Hollis, and she just barely rights herself, using my chest for leverage before snatching her hands away like my shirt is on fire. I take two giant steps back, my breath coming in short pants perfectly matching those coming from Hollis.

"What the hell happened in here?" Miller's eyes scan the room and my gaze follows. The place is a neon night-mare, glitter covering every inch of the desk, chair, and surrounding floor. "Dude, did you just shoot a load of glitter?"

I move to slam the door in my brother's face but think better of it at the last second. The last place I should be in this world is in a room alone with Hollis Hayes. The woman is a viper, and she's out to ruin my business—the one I worked tooth and nail to grow and nurture.

What the hell was I doing even touching that woman?

I nudge Miller to the side and turn toward Hollis while my thumb hooks to the door. "Out." I don't dare look at her. Hell, it's in the realm of possibilities that she put some kind of curse on me. What else could explain my complete and utter lapse in good sense? I'm the guy who keeps his eye on the ball while everybody else falls apart. People are counting on me, and here I am risking half the family's livelihood by letting my dick do the thinking. That's Miller's territory, not mine.

Hollis doesn't even hesitate. She stalks past me, letting her elbow dig into my ribs as she passes, a trail of glitter fluttering to the floor in her wake. "My pleasure," she spits behind her.

Jesus, I've got to get my head together. Because that can never, and I mean *never*, happen again.

CHAPTER
SEVEN

ALL THAT GLITTERS IS NOT GOLD

CASH

"HEY, if it isn't twinkle dick." I'm greeted by my brother Denny when I walk into Mama's kitchen.

I don't bother asking what he's talking about because I knew full well Miller would activate the family grapevine as soon as he left my office this afternoon. Denny stands from his chair and comes in for a half shake/half hug.

"Hey, Rosie," I greet his girlfriend, who's stirring something that smells like soup in a big pot on the stove. She used to follow my brother around like a puppy when she was a kid, but Denny's the one panting after her now. Poor girl. She's practically a saint. At least there's one person who won't throw my ill-advised make-out session with Hollis the Horrible in my face.

"Hey, sparkle sausage," Rosie throws over her shoulder with a wicked grin and a flip of her dark hair.

Et tu, Rosie?

Denny snickers and slips her a high five on his way

back to the table. "I guess we don't have to ask what you've been up to."

I ignore them. One, because it's the only way to get these asshats to shut up, and two, because nothing about what I've been up to today is worth talking about. They may all know about my Hollis slip-up, but not even Carter knows yet that the health inspector's report is real and we're likely up shit's creek.

My assumption was that Hollis would back off once she had her fun, but now I'm worried she was being truthful when she claimed not to be the one behind it. It's the first time I can remember actually wishing for her to prank me. So I'm not involving any of my family until I know for certain what's going on.

I know it makes little sense that I'd coddle Carter like this, with him being not only my business partner, but the oldest of my siblings. Yet here I am doing just that.

Mama calls it older child syndrome, claiming it's common for the older siblings to do their level best to maintain order in the family dynamics and keep everyone where they should be. I don't particularly relish the role, yet that never stops me from being compelled to take on the mantle—all the more since our dad died a few years back.

I was working a job in Winston-Salem at the time—just some short-term gig I thought might turn into something —and it never even occurred to me *not* to move back home and do what I could to ease my mama's pain and burdens. My baby sister, Lynn, was only thirteen at the time, and Miller was in the internship phase of his long career as a teenage delinquent, so there was plenty of shit that needed my attention. I moved back into my childhood home and did my level best to shoulder any responsibility I could that might help Mama and the family out.

Carter was living large in Washington D.C., working as a legislative aide for some congresswoman. He hired a fancy lawyer to sue the hospital for botching Dad's care and killing him. No other explanation for a perfectly healthy fifty-year-old man going in for gallbladder surgery and never waking up. I got a job working nights as a bartender at a local brewery so I could be available during the days. I handled all the household financials, played chauffeur to Lynn and her friends, as well as being executor of Dad's estate, as it was. His few assets went directly to Mama, but there were plenty of loose ends to tie up—especially since he'd run up some credit card debt. It took the better part of a year to cover everything, and another eighteen months to reach a settlement with the hospital. We got enough money to pay the remaining debts, and disciplinary action was taken against a doctor and a nurse.

But Mama didn't pay attention to any of it since nothing anybody said or did could bring her husband back. The phrase, "Whatever you think is best," became her mantra during those two and a half years—not that she withdrew from life or family, as a spouse might do in her situation.

In fact, she went the opposite direction. Dad's passing turned her from a run-of-the-mill oddity and lover of life to an insanely enthusiastic optimist who never met a stranger or a moment she didn't want to celebrate. Mama treats every day as if it might be the last one on Earth, something I'm sure we all should do, but who has the time —or patience? As a result, she's earned herself a bit of a reputation in our corner of the Blue Ridge Mountains for being off her fuckin' rocker. I'd never ask her to change, but that doesn't mean I don't get frustrated feeling like I single handedly hold the family's future in my hands sometimes.

And if this health code violation bullshit sticks—which it can't since we *just* passed an inspection—I have zero idea where we're gonna get the money for all the upgrades they're demanding in the next three weeks.

Opening a brewery was always something Cart and I talked about doing when we spent summers home brewing beer with our dad in the detached garage. Carter came into the Blue Bigfoot partnership when he was working in D.C., so he put up cash and cosigned loans in exchange for me doing day-to-day operations. He seemed pretty flush and talked about an emergency fund he had, so I never thought much of it until he came home broke and moved into the attic. That emergency fund of his is long gone.

I spent the afternoon staring at Blue Bigfoot's accounts —checking, savings, credit cards, business loan—all telling me shit I already knew. There's no way we can get another business loan, and nobody I know has $25k sitting around under their mattress. Though I'm not inclined to spend a dime doing needless renovations even if we did.

"Finally." Mama throws her hands up as she crosses the threshold into the kitchen. "I thought you'd never get home. I left some soup on for you." She pulls me into a quick hug, her curly brown hair blinding me. "You work too hard."

"Hey, Mama." I release her and bend down to pet Mango, who's followed her into the kitchen. Most people are panicked when they first meet Mango, which is under-standable given that he's a skunk—and a spoiled rotten one at that. But his scent gland has been gone since Mama rescued him from the side of the road as a baby. She still claims Bigfoot accidentally stepped on Mango's mother, and nobody argues any different.

"I don't think what he's been doin' can be called 'work.'" Denny grins as he flashes air quotes.

I flip him the bird. "Don't you have a love nest to get back to?"

Miller waltzes in and goes straight for the fridge, his boxers sticking out above his low-slung jeans. "Yo, I think you've got a little something right there." He gestures to his cheek and shoots a smirk at me.

"Oh? I think you've got something right there, there, and there." I point to the various spots where his piercings shine brighter than any piece of glitter ever could. I swept up what I could from the office, but that shit is still gonna be showing up in cracks and crevices a year from now.

Mama ignores us all, her brows pulling together. "Did Carter come home with you?"

"No. He left before I did." It shouldn't surprise any of us that he's MIA. The dude hasn't been himself since he returned home to Asheville a few months back. One day, he just showed up and declared his partnership in Blue Bigfoot was changing from remote to in-person. Not that I don't appreciate the extra set of hands—or his brewmaster talents—but nobody knows why he ditched his posh job and came home—not even Mama. If she can't get him to talk, nobody can, so we've all silently agreed to leave him be about it until he brings it up.

But nobody's leaving *me* be, it seems.

Mama arches a brow. "Perhaps he was intimidated by you and your glitter stick," she says, sending every asshole in the kitchen into fits of laughter.

Twenty minutes and several new nicknames later, I'm sitting at the table alone with a bowl of Mama's butternut squash soup when Miller wanders back in. He turns a chair backward and straddles it across the table from me.

"I think y'all have exhausted the entire Urban Thesaurus on nicknames for my dick," I tell him as I bring another spoonful to my mouth. I swear Mama should sell this soup, it's so damn good. Lynnie calls it "a hug in a bowl," or something like that, and she's not wrong.

Miller grins. "I still think shimmer schlong was the best. Who knew Rosie had it in her?"

"I guess she ain't the shy little girl from next door anymore," I respond. The Carmichael family has lived next door to us since we were all in diapers. Mama and Adrina—Rosie's mom—are best friends, and everybody is like family to each other.

Instead of making another joke, Miller swallows and folds his hands on the table, telling me I'm not gonna like his next words one bit.

"I've been meaning to thank you for earlier this week," he says, surprising the hell out of me.

"Believe it or not, you're doing a half-decent job, so no need."

He runs a hand through his messy hair and clicks that tongue piercing. "No, I mean for having my back with the neighbor—Hollis."

The fact that he doesn't work in another joke at the mention of her name tells me he's being dead sincere.

"I didn't want to say it in front of her," he continues. "But that Hadley chick is one hundred percent certified nuts. She was telling me their dad has all sorts of connections with politicians and police, and he could make anyone disappear or some shit. Crazy stuff. And total bull-shit, I'm sure." He chuffs out a half-laugh.

It's not Miller's usual M.O. to express gratitude, so this conversation is not only surprising, it does my heart some good on what's otherwise been a shitty day.

"No problem. Family first, right?"

He nods his agreement, and I point my empty spoon at him.

"Just do me a favor and stay away from the society set, yeah? The last thing we need is an abduction or a prison sentence."

"Noted." Miller shrugs. "To be completely transparent, I did my share of lying to her too. She might have been under the impression I own Blue Bigfoot." His nose wrinkles as he looks anywhere but my face.

I raise an eyebrow, but I'm not about to give him a hard time—not now, at least. We've all said things to impress girls.

Miller spares me a glance, and when he sees I'm giving him a pass, he's quick to hurry on. "You and Hollis, huh? I gotta say I can see the appeal. The way you've been talking about her, I thought she'd have horns and a tail, but she's hitting that sexy librarian vibe hard."

"The only vibe that woman has is the serial killer kind," I lie.

"Whatever you say, bedazzle dong—sorry," he cuts himself off when I start lunging in his direction. "You should definitely hit that though. Then we can use her dad's connections to meet the president—or at the very least, get someone in local government to expunge my arrest record."

Twenty-one-year-old Miller's got nothing on the nine-teen-year-old version. He got himself arrested on a drunk and disorderly, was forced to pay a fine he couldn't afford, and spent six months doing community service. There's nothing quite like rolling down the highway seeing your brother in an orange vest picking up trash on the median.

"I thought we agreed never to talk about that." I send him a glare and drop my spoon into the empty soup bowl.

He snaps his mouth shut, but opens it right back up to say, "I guess I still owe you another thanks for bailing my ass out back then."

It's true he never paid me back, but if I kept score around this place, it would be too depressing to live. "You can thank me by getting to work early and washing down the picnic tables. Now that the sun's out, we'll be using the patio a lot more." I stand and take my bowl to the sink.

"On it," Miller replies, rising from his chair and heading for the stairs.

I watch his back until he turns the corner. Our conversation was, dare I say, downright *pleasant*—a fact that has me wondering again what in the hell is going on with my brothers.

CHAPTER
EIGHT

DON'T BE SO SHELLFISH

HOLLIS

"STUPID, STUPID, STUPID!" I mutter to myself as I all but throw dog treats into the decorative basket perched on the counter.

I can't *believe* I let that psychopath touch me! It's been almost twenty-four hours, and I'm still fuming—at him, at myself, and at God for giving Cash Brooks magic hands and lips that have no business being that soft.

My mind replays his tongue's sensual slide past my lips and his strong fingers digging into my butt while he devoured me.

No! I throw another treat.

Why can't I turn this awful rerun off? Cash is the last person or thing I want to be thinking about right now—or ever.

I flex my finger where a bandage covers one knuckle. Dammit! I'm blaming him for that too. I was so distracted when I was grooming my last client that I cut my finger with my trimming shears. Buttercup, the bichon, is way cuter than my stupid neighbor who deserves zero of my attention.

A treat misses the basket and falls to the floor, where Marco and Polo scurry from their bed to claim it. I brought them with me to work this morning, thinking I could use both the distraction and the moral support. But so far, they've just slept and chased each other's tails. They're entirely unhelpful in erasing the memory of my neighbor pinning me to the wall and making my head explode on an otherwise mundane Thursday.

This is ridiculous. I am a grown woman in control of my own body and mind. I've got this.

I return to my fuzzy black chair and close my eyes, taking a deep breath to rein in my emotions. *Breathe in. Breathe out. Breathe in. Breathe out. You're becoming calmer with each exhale.*

My heart begins to settle down in my chest. This is good. I can put my meditation skills to use. There's no reason for me to think about anything I don't choose to.

You're on a tropical island on a white sandy beach. The sun warms your skin as you lie on a soft chaise and listen to the ocean's rhythmic waves.

Thaaaat's right.

Now feel the light breeze ruffle your hair and skim across your skin. A shadow falls over you—but that's okay because the sun can be too hot sometimes. A low voice whispers in your ear, "I know you're wet for me, Hollis."

"Aaaahhhhhgggg!" My eyes pop open and I scream, clutching my chest and hurling my head forward between my knees. Marco barks in alarm.

How dare Cash show up in my meditation scene?! And naked, nonetheless! (Oh, did I forget to mention that part?)

Polo trots over and paws my leg, so I pick him up for a snuggle and then look deep into his brown eyes.

"I'm totally screwed, aren't I?"

His only answer is a burp.

"You always know just what to say." I kiss his head.

Enough of this. So I kissed the guy—so what? Actually, *he* kissed *me*. I was only being polite by kissing him back. And, yeah, it's been a while since I've been with a guy, but I've been very busy. Opening your own business is no small feat.

Something I'm sure Cash knows. And something he's certainly aware *I* know.

How dare he accuse me of sabotaging his business? I would never do such a thing to a fellow small business owner, no matter how much I dislike him. The rest of his family seems decent enough from the few members I've met, so how could he think I'd go so far as to destroy a family's livelihood and risk his employees' jobs? Oscar and his wife have a baby on the way, and last time I ran into Jodi, one of the servers, she was drowning in student loans.

Is that what he honestly thinks of me?

A chill spreads over my skin, forming goose bumps in its path. This isn't fun anymore.

I start when my phone rings from the counter, but it's a welcome distraction, doubly so when I see it's my friend Rylee calling.

"Hey! What's going on?"

"Oh, I don't know. I guess maybe I got that promotion at the paper or something." She feigns nonchalance.

"You what?! That's amazing! Congratulations, Rylee!" She's been gunning for this promotion for ages, and nobody deserves it more than her.

She laughs into the phone. "I swear I almost jumped over Andrew's desk and laid one on him."

"If you had, I would take it to my grave and never tell Dean," I tease as Polo wiggles in my arms. I set him back on the floor where he promptly attacks his brother's tail.

"Hell, Dean would be the first one to condone such behavior—he's got to be sick of me whining about writing restaurant reviews."

"I will still never understand Andrew putting you on food reviews. I mean, I know you guys were understaffed, but I've seen you put mustard on an Oreo." Rylee and I have known each other since high school but only reconnected last year when we ran into each other at a concert. She hadn't changed at all.

"Ha! One of my better combos, I must say. Anyway, no more undercover eating for me. One bout of food poisoning is my quota for the year. I'll never eat an oyster again."

"Considering we live a good five hours from the ocean, that's probably for the best. What restaurant was that anyway? You never told me." My heart's already getting lighter. Cash *who*?

"The Sandpiper. Never again."

I groan. "Harry knows the guy who owns that place—somebody Rhinehardt. They play golf together." I bark out a laugh as a memory surfaces. "Oh my god! He came to our house for dinner last summer and was talking about how the health department was giving him trouble!"

"And you couldn't have told me this before I ate there?"

"I didn't know!" I defend myself as I grin into the phone. "Maybe you should blame Harry instead. He told the owner he'd pull some strings and smooth things over."

Rylee groans. "That sounds like Harry. He should be the mayor—he knows *everyone*."

"I know, right?" I roll my eyes.

But they halt mid-roll, and I straighten, a thought striking me.

The health department.

And Harry.

Harry, who does crazy shit when somebody he loves has been wronged.

But Hadley came clean.

Didn't she?

Crappity crap!

My thoughts ping-pong around my brain as I try to discount the notion, and I miss what Rylee says next.

I'm being paranoid. Even if Hadley hasn't fessed up to him yet, why would Harry have a beef with Cash and Carter? It makes no sense.

Still, it all feels like too much of a coincidence to just brush aside. I'll sleep better if I rule it out.

"Hey, Ry, I'm sorry, but I have to run. Congrats again. I'll call you tonight, okay?" I hang up before she can respond, snatching my purse from under the counter.

"Come on, boys. Now." There's no time for my usual patience with the dogs. I need to close up shop and get over to my parents' place.

I hope to hell I'm wrong. But if I'm not, Hadley's going to need better bodyguards than the Logans.

CHAPTER
NINE
WINTER IS COMING

HOLLIS

LUCKILY FOR MY SISTER, she's not home when I push through the front doors of the stucco and stone residence. Neither is my mom. But it's just as well because it means I can talk to Harry alone without anyone else inserting their opinions. I drove over here on autopilot after dropping the dogs off at home, telling myself the whole way that there is no reason to think Harry would take something he thinks Miller did out on the entire Brooks family. That's like *Game of Thrones* level revenge when Harry is more of a *Downton Abbey* kind of guy. It's preposterous, really. When I've finally managed a level head, I find him in the kitchen sneaking a slice of cheesecake from the fridge. See? He's no vindictive lunatic, just a normal guy.

"Hey, pumpkin." He raises both hands, an empty dessert plate in one. "You caught me."

My smile is almost at its usual strength. "Did you have a good round?" He's undoubtedly just come from golf, with his pink cheeks, windblown hair, and uniform of designer golf shirt and slacks.

"Beat my best score this year so far." He smiles, transferring the slice to the plate and closing the refrigerator door. "It's good to see you—it's been too long."

"I've been busy."

"With the shop, I know." He nods, his tone telling me what a struggle it is not to say more.

I offer him a thin smile and shrug. "So, who were you playing with today? Mr. Rhinehardt?" It's an innocent question.

He sinks a fork into the cake. "Not today. This round was with some guys from the office," he finishes, bringing a forkful to his mouth and moaning as he gets his first taste. I look away because nobody needs to see their dad make that face.

"What are you up to today?" he asks around his bite.

"Nothing much. Had two new clients call in." Clearly, my marketing efforts are working because new people are calling for appointments every day. "And, uh, I had kind of an interesting conversation with the guy who owns the brewery next door," I say as casually as possible.

I take a seat on a stool at the kitchen island across from Harry, not allowing myself to look at his face until I'm fully seated. There's that small part of me that's still afraid of what I'll see. When I finally lift my eyes, my breathing falters because his face has gone stony.

"Why in God's name would you put yourself in a room with that criminal? It's bad enough you're right next door, Hollis!" His eyes narrow, and his jaw locks tight. "He didn't hurt you, did he?"

What? "No! Why would you think that?" Good lord, I never thought I'd see the day when I'd be defending Cash

Brooks's honor, but here we are. "He might be grouchy, but he's no criminal." Unless grinding his hard-on into my clit is a criminal offense, in which case, bring on the handcuffs. Dammit!

"*Oh, Holls,* you're way too trusting. The man has a criminal record, and he took advantage of your sister!"

"Wait, what?" I wrinkle my nose. I'm going to kill Hadley. "I'm talking about *Cash Brooks*, the owner—well, one of them. Are you talking about Miller?" Who didn't, in fact, take advantage of anyone, by the way. One issue at a time, I guess.

"Yes, of course. He's not going to get away with this, even if the law is *technically* on his side."

"Whoa, slow down, Harry." Does no one in this family communicate?

He's shaking his head, so I hurry on before he can cut in.

"Miller didn't do anything to Hadley." My brows draw tight, and I look him straight in the eye. "I talked to him, and it was all pretty innocent—just a few kisses. Hadley made it up because he hurt her feelings. That's all. I'm sure if we just sit her down—"

Before I can continue, he drops his fork to the countertop with a *clang*. "He lured your baby sister into trusting him and laid his hands on her! She's an innocent child!"

I so do not want to be the one to break it to Harry that his little angel disposed of her V-card two years ago and has never looked back.

"I know Hadley's upset, but Miller said they never even dated and certainly never…" I make an ambiguous hand gesture, hoping he gets my meaning. The words "Hadley" and "sex" in the same sentence might have his ears pumping steam like a cartoon character, so I can't imagine what a more precise hand gesture might elicit.

"These predators always lie," he insists, his tone communicating that his word is the last on the subject as he picks the fork up again. His paunch is becoming a bit more pronounced these days, I notice.

"I *really* don't think he is, Harry, but they're both adults," I insist, the full implications of this misunderstanding thudding like a brick in the pit of my stomach. "And on the off chance I'm wrong, it's important for you to know Miller Brooks does *not* own the brewery. *Cash and Carter* Brooks own the Blue Bigfoot and have nothing to do with this, apart from being related to Miller." I need to get this message across loud and clear if there's even the slightest chance he's involved in this health inspector fiasco. Then I can worry about Miller's neck.

But Harry's not listening. "Don't believe a word that bastard says." He picks up his plate of barely-touched cheesecake and strides to the sink where he tosses it inside. I hear the plate shatter. "Now he's got *you* wrapped around his finger too."

"No, he doesn't! He's just a kid—like Hadley. When Hadley gets home, we can—"

Harry whips around and points at me. I can't remember a time when I've seen him so angry. "He's *nothing* like Hadley—or you. He's a predator who put his hands on a young girl, and he *will* pay the consequences for that."

My pulse is a bass drum in my ears. Nothing I say is making the slightest dent. My fears are being realized—his words are all but a confession, aren't they?

"What did you do, Harry?" My voice comes out as a

croak over the lump in my throat, my fingers sweating as they grip the edge of the marble countertop.

He watches me for a long moment and then exhales, his shoulders losing their tension as he approaches the island again. He pauses there, gathering his composure. "It's nothing you need to worry about. We can talk more when your mother and I get back from our vacation. And I'm sorry I raised my voice."

"Harry."

"When you're a parent, you'll understand, Hollis. Until then, leave it to your mom and me, okay?"

"No!"

His brows arch as I spring to my feet.

"Even if you don't believe Miller—or me—leave his family out of it. Please tell me you're not taking this out on them by using some of your connections like you did with Mr. Rhinehardt."

His head jerks back. "What is *that* supposed to mean?"

Shit, I've gone too far. His stubbornness multiplies like horny rabbits when he's being challenged.

"I don't *use* anyone, Hollis." His lips thin. "Unlike some men."

This is careening off the cliff faster than I can pump the brakes.

"Harry—"

He cuts me off again. "This conversation is finished. You're simply going to have to trust that I know what's best for this family." With that, he strides from the room, leaving me with nothing to do but assume the very worst.

Well, that and shove an enormous slice of cheesecake into my mouth. Sometimes a girl just needs to eat her feelings, okay?

CHAPTER
TEN
SO SO BAD

CASH

"I KNOW I've been a bad girl." Hollis lifts her eyes to me from the spot where she's kneeling at my feet. She gently grips my balls with one hand while the other slides up my stiff cock, and the soft skin of her thumb brushes my most sensitive spot, just beneath the tip.

I groan and thread my fingers through her silky blond hair. "You've been so, so bad," I respond, hardly recognizing my own voice.

The corners of her mouth curl seductively as she gazes up at me. "Let me make it up to you."

Her chin falls, and I feel the hot rasp of her tongue over the head of my cock before it's enveloped by her damp lips. I drop my head back, my fingers twisting in the curtain of silk as I hold her exactly where I need her.

"Fuck. Hollis."

Her tongue sweeps the underside of my shaft before she takes me in her mouth again, pulling me deeper this time. I don't think I've ever been this hard in my life.

"Just like that," I moan as her lips and tongue glide up and down my cock, setting a rhythm that has starbursts exploding behind my eyelids. This is next-level head.

"Where are your glasses?" I inexplicably ask. Is that even my voice? Shut up, you jackass! Who cares where her fucking glasses are?

She releases my dick with a pop, and I gaze drunkenly down at her. Her full tits are visible now, tipped with tight pink nipples that brush my thighs as she moves to stand.

Hell yes. The only thing I want more than this blow job is to sink deep inside her and get a taste of her skin.

But as I release her hair and move to cup her breasts, something tickles my nose, and I swipe at it, smacking myself in the face and jarring myself awake.

I blink rapidly, barely catching sight of the retreating black and white tail before it disappears into my closet.

I exhale a heavy groan and lift the covers to see the tent in my boxers. It takes my bloodless brain a few seconds to recall that I just had a sex dream about Hollis Hayes.

Shit.

This is not what I need right now.

"No!" I scold my penis. "Stop getting ideas, you asshole."

There is way too much shit to deal with to waste any time having these kinds of thoughts about my neighbor. I drop the covers and glance over to the bedside table to see the clock showing 6:26 a.m.

Since I know I won't be falling back asleep, I may as well get in a run and maybe a workout. If I exhaust my body, it won't have any energy left for inappropriate thoughts and hard-ons.

Five minutes later, I've tamed my unruly cock, and I'm pulling the back door of the house closed behind me. The house is part of a small, hidden enclave of older homes with property backing up almost to the Blue Ridge Parkway in East Asheville. Its elevation is a thousand feet higher than the city proper, but we don't have the sweeping views like the multimillion-dollar homes dotted along the mountain ridges. Instead, our view is of the forest, but we've got hiking trails, good neighbors, and it's only a little over twenty minutes to get downtown.

Developers come sniffing around now and then, but the land is useless unless all the families agree to sell, and that ain't happening in my mama's lifetime—or Adrina's and Wes's. Not to mention our neighbor on the other side, a reclusive old guy named Winston, who we only glimpse when he's smoking his pipe and birdwatching out on his back deck—usually in just his skivvies.

When we were kids, we used to explore everywhere, actively trying to get ourselves lost in the woods so we could be real adventurers. But our dad would always find us somehow, particularly when there were chores that needed doing.

A smile crosses my lips at the memory as I veer right, my feet pounding the path of a well-worn hiking trail near the property. Everyone apart from Mango was still asleep when I slipped out, and I knew Mama would be happy when she spotted Carter's car in the drive. I didn't even hear him come in last night and climb the creaky steps to the attic.

I formed the beginnings of a plan before I nodded off last night, the first step of which will have me waiting outside the Health and Human Services office when they open at nine.

The more I think about it, the more I'm convinced this is either some huge mistake or, more likely, it's Hollis's work after all. But if it takes me admitting she's the biggest evil genius in the state to make her undo whatever she'd done, I'll happily do it. That girl is operating on a level I can't hope to match, as much as I enjoy torturing her.

The inspection citations themselves are absurd. I've been working in bars and breweries for most of my adulthood, and I've never seen this level of bullshit. Once I show up at their office with all my paperwork, this will be over.

A robin swoops down a few feet ahead of me as I round a corner going downhill, and I take it as a sign that everything will work itself out by the time Blue Bigfoot's doors open at noon.

TURNS out robins aren't great predictors of luck.

It appears the inspector who came to Blue Bigfoot is a regional manager or some shit and doesn't even work out of the county office. There was something else about an anonymous tip and new standards rolling out, and basically a bunch of words that only amounted to one thing. I am up shit's creek with no paddle, no life vest, and no fucking clue how to swim.

"Anonymous tip," I mumble to myself as I push through the department's doors and stalk out to the parking lot. I'll bet my last dollar Ms. Anonymous has a first name starting with H and a wicked penchant for driving me nuts. The funny thing is I actually believe her that she doesn't want to ruin my business. A few hours of sleep gave me a little perspective on that. But that doesn't mean she didn't make the call that sent the dominoes falling—even if her only intent was to have me suffering a few moments of panic.

It's time to tell Carter.

I know it is.

But whatever is going on with him is obviously messing with his head. The Carter I know is self-assured and charming, wicked smart, never impulsive, and a magician when it comes to managing conflict. He uses one hand to distract you with how sincere and forthright he is while the other one pulls everyone's strings like a puppet master manipulating the situation to his desired end. I'm not saying he's selfish. He just knows exactly how he wants things and how to get there. That's why he'd make a great politician.

But that Carter is temporarily on vacation while this new one wanders around distractedly in the same clothes for days, disappears at random, and doesn't seem to be concerned with cause and effect. His slick bullshit used to bug the hell out of me when we were kids, so I don't know why I'd wish for its return. Yet, I do.

No, if I involve him, it could end up being the straw that breaks that disoriented camel's back.

And then there's the other part.

The part I didn't tell Hollis.

The part Carter witnessed and will throw back in my face, as well he should.

When I said I clocked Hollis's stooge the moment he walked into the brewery, I meant it. I was sure that guy was a fake, and I wanted nothing more than to shove it in her face that she couldn't pull one over on me.

Which, unfortunately, means I didn't treat that guy with one iota of the respect I would have if I'd known he was the real deal. In fact, I acted like a complete asshole and lunatic. I cringe at the memory of me telling the guy we only piss in the fermenter a couple times a week. Shit.

Hollis has me so wrapped up in our little war—in besting her—that I forgot about the number one priority—the brewery. That's all that matters because that's what my family needs. Not one-upping the neighbor, or making out with her, or dreaming about her sucking my cock. I let her pull my eyes off the prize, and that's nobody's fault but my own.

I don't want to admit to Carter that my own arrogance is what ultimately got us into this mess.

I pull the report from my back pocket and unfold it as the March breeze ruffles the papers in my hands.

This is my reality now, and I need to face it. It's like they say, the way to eat an elephant is one bite at a time.

In addition to the trumped-up violations in staff hygiene, contaminated draft lines, and temperature inconsistency, they're demanding a list of equipment replacements.

Water filtration system upgrade. That one will cost us around four grand.

Installation of a keg-washing system. As if doing it by hand is somehow unusual or unsanitary. Six grand.

Replace low-temp dishwasher. Another six grand.

Run new lines for soda and kegs, new cooler gaskets, replace drain grates. Those will add up to a couple-k.

Replace glycol chiller. Which rounds us out to about twenty-five-k with a five-k price tag.

And, oh yeah, bi-monthly pest control I don't even want to think about since the once-a-month package we have now is already costing me two thousand dollars a year.

I skim a few more notes I made and then do the math again, but it tells me what I already know.

Denny can help with some install if he's got the time, and I can ask my old boss down at Rabid Rocker Brewhouse if he's got a bead on any second-hand equipment or deals. Assuming I can scrape a few bucks off by using personal contacts and picking up some gently used gear, it's still gonna be at least twenty or twenty-one grand.

My fingernails scrape my chin as I run my hand over it. Where in Drunk Larry's name am I gonna magically come up with that kind of cash?

I wonder for a second how much my car is worth but then glance up at it sitting in the parking lot with duct tape on the side mirror and rust creeping up from the underside. Scrap that.

I should get back to the brewery. Oscar's not due in for another couple hours, so I left Miller a note to let himself in if I wasn't back and Cart was MIA. I ran through the alarm system with him last week, but I'll probably be getting a call from the security company any minute now when he trips the alarm.

But I can't go back there and stand in the middle of the dream I worked my ass off to build, knowing I'm doing nothing to save it.

No, that's not me. I've never taken anything lying down, and I'm not starting now.

"You think you can break me?" I ask the clouds above. "Not today."

Twenty minutes later, I'm driving by the firehouse Denny and the rest of the water rescue crew use as their home base, so I decide to pull in.

"Yo!" the man himself yells from one of the bays, a net

bag of PFDs over his shoulder. Denny should have been born in the water for all the time he spends on it.

"Hey, man," I respond, climbing out of my driver's seat and closing the distance between us. "You doing exercises today?"

He throws a thumb back toward the open bay. "Got a couple new volunteers, so we're gonna throw 'em in the deep end." If his grin is anything to go by, I feel sorry for the poor souls.

"Yeah? Then I won't keep you. I need to run a new filtration system and a few other things down at the bar the last week of the month, and I wanted to hit you up— see if you've got some time."

He shrugs. "I don't see why not. Rosie's busy as hell with her new job and her Etsy shop, so she'll most likely appreciate me getting out of her hair."

"Okay, cool. Thanks, man. I'll let you know when I have more details." Denny is generally handy, and it's not a one-person job. I'm not about to ask Carter.

"How much does it pay?" Denny straightens and squints at me, but I've still got him by three years and maybe an inch or two in height.

"Beer, same as last time."

"Just checkin'." He shrugs, hitting me with the same shit-eating grin he used when he and Rosie's brother, Luca, tried getting me to buy beer for them as teenagers.

One of his coworkers calls his name, and he takes off for the truck with the life vests and a two-fingered wave in my direction.

"Thanks, man!" I yell after him.

I still need to stop at Rabid Rocker to see if I can get a few contacts, and then I'll head back to the brewery to make calls.

See, I can totally manage this on the down low. Nobody needs to know what's going on until it's over—just a few improvements that I can pretend aren't costing me a boatload of green I don't have.

At least I'll have my head buried in so much work I won't have time for even a glance Hollis's way.

I knew there had to be a silver lining in there somewhere.

CHAPTER
ELEVEN

THERE'S A SCIENTIFIC NAME FOR THAT

HOLLIS

"HADLEY, if you don't call me back, I swear I'm cutting up all those tiny shirts you call dresses!" I whisper-hiss into my phone just as the bell rings above my door. "Call me!"

I shove the phone under the counter and paste on my best customer service smile. "Hello! Welcome to Happy Tails Salon."

The woman doesn't hear me, however, because she's distracted pulling on a leash while one foot holds the door open.

I rush over, still planning Hadley's murder in my head. After the blow-up with Harry last night, I left him a note asking him to reconsider and to call me. It seems my entire family is ignoring me now.

I grab the frame of the door. "Here, let me hel—" But my mouth freezes when I catch sight of the animal straining on the other end of the leash. "Is that a skunk?"

"Why, yes," the woman says, turning to me with a

friendly smile and shock after shock of curly brown hair poking out from beneath her knitted cap. "Mango's just a little shy sometimes, aren't you, my little baby?"

Mango? Oh, god. This is my one o'clock. "Umm," is all I can come up with. When she filled in the online client profile with "unknown" as the breed, I took that as universal code for a pit bull mix. Not a skunk.

The woman crouches down. "Come on, baby. I have a whole pile of sunflower seeds waiting for you when we're done," she coos. And she must speak skunk because the little critter trots his way right through the door, allowing his owner to scoop him up and stand.

"This is Mango," she says, beaming with pride and adoration. "And you must be Hollis."

I return her smile because, yes, she's a customer, but it's also not very often people stop to learn my name. I'm usually just the Happy Tails lady or the dog groomer or "hey, thanks."

"I am. It's nice to meet you…"

"Ginny," she fills in. "Ginny Brooks."

My smile drops like the Hindenburg.

Ginny Brooks laughs. "I can see you've met my boys."

I try to recover as gracefully as possible. "Yes, I have. They're very…" Dammit, there must be something redeeming to say about Cash. "… tall," I finish.

Ginny watches me, not trying even a little bit to hide her amusement. "Their father was six feet tall by the time he was fourteen. He passed a little over five years ago," she shares like she's telling me the temperature outside.

"Oh, I'm so sorry." God, Miller must have been all of sixteen. How awful. "I didn't know."

"Well, why would you, dear?" She shrugs and smiles down at the skunk nestled in the crook of her arm.

"Mango here loves a good bubble bath, so I thought I'd treat him to a spa day."

It's true. She booked the whole package—ultra smooth coat conditioner, doggie cologne, nail trim and polish, deluxe bow or bandana. Our "Doggie on the Town" special is our best-seller. I rent a small sign just outside the dog park advertising it, and my return on investment is huge.

I glance at Mango the skunk again. This is what I get for not reviewing the entire intake sheet *before* clients arrive. I hurry behind the counter to bring up his form and file, and yup. Right there on the proof of vaccination letter from the vet it says, "Mephitis mephitis, (striped skunk)" Luckily, right under that, it lists rabies vaccinations going back three years.

Well, there's a first time for everything.

"So, is there anything I should know, Mrs. Brooks?" Typing fingers at the ready, I glance up again.

"Oh, call me Ginny. Well, let's see." She thinks for a few moments, giving me time to look for some sign of family resemblance. Maybe it's the smile. Or the chin? No. Cash's chin is much more square, masculine, sexy. And his lips, they're definitely fuller with a—

Ginny cuts off my musings. "He's a little temperamental," she begins.

I don't think I've met a new client that didn't meet that description, so my fingers stay still. "Okay."

"But he doesn't mean to be testy, I promise you."

I send her a reassuring smile. "Believe me, I understand. Most of them are like that." Note to self, watch the teeth.

Ginny purses her lips playfully. "I know. His father would do the same thing, and then ten minutes later, he'd get all affectionate, and it was just impossible to stay annoyed with him."

Wow. I've never met anyone who lived with one skunk, let alone a whole family. I have to admit, Mango is pretty darn cute with that pink nose and tiny white stripe running down the center of his face.

"But it's only because he's frightened—he's afraid to let people too close, you know what I mean?"

"Absolutely. No worries. Does he bite?" I've had a couple fear biters before, but I've found if I give them room and some time to get to know me, they relax.

Ginny laughs and leans closer. "I knew I'd like you."

My brows draw together at that response, but I interpret it as a "no" to the biting question and type that in.

"And how old is he? Do you know?"

"Well, I should hope so." She laughs again. "I was only in labor with him for forty-five minutes, but it's not somethin' a mother forgets. Even from the first day, he was trying to make things easier on me."

She sighs and settles in like she's preparing for a long ride. "Do you know he got his first job at fourteen bagging groceries? He'd spend his paycheck on treats for his siblings or stick some of it in the family rainy day jar when he thought we weren't looking. And he never once got in trouble at school. Not once." She taps the counter with an index finger. "When he was in high school, he'd help his dad doing repairs on the house on the weekends. Said he liked learning how things work, but I knew he was bein' sweet." She's looking at me like Michael B. Jordan himself just walked up behind me.

But my jaw is on the counter by this time, of course, my brain trying to play catch-up. "I'm sorry," I cut in. "But are you talking about… Cash?"

"Well, of course, dear."

"I…" That's all I've got.

She continues like she's delivering a sermon. "And then when his father passed, he was the one who made all the arrangements—wouldn't even let me set foot in the funeral home until the morning of the service. It was beautiful." Her head tilts back until she's looking at the pipes of my industrial ceiling. "And now he's got his own personal guardian angel up there, keepin' him out of harm's way."

Her chin drops down again, and her eyes meet mine; they're the exact same brilliant blue Cash's are. "Not that he doesn't do his level best to mess things up, mind you. Sometimes that boy is his own worst enemy." She sighs again and scratches Mango on the head before finishing, "He needs to take a break, enjoy himself, have some fun, you know what I mean?"

If I'm not mistaken, Cash Brooks's mom is trying to get me to bang her son. *Sweet Jesus.*

"Sure," I agree—not with the idea of my involvement, but yeah, it sounds like the guy could use some loosening up. Are all those things she said about Cash true?

"Well, I'm so happy we had this talk, and it's been such a pleasure meeting you. You're just as sweet and lovely as I knew you'd be."

"Uh, thank you." Where in the world did she get such a mental image of me? It certainly couldn't have been from Cash. I'd be unsurprised to learn that he refers to me as the devil incarnate—it's how I often refer to him, after all.

Ginny hands Mango over, and I'm surprised by how silky his coat is. And he's a snuggler. Who knew skunks were so cuddly?

"I'll be back around four. Thank you, Hollis!" she calls behind her as she scoots out my door.

I look down at my charge as I pet his tiny head. "Well, Mango, it seems we have a dilemma on our hands."

It's true.

We make our way to the grooming side of the salon, and I latch the swinging half-door before setting him on the floor to sniff around. As I'm sifting through my shampoo options—maybe coconut would be good—I let my mind go where I've been avoiding all morning.

I need to suck it up and help my neighbors with this health inspector fiasco.

It was bad enough when it was just Carter, Miller, and the other staff who my parents were messing with (Cash doesn't really count because the jerk genuinely thinks I'd stoop this low for the sake of a stupid rivalry). But now I've met Ginny, who apart from making way too many assumptions, seems like an extremely nice lady. And her husband—Carter and Miller's father—is dead! I'm choosing to believe Ginny slept with the evil mailman to conceive Cash.

I mean, come on! There's no way I can't step in and help.

Hadley, the little schemer, left for spring break this morning, and my parents decided it would be the perfect time to skip town themselves. So they're now on a plane to Lake Como. I'm pretending everyone's phones are stuck in airplane mode so my head doesn't explode all over my salon.

I pluck the bottle of coconut shampoo from the shelf and turn to help Mango into my tub. But he's not there, sneaky little boy.

"Mango?" No response.

He must be hiding behind the shelves.

Not there.

I peek into the tub in case it turns out he's as big a fan of baths as Ginny claims, but nope.

"Mango?" I call again. Crap. How have I lost Ginny's skunk in thirty seconds?

Not only is my family trying to ruin the Brooks' family business, but now I've lost their damn skunk! A thorough search of the entire shop comes up empty, and I'm approaching tears when I finally spy a tiny tuft of black fur stuck to the return vent. The return vent that I've never noticed until now is missing a screw in one corner.

Crap on a cracker!

I drop to my knees. "Mango!" I shout into the vent. "Come back!"

"Hollis?"

I nearly concuss myself on the corner of my grooming table when I turn to see who snuck into the shop without me noticing.

It's Carter Brooks.

"I heard you yelling. Something wrong?"

"Carter, thank god." I stand and hurry to the partition. "I lost your mom's *baby*."

"I assume you're not talking about my sister," he replies with more calm than the situation warrants.

"No, I'm talking ab—wait, you have a sister?"

He nods "Lynn. She's away at school."

"Huh. So there are four of you. Your mom's a braver woman than I thought."

"Five. I'm assuming you haven't met Denver yet." This is the most I've ever heard Carter speak, and I notice a set of identical dimples hiding behind his scruff. He could probably kill a girl with a good flash of those dimples in the right lighting.

"Five?" Ginny is a saint. Or crazy. Or maybe her

husband was just super hot and she couldn't help herself. By the looks of her boys, I'm thinking that might be my answer right there.

"You okay?" Carter asks, and it takes me a minute to snap out of it and remember my crisis—well, the latest one, at least.

"Oh! Right! I lost Mango." I grit my teeth, waiting for who knows what kind of reaction. But the one I get is most unexpected.

Carter laughs, and I swear angels start singing somewhere. I've never seen more positive energy from him than a half-smile in the last four months. Who knew he had all of *this* tucked away?

But this does little to solve my problem. "Why are you laughing?"

"Because my mama is the worst busybody in all of North Carolina. She brought Mango in for grooming?"

"Yes!" There's not enough space in my brain to dedicate to Ginny's ulterior motives or what mistaken impression she got about the nature of my feelings toward her son—which consist of a single feeling, just to be clear. A feeling that can be summed up in one word: violent. "And now I've lost him!" I get back to the point.

Carter simply shrugs, but his grin stays put. "He'll turn up. He always does."

"You're not even the least bit concerned that he could be sucked into the air conditioning unit or something?" I point to the vent and the evidence of Mango's jailbreak.

"Nah. He's probably next door scaring a customer by now."

"Oh my god," I mutter, pushing through the half-door and right past Carter on my way to retrieve the little troublemaking Mephite mephite, or whatever it's called.

It seems Carter follows in my path, because the moment I walk through the doors of Blue Bigfoot, his voice comes from right beside me. "See. Right there."

I follow the direction of his finger, and sure enough, Mango is perched on one of the barrels they use as drink tables, tearing up a coaster.

"Oh my god. Carter, thank you!" I step slowly toward the skunk, so I don't scare him away, and he allows me to pick him up with no fuss.

Carter looks at me holding the skunk and blinks a couple times before his face resumes the preoccupied expression I've come to know these past months.

"Hey, Carter," I say before he can retreat to the beer-making room—and into himself. Now is as good a time as any, I suppose. And since there's no way I'm dealing with Cash, it'll have to be Carter. "About that mess with the health inspec—"

"Hollis!" I'm cut off by Cash, who appears at his brother's side out of nowhere. I ignore him.

"As I was saying." My tone is pointed. "I need to tell you—"

"You don't need to talk to Carter," Cash butts in again.

Carter and I both turn to scowl at Cash. He looks ragged, those circles from the other day having taken over more real estate under his eyes.

"Mind your own business." I frown at him.

"We're just talking," Carter says in a slightly nicer tone.

"No. You can't te— No. I need to exp— Just… no," the maniac stutters and shakes his head.

Good lord. "Do you need a nap? Or maybe some warm milk. A pacifier?"

Cash shifts on his feet and opens his mouth for more

drivel to spill out, but Carter blocks him with his hand. "Hey, man, let the woman talk."

I perch my free hand on my hip in solidarity. "As I was saying, Carter," I begin again.

Cash's eyes flash wildly from me to Carter, then back to me again, and I can see the exact moment he comes to a decision about whatever has him blabbering all this nonsense. Unfortunately, his decision has him charging right up into my space—fully ignoring both the skunk in my arms and his brother two feet away—and attacking me with his mouth.

Here we go again.

CHAPTER
TWELVE

THAT'S MR. PRINCESS TO YOU

CASH

HOW DO I keep getting myself into this situation with this woman? When it was clear she was about to spill the truth to Carter, I was desperate to make her stop. And the only thing I could think of to shut her up was to make speech physically impossible.

Her lips are as soft and accommodating as I remember. I'm preparing for her hands to shove me away, but when her free one lifts to my chest, it gets distracted feeling me up. Just like my rational mind gets distracted by the feel of her warm breath over my skin. What is it that makes my mind stop functioning when she's nearby?

Before I know it, my arms snake around Hollis's waist and I'm pulling her to me. Her breasts settle nice and soft against my chest while I slide my tongue past her lips for a deeper taste. She moans into my mouth, and it has my dick standing at attention. He's such an easy mark.

I'm vaguely aware of someone muttering something nearby, but all my attention is centered on tasting Hollis's sweet mouth and running my hands over her hips and around to her ass. Images from my dream this morning surface, and the idea of Hollis on her knees in front of me, combined with the feel of her in my arms right now, has me damn near coming in my pants.

"Again?!" a loud voice pierces my consciousness, and Hollis pushes off my chest. "What did I ever do to you?" Miller grimaces at me from a few feet away, a broom and dustpan in his hands.

My eyes flash to Hollis, and she's glancing around the room, Mango hanging limply from her left hand at her side. Her cheeks go from pink to red when she finds a handful of customers grinning our way.

She pulls Mango to her chest with both hands and flees to the sidewalk.

I chase after her without thinking. "Hollis! Wait!"

She doesn't turn until we're right outside the door to Happy Tails, where she rounds on me and snarls, "What the hell was that? Are you trying to scar your family pet for life?"

I throw my hands up. "It was the only way I could think of to get you to shut up and scare Carter away."

"And why, pray tell, was that so important? Carter and I were having a perfectly nice conversation until you and your wanna-be-big-dick-energy entered the room."

"What is that supposed to mean?" Is she implying my dick is tiny?

"You stormed in like a whiny possessive boyfriend and—"

"No, I didn't," I interrupt.

"Whatever." She huffs and wrinkles her nose at me, tucking Mango into the crook of her arm. He smacks his lips in contentment. "If you must know, I was offering my help with the health inspection issue."

I cough out a humorless laugh. "Guilty conscience keeping you awake at night?"

"Better than the itch of genital herpes that's no doubt got you tossing and turning," she bites back.

"Funny." My hands hit my hips. "We don't need your help."

"Really?" Her free hand mirrors mine and her neck does that shifting thing girls do. "Why don't we ask Carter?"

"No!" I shout, lunging in her direction before I can stop myself.

She looks at me like I just invited her on a date to a sewage plant. "Did you suffer a head injury this morning?"

"No." My fingers rake through my hair in frustration. "Shit."

"What? Just spill it."

I inhale and hold it for a second. Then… "I haven't told Carter about the inspection being real."

"What?! Why not?" she screeches. A glance around reveals Oscar and Kelsie watching us through the glass doors to Blue Bigfoot's patio. They scatter as soon as they're made.

"I thought you guys were partners," Hollis continues as I guide her farther down the sidewalk and outside the scope of prying eyes. Miraculously, she doesn't bite me.

"We are. It's just… complicated."

She absently pets Mango's head, and the little traitor leans into her hand while she has a silent conversation with herself. This new evidence of multiple personalities is unsurprising. "Fine," she bites out. "I guess your relationship with your brother is none of my business."

"No, it's not. Thank you for recognizing that," I bite back with more aggression than I intended. "Now, if you'll run along and wash my mom's skunk, I'll get back to the mess you made of my life's work."

Her lips twitch. "I'll bet that's a phrase you never thought you'd hear yourself say."

I can't resist the hint of a smile that breaks through in response before sanity rushes back.

"Look." Her smile drops as well. "As much as I'd love to get out of your toxic splash zone, I can't."

"Oh? Already addicted to me?"

Hollis lifts a hand to cup her ear. "Sorry, did you just admit being 'a dick to me?' Admitting your problem is the first step."

"Leave." I point to her door.

"This is *my* sidewalk!" She glares at me and then straightens until she's a good inch taller. "I'm helping with your business issue if you want me to or not."

"We don't need your guilty conscience or your blood money."

"I'm a dog groomer, you chowderhead, not a warlord with a diamond mine."

"You know what I mean."

"Not really." She looks down her nose at me, which is impressive given our height difference. "You know I'll bet Carter would be happy to accept my offer." She moves to step around me, and I snake an arm out, grabbing her by the waist.

"Wait."

"Yes?" She tilts her head, her hair sweeping her cheek and her tone sickly sweet.

"I'm not taking your money." She may have me over a barrel, but I need to be crystal clear about this.

"I'm not offering it."

"Then why are we still talking?" I should get a Nobel Peace Prize for not strangling her.

She shakes my arm off. "I was offering to help you with some marketing. You know, drum up a little extra business—earn some cash to throw at your problem."

"What do you know about marketing?"

Her jaw drops like I just suggested she do her Christmas shopping at Dollar Tree. "How do you think I'm killing it here?"

I shrug. "I figured mommy and daddy bankrolled you."

She purses her lips and mutters something about self-righteous dickheads before pasting on one of her saccharine-sweet smiles. "How much do you need to raise to make it go away?"

"Twenty-k. Minimum." I'm curious to see how she reacts to that.

Her eyes go round. "What? Twenty thousand dollars?" She bites her lip, and my fingers twitch.

I need to keep my focus, so I stare her down. "I don't think a bake sale is gonna cut it, princess."

Hollis straightens again, that familiar defiance back in spades. "You're on."

"This is pointless. I don't have time to waste." My hands go to the back of my neck where a tension headache is forming.

But she leans in and pokes my chest, leaving a burn I can't explain away. "Face it, *princess*. You're stuck with me."

This is possibly my greatest fear coming to life.

"And since you already mauled me in front of your brothers, no one will think it's odd we're spending time together."

I get another of those fake-ass smiles before she traipses past me, the ding of her stupid bell signaling her departure.

"That's Mr. Princess to you!" I shout to no one in particular. I'm beginning to lose it.

Hell, now that Hollis's back is up, she'll likely raise twice what I need just to spite me.

I should be welcoming all the help I can get, and if it were coming from anybody else... that's a lie. I'd have difficulty accepting help from anyone, but does it have to be Hollis?

I drop my hands and trudge back to Blue Bigfoot with a sigh of defeat.

But a tiny smile curves the corner of my lips without my permission when I remember her shocked expression as I went in for that kiss.

She's into me. I know she is.

I just need to remember she's the enemy.

CHAPTER
THIRTEEN
BALLS

CASH

"HEY, just to be clear, I wasn't moving in on your girl," Carter announces from across the bar top.

It's been two hours since fighting with Hollis on the sidewalk, and she hasn't stopped blowing up my phone since. I glance up from her latest incomprehensible text. "What?"

"Hollis," my brother clarifies.

I start to wave Carter off with a smart comment at Hollis's expense and stop myself just in time. Right. It's supposed to look like we're into each other now. "Oh. Okay, cool," I manage, dropping my eyes to my phone again.

"Everybody knows you two have had a thing for each other since she moved in."

"What?" I'm surprised my neck doesn't snap from the whiplash. "No, we..." *Shit.* "...Okay." My voice is strained. I can't help it. He's making this shit up to bait me, and I ain't fallin' for it—although screwing with me is unquestionably something the old Carter would have done, so that's something at least.

"You alright?" He leans in closer, elbows to the bar. If I'm not mistaken, he may have shaved this week.

"Yeah. Just distracted." I lift my phone as evidence before typing out a text.

ME:

> What is this supposed to mean?

HOLLIS:

> Exactly what it says. You can read, can't you?

ME:

> It would be just like you to make fun of people with disabilities

HOLLIS:

> We don't say "disability" anymore. It's "differently abled."

ME:

> Thanks for the TED Talk. And, yes, I can read. You, on the other hand, could use some help getting to the point.

HOLLIS:

> Good god.

My phone rings, and of course, it's the she-devil herself. "What?" I survey the taproom. The crowd today is decent for a Saturday, but I'm gonna need more than decent to raise the cash I need.

"You know, I still can't believe Ginny is your mother. You act like you were raised by vultures."

"I hear they're particularly industrious."

"They can smell rotting flesh from a mile away, and they regularly pee on themselves instead of bathing."

"Fantastic. You care to get on with it?" The only good thing about conversation with Hollis is that we're both fluent in sarcasm.

"It's marketing 101. Give the customer what *looks* like a great deal, and they'll hand over their money."

I signal Oscar to take the group of three who just sat at the bar, and I tuck the phone between my ear and shoulder as I grab three pint glasses for him. "What kind of deal are we talking about?"

"Free beer."

I pause with the last glass in my hand. "I thought we were supposed to be *making* money, not giving it away."

"We are, dummy. I'm sending you a link."

By the time I get off the phone with Hollis, I have to concede that her idea doesn't suck. The plan is to offer gift cards for customers to buy at the bar. For each fifty-dollar card they buy, they get a free beer on the spot. Then they can use their gift card instead of cash or credit on their next visit.

"How many times have you found an old gift card lying around that you forgot you even had?" She didn't wait for me to answer. "That's cash in your pocket. And even if seventy-five percent of people use the entire card's value, it will be AFTER you get the cash to pay for this urgent stuff. It'll be spread out over time."

It takes me all of fifteen minutes to upload our logo and order the cards for two-day delivery. If we can sell a hundred cards, that'll be five thousand bucks minus the cost of the free beers—which isn't all that much in raw materials.

I'm beginning to regret not making more of an effort

with Hollis from the start. If I had, I wouldn't be in this position in the first place, not to mention she might have shared her marketing ideas with me earlier.

After I wrap up with the gift cards and Hollis has mercifully stopped texting me, I make a couple calls to suppliers and do the payroll, mentally adding whatever's left over to what I've lovingly come to call the FUBAR Fund—since everything about this is indeed fucked up beyond all recognition. Then I tell Oscar I'm running out for a bit. I like to give him shit, but he's the most reliable guy I've ever worked with, and I'm not about to mess with his income. He and his wife have a baby on the way, and hearing him tell it, babies have expensive taste.

My old boss at Rabid told me about an auction taking place in two weeks that's supposed to have some equipment from a defunct brewery down in Henderson County. I shared a little of what's going on—mostly to get his take on the required upgrades—and he told me it was bullshit and to fight it. I told him I would if I had the resources or time and that he might want to watch his back too. Then I went to get an early look at the auction items to see if it's even worth bothering with.

The forty-minute drive is time well spent because they've got a practically new keg washer and a glycol chiller that'll do nicely. This brewhouse only did distribution—no taproom—likely because the location was terrible. Not much thru traffic and just far enough off Highway 64 to make it not worth the special trip. Particularly when Asheville is right up the road and is the second-biggest craft brewing city in the country, per capita. We've got a little over one brewery for every three thousand citizens, which tells me we North Carolinians are doin' something right.

My phone dings with a new text, and I know I shouldn't check it while driving, but I do anyway.

HOLLIS:

> I'm emailing you a short list of local musicians who will play your patio for tip money.

We've had Kelsie's band play a time or two, but it's hard to say if they helped or hurt business. Luckily, she's a better bartender and brewer's assistant than a singer. I've been meaning to find a group or two that'll be a good fit, but I only have so many fingers to plug all the holes in the dam.

And given that I have eighteen days left to save my brewery, I should probably show more gratitude for Hollis's help than I am.

Since I'm about to drive right past the senior center on my way back, I make an impulsive decision to stop so I can text Hollis back and pop in to say hi to Mama. Somebody needs to set the record straight with her about whatever the hell she's imagining is going on between Hollis and me.

ME:

Thanks

There. That oughta do it.

The dots dance in their little bubble for a good fifteen seconds, so I'm surprised when her response is so short.

HOLLIS:

???

ME:

What?

HOLLIS:

> That's what I was asking!

For the love of Larry. What the hell is she talking about now?

I get out of the car and shove my phone in my pocket.

The senior center sits in a low building surrounded by mature trees and a walking path. Mama's been working here since before my dad passed, and she rarely misses a day. We always say she's a good fit because the only person who likes talkin' more than her is an elderly individual in need of a listening ear.

Plus, it keeps the rest of us sane when she gets one of her "grand ideas." She's planning a day trip in April to try catching sight of Bigfoot over in Dupont State Forest. Better the senior citizens than me. I may be fond of the concept of Bigfoot—hell, we named the brewery after him —but I'm a bit too practical to take all the lore seriously. I leave that for Mama.

I find her in the activity hall stacking chairs and talking to a short girl with dirty-blond hair in a painter's smock.

"Hi, darlin'. What are you doing here?" Mama sets a chair down and greets me with a kiss on the cheek.

"Just driving by and thought I'd pop in." And have a word with her about how Mango made his way into Hollis's arms earlier today.

"Cash, have you met Lizzie? She runs the art program here."

I offer my hand, but Lizzie raises her palms. They're covered in blue paint. "Unless you want blue hands, I'll just go with a wave."

"The guests absolutely love Lizzie." Mama beams.

"They love painting naughty pictures, that's what they love," the girl responds with a mischievous grin.

No wonder they get along.

I pick up the chair my mother abandoned. "Listen, can I have a quick word?"

We both nod goodbye to Lizzie before she waves again and walks away. I do a double take when I see she's got a huge green palm print on the ass of her jeans.

"Her boyfriend plays for the Arrows," Mama explains, though it does little to clear anything up. "What's up?"

I drop the chair on top of the stack and reach for another one.

"It's about…" Damn, how am I gonna maneuver through this? "Hollis." I go with the direct method.

Mama's smile ratchets up to an eleven. Terrific. "She is such a doll. I took Mango in for a spa day earlier, and I can see why you fancy her so much. Do you know he smells just like a pina colada now?"

"Yeah, uh, about that." I don't want Mama getting her hopes up—she's been on me to make more time for my personal life for years, and she's the type who gets invested fast. She's even cozied up to a couple of Miller's past hookups—hell, she went Christmas shopping just this past December with one of his exes.

I swear, if Denny and Rosie ever break up, she'll likely make such a fuss they'll get back together just to shut her up.

"It takes a special person to work with animals," she informs me as she starts on a new stack of chairs. "You need great patience, not to mention the capacity for unconditional love."

Like a band-aid, I tell myself. "Mama. Hollis and I are not together."

She halts and turns to me. "Well, I know that."

"You do?"

She lets out an amused huff. "Of course. You're both 'tryin' before you're buyin'' and all that."

Dear god. The air quotes somehow make it even worse.

"Okaaaay." I stall and grab the last two chairs at once while I choose my next words. "But… I'm not really in the market for… buying. Or trying, for that matter." Who has the time?

"We'll see." She folds her arms over her chest.

"No. No." The metal chair legs thump on the linoleum as they drop back down. "There are no… sales transactions happening. No transactions of any kind, in fact." My tone is meant to brook no arguments, but it has no effect on her.

"Well, it's like your dad used to say, sometimes you have to spend money to make money, and you can't very well do that without transactions of some kind, can you?" she replies as if I'm instinctively supposed to follow her train of thought.

"Are we still talkin' about women?"

She ignores my question. "Did you know that Lizzie and Gunner met when they were locked in a basement together by chance?"

"How could I possibly know that?"

"Sometimes things just happen." She shrugs. "All I'm saying is you should be open to the unexpected. Maybe try somethin' new. Not knowing the outcome when you try somethin' is the best part! And while you're at it, maybe let some of those balls you're juggling fall to the ground. They're not gonna break."

Ha! Easy for her to say! How does she think the leaky

pipes get fixed, or the gutters get repaired, or Lynnie's car insurance gets paid?

But there's no point in arguing, so I don't. Instead, I take a breath and let it go. "Wait, is Lizzie dating Gunner Nix?" He's the star of our new Major League team here in Asheville.

"Of course." She says this in a way that is quintessentially Ginny Brooks. She doesn't care if you're LeBron James or the street sweeper; she'll treat you the exact same way.

"Holy shit." I drop the last two chairs on a stack.

"Holy orgasms is more like it—but you didn't hear it from me."

"Don't. Please. I beg you."

Her hands go to her hips this time. "Despite what you might think, I know more about sex than you young people do."

"Can we not?"

"You're the one who brought it up." She waves me off and steps over to a rolling cart topped with a home theater projector.

"Fine. Whatever." I follow her. "Look, I just don't want you to be disappointed when Hollis and I go our separate ways. That's all." See, I followed an impulse in stopping in here—just like she's encouraging me to do—and look where that got me.

The soft smile is back. "That's awfully sweet of you to be concerned, but everything will work out how it's supposed to." She says this with the confidence of a genuine psychic.

I don't understand how she thinks this way. "How can you say that with any conviction? I mean, with everything life has dealt you?" I spend every day just trying to prevent the other shoe from dropping. How does she escape worrying about it?

"A loving marriage, five wonderful kids, food on the table, the sun above, and more friends than any one person can ask for."

"You know what I mean."

She stops fussing with the projector cord and grabs both my hands in hers. "Darlin', your father dying doesn't take away from the relationship we shared. I wouldn't trade my life for anyone's."

My throat gets thick, and I don't know what to say, except, "Love you, Mama."

"I love you too, Cash." She gives my hands one last squeeze and then picks up a red envelope. "Now, *Boogie Nights* isn't gonna return itself to Netflix. I need to drop this with the morning mail."

Aaand that's my cue to get back to the evening shift at the brewery.

HOLLIS

"HAVE you ever seen that movie *The Full Monty*?" I glance over at Cash from the driver's seat of my mom's Escalade. I figured she wouldn't care if I borrowed it—especially when she's having a grand old time in Italy, drinking wine and eating all that amazing food.

Cash's eyebrows almost meet in the middle as he searches for an answer to the very simple question.

"Don't hurt yourself. It's just a question."

I'm on high alert this morning after Cash's unsettling text from Saturday. Hearing the word "thanks" from anyone else wouldn't send me into the same tailspin his text did. He's obviously trying to lure me into a state of false security. That must be it, because the alternative is too bizarre to contemplate. Cash Brooks being civil and polite? Ha! There will be igloos in Satan's fiefdom before that happens.

"Is it a Monty Python movie? I thought I'd seen all of

those." He's still rubbing those two brain cells together in the passenger seat.

"There's no python, just monty." I wave a thank you to a driver who lets me merge onto I-26.

"Wait, you've never heard of Monty Python?" He sounds like I just told him I'm a flat-earther.

"Don't be a moron. Of course I have. 'My hovercraft is full of eels,' isn't yours?" I glance his way again.

He looks mildly impressed, despite the effort I'm positive he's expending to hide it. "No. I've never heard of the other monty thing. Why?"

"Hear me out." I'm not being serious—well, not entirely—but we've been driving in silence for the last ten minutes, and I'll lose my mind if I have to endure one more minute of a stewing Cash Brooks. If I thought an irritated Cash was unbearable, a pensive one is much worse. Who knows what's lurking inside that demented mind? This would have been so much easier with Carter.

"It's about these guys in the UK who are laid off and hard up for money, so they decide to put on a male review to raise a bunch of cash."

"A male review? What is that?"

I try and fail to suppress my grin. "A strip show. Fully naked, a.k.a., 'the full monty.'" An exaggerated eyebrow wiggle punctuates my explanation.

"Have you lost your mind?"

Ah, welcome back, irritated Cash.

"What?" I check my blind spot and change lanes. "Carter's hot. And Miller's got that bad boy thing going for him. It could totally work." There's no way I'm verbalizing any of my thoughts concerning Cash's general hotness. My thighs clench every time my mind flashes to those two kisses we shared. My vibrator has been getting quite the workout this week—even though I curse myself every single time I pull her out.

I look over again so I can enjoy Cash's cringe face, but it's more offended than irritated now.

"What do you mean, 'Carter's hot'?" He mocks my voice and does a crap job of it.

"Just what I said. He's hot." I shrug, knowing the more casual I sound, the deeper the creases in his forehead will get. "You know, smoking, tasty, fine, highly doable, stupid hot, boinkworthy, bangdorable." I tick them off on my fingers, abandoning the steering wheel for a moment. "Have you seen the man's dimples?"

"Enough. Okay, I got it! *Jesus*. Watch the road, will you?"

It's impossible to hold my laughter in.

"Let's just pick up this dishwasher and be done with it," he groans.

Before I went to the shelter yesterday for my usual Sunday animal fix, I stopped by the brewery to pay a pretend visit to my pretend boyfriend. Well, that and discover the subtext of his "Thanks" text. I overheard Cash on the phone trying to borrow a truck to pick up a used industrial dishwasher he'd found through someone or other. And since my parents are out of town, their vehicles are just sitting at the house. I told him it would be no big deal to borrow an SUV and help him out before opening time at the salon today.

After the expected initial protests, he agreed to the ride but insisted on paying for gas. I told him he was every woman's dream come true.

So here we are on our way to Weaverville for said appliance, and it could be going better. I shouldn't be riling him up just because I'm feeling out of sorts. But…

"What's the matter, Cash? Jealous of your big brother?"

He answers with a loud scoff and turns the radio up. "Someone You Loved" by Lewis Capaldi is playing, and you can't not sing along to that.

When the song ends, the deejay starts talking, so I turn it down again.

"Your voice doesn't suck," Cash mutters.

My gut reaction is to bite back with a smartass comment, but instead, I glance over to check his expression. He's looking out the window so I can't see it.

"What was that?" I need to see his face to figure out how to take his comment.

When he turns, some of his armor has dropped. It's unnerving. "I said you have a nice voice."

Damn, he's handsome. But he looks tired again. I have the strangest urge to reach over and squeeze his arm—but I don't, of course.

What I do instead is repeat the same word that's had me feeling discombobulated since Saturday. "Thanks."

We fall silent again, but this time I'm not feeling as apprehensive.

Cash gives me more directions, and we pull up to a warehouse with a few semi-trailers and a handful of vehicles parked outside. He lifts his butt from the passenger seat and pulls out a wad of bills from his back pocket.

"Where did you get that?" Despite what I know he thinks of me, I'm not used to having stacks of cash hanging around. Spending half my childhood moving around and existing in a constant state of financial insecurity, I have a complicated relationship with money.

He opens the door and shoots me a smile so unexpected it strikes me speechless. When he adds a wink, I worry I might pass out. "Robbed a bank. Keep the car running," he teases before shutting the door behind him. I watch his ass in those jeans until he disappears inside a large open bay. Only then do I gasp for oxygen.

Damn, that boy is fine. I'd never admit it to him, but he's more attractive than all his brothers put together—of that, I'm confident, even if I haven't met one of them.

I pull my phone from my purse to see if Hadley finally tried reaching me. I still haven't managed to get my parents on the phone either, and even if I manage to, there's no reason to think things will go any differently from the last time I pleaded with them.

My complete and utter distraction means that I jump in my seat and squeak when Cash knocks on my window a few minutes later. "Can you open the back?"

I nod and jab at all the buttons until I get the right one. *Let's keep it together, Hollis.*

After a series of grunts and groans, Cash and another man manage to get the giant appliance into the back of the Escalade and close the tailgate.

"All set?" I ask when Cash returns to the passenger seat. My voice is awkwardly cheery, overcompensating for my freakout from minutes ago.

"Yup," is all he says, so I put the car in reverse and begin the drive back to the River District.

But of course I can't stay quiet. "So, where *did* you get that money?" It had to be several thousand dollars.

"I told you," he responds in a teasing tone, but he's not looking at me.

"Haha. I know you didn't rob a bank because I read the news every morning and there haven't been any reports of flannel-clad bank robbers."

This gets a ghost of a smile from him. "If you must know, I sold something."

"What did you sell?"

"Do you always ask this many questions?" He's come full circle to irritated Cash.

I frown as I make a left at a stoplight. "Sorry. Jeez. I'm just making conversation."

"Well, I'd rather not talk about it if that's okay with you."

Crap. I hope it wasn't something sentimental. Is he over there thinking again? The boy is going to hurt himself.

Oh, God, please don't let it be something his dad left him. What if it is? I'll have to find out what it is and then hunt it down at some shady pawn shop. I'll send Hadley the bill.

Since he's not sharing, I switch to something else. "So, we can cross dishwasher off your list. What's next?"

This gets his attention.

"There's an auction for some equipment from a foreclosure down in Henderson County the weekend after next. I went and checked it out the other day, and they've got a keg washer and a glycol chiller that'll work. The only problem is I need cash for it."

And he doesn't have anything else to sell. He doesn't need to say it.

"Okay, then we'll raise the cash. Those gift cards are coming in today, so you can start there. Then we can move on to phase two."

"I'm sure I'll regret asking, but what is phase two?" He raises a hand up between us. "And if it involves my brothers getting naked in public, you can just quit right now."

The look on his face has me laughing out loud. "We can

table public displays of penises for now, but what about a different kind of sausage fest?"

"Just kill me now, will you? I'm not sure I'll survive this project together."

I'm feeling oddly optimistic. "Chin up, Mr. Brooks. We're just getting started."

CHAPTER
FIFTEEN
PEACE OUT

HOLLIS

"I'M ALMOST THERE," Cash pants, sweat running down his temples.

"Hurry," I urge, my own voice breathless from exertion. "I don't know how much longer I can hold it."

"Come on, baby, just one... more... there!"

I collapse onto the floor of my office, chest heaving and body limp. Cash slides down the wall next to me and swipes a hand over his damp forehead.

"What happened to 'biceps of steel?'" He smirks at me, eyes twinkling in a way I don't find unattractive.

"I said I was used to lifting eighty-pound *dogs*, not gazillion-ton dishwashers."

We both look over at the giant appliance taking up my entire office. I offered to let him store the dishwasher here until he's ready to install it—or tell Carter what's going on, whichever comes first.

I'm supposed to open my doors in twenty minutes, but

a nap is sounding so much more appealing. Thank goodness Josh is coming in today.

I pry myself off the floor and go to the grooming area where I keep a stack of clean towels.

"Here." I toss one to Cash. He catches it with the ease of a guy whose control of his body is absolute.

"Thanks." That's two in under forty-eight hours. I might need to call the Guinness people.

I bring my towel to my neck and swipe it around so I can wipe the sweat from my nape. When I look up, Cash is watching me. And it's not in the casual way you might watch your grandma knitting a scarf. It's a look that says he's getting ideas Grandma would not approve of one bit. My thighs clench.

"So." I let my hair fall back in place and adjust my glasses. My good sense deserts me when he looks at me like that. "What do you think about my idea?"

"Your idea?" he asks in a distracted tone before blinking and focusing on my words instead of my neck—my neck that's covered in goose bumps now, thanks to him. "Oh, right. The sausage thing."

I wasn't kidding about the sausage fest. Well, not completely. Blue Bigfoot doesn't do food service, but that doesn't mean they can't, and they already have a popcorn machine and chips and salsa for purchase. So I figured a themed event with some easy-to-serve grub would be a draw and bring in more money. And I just happen to know somebody who considers herself quite the foodie. Or not.

"I thought I escaped the food scene?" Rylee complained when I called her last night on my way home from the shelter.

"No need to relive any nightmares, I promise. I just

need the name of that sausage place you said made an elk sausage that 'had you hot for an elk ride.'"

Rylee snorted. "You should hear what Dean said about the smoked wild boar sausage. Hold on. Lemme get the info."

Old staples with unique twists are all the rage these days. We can get fancy-sounding sausages made from elk, venison, bison—you name it—at a super reasonable price, then doctor them up with gourmet toppings and a nice roll and charge a premium. Rylee raved about stuff she got to try—goat cheese, bacon jam, figs, caramelized this, pickled that. Serve it with a side of chips and some tongue-in-cheek promo about sausages, and voilà! It's like free money. All we need is volunteers to prep, and I'm sure one of those strapping Brooks brothers knows how to work a grill.

"I think it's good. I just don't know that it's gonna get us where we need to be," Cash replies as he gets to his feet and unfolds his towel. He looks like Mr. January, fresh from chopping down a giant sequoia and ready to pose for his sexy calendar photo shoot.

I look away. "Maybe." Although it could be a great moneymaker over time, it is a lot to ask for a single day. And we're running out of time to raise cash for that auction. Twelve days is not long when you're talking about this kind of money.

I guess it's a good thing I dropped those earrings off with an appraiser even before I pushed my help on Cash. I'd fully intended to find a way to return them to my mom, but if worse came to worst, I figured it would be best to have money on hand to bail the guys out of this fiasco. Of course, that was before I knew how much they needed.

I know he thinks I'm made of disposable cash, but I

used my entire savings to open Happy Tails, and all my money is tied up in it, so I'm of little help. I mean, sure, I could scrape together a little bit, but I was counting on those earrings as our safety net if I couldn't get Harry to back off.

Although, convincing Cash to take the money will be like getting a cat to cuddle on your schedule instead of hers. Mr. Darcy's got nothing on Cash Brooks when it comes to pride. The man is beyond stubborn. Not to mention grumpy, self-righteous, inflexible...

He walks my way as he wipes his face and hair with the towel.

And so freaking hot.

I swear, the sight of Cash ambling my way with mussed hair and relaxed features has me picturing him stepping from a steam-filled shower in that towel and nothing else. I know if I glance down right now, my nipples will be waving hello through my top.

I'm proven correct when Cash homes right in on those little traitors. His eyes catch fire, and—why is it suddenly so hard to breathe?

It's time for that lecture I keep giving myself, but I'm having trouble remembering exactly how it goes. Something about bad ideas and not being stupid and not letting his lips distract me. I'll tell you, though, his lips are more perfect than Michelangelo's David statue, which damn near impossible, yet it's absolutely the case. But where David's lips are cold, solid stone, Cash's are warm, soft, supple. Such a delicious contrast to the bite of his scruff against my skin.

Just one tiny reminder will be no big deal. One press of my lips to his and I can lay this distraction to rest.

Just. One. Little...

I close the short distance between us, dropping my towel to the floor and driving my fingers through his sweat-dampened hair. His lips capture mine in a brutal kiss that's a far cry from the gentle taste I promised myself. He devours me. His tongue in my mouth, his stubble across my chin and cheek, his fingers digging into the skin of my hips and then sliding up my back to pull me roughly into him.

It borders on savage, and it could not be hotter. I have no control over my body. My fingers scratch and pull at his hair and his shirt while my legs try to climb up his thighs. He doesn't hesitate to grip my butt in both hands and lift me so my legs can wrap around his hips and bring his hard length up against my blazing core right where I need it.

I hear the clatter of metal hitting the floor, but I don't care what it is. All I care about is the hot pulse between my legs and the feel of his tongue as he feasts on my mouth. My back hits a wall, and Cash is peeling my legs from around him. I whimper into his mouth when I lose the pressure of his cock against my clit, but then his warm fingers push past the waistband of my leggings and panties, and he parts me.

"Fuck, you're wet," he groans against my lips, and I suck in a gasp as he circles my clit, and it swells to allow him access to every one of its nerve endings.

"Cash," I pant.

"Say it again," he demands, and when I do—I'm powerless over my body, my mind, everything—he gives me exactly what I need but couldn't find the words to ask for.

His fingers slide through my wetness, and he delves two of them inside me. My walls grip him, and my head drops back on a moan.

"Jesus, you're so tight." He strokes me long and slow while I squirm, grasping a fistful of his T-shirt in one hand and the strong curve of his shoulder in the other. But his arm around my back keeps me upright all on its own.

He's so solid and warm, and he smells like clean sweat and soap. A headiness flows through me as I let him take over and bend my body to his will.

"Cash," I moan again. It appears to be the only thing I'm capable of saying or doing while his fingers caress me and pull me into a pleasure trance. I can feel the hot tension building where he strokes in and out while his thumb tends expertly to my clit.

The pressure inside me intensifies the more he coaxes me with his hands and his voice. I'm throbbing everywhere at once.

"That's right, beautiful. Come on. Come all over my fingers. I want to feel you get there."

It doesn't take long for my body to obey, and I tip over the edge, white spots exploding behind my eyelids as I pulse wildly around Cash's fingers. My knees give out, my body sagging into his strong arm around my middle.

He milks my orgasm with his fingers until I can't take anymore. That's when I realize my eyes are watering, and my entire pelvis is undulating and tingling. As I lounge there like a noodle, waves of pleasure still echoing through me, I can hear Cash murmuring quietly against my temple. An overwhelming contentment washes over me, and I smile lazily into his neck.

That is, until a fuller comprehension of the situation starts to unfold in my addled brain. I think Cash Brooks just finger-banged me to the best orgasm of my life.

And if that weren't enough, when I blink to acclimate

my eyes to reality once more, he draws his head back to look at me, then pulls his hand from my panties and slides his two wet fingers into his mouth, sucking my taste from them while his eyes never leave my face.

My body bursts into flame again, and my head goes light.

A quick succession of knocking sounds has us both turning to the front of my shop. There's a woman in a visor and a sleek ponytail shading her eyes and peering into the store from the other side of my glass door.

I suck in a sharp gasp and send myself into a coughing fit as I choke on my own saliva and struggle to put my feet squarely under me.

I just let Cash put his hand down my pants and make me come in front of the entire city of Asheville! Well, sort of.

Talk about bad decisions—what the hell is wrong with me?

I stagger through the shop to the front door, after-shocks still making me twitch, and I hear what sounds suspiciously like a laugh coming from behind me.

"I'm so sorry. Did I catch you working out?" the woman asks in a cheery voice when I flip the lock and swing the door open. "Today is my cardio day too."

This time, I hear a guffaw.

I can only imagine what I look like, so I just nod weakly and usher the woman in. She goes on about a specific collar she's looking for, but I only hear half of what she says. Because the majority of my attention is stuck like Gorilla Glue on the man making his way toward us from the grooming area.

As if I need more proof that the universe is unfair, he looks like he just finished that calendar photo shoot and is on his way to bang his model girlfriend. How does he do that?

Cash graces my customer and me with a smile and a flash of those hypnotic blue eyes before throwing out a casual, "Thanks for the snack, neighbor. It was delicious," on his way to the door. It takes every ounce of control I have not to gape at him. Even more when he catches my eye over the customer's shoulder seconds later and casually throws up a peace sign—using the same two fingers that were just inside his mouth—and me.

I am in *so* much trouble.

CHAPTER
SIXTEEN

GOAT FARMERS CAN BE
SEXY TOO

CASH

HOLLIS IS AVOIDING ME.

I shouldn't be surprised. I'm sure she's been beating herself up all week for giving in to a moment of weakness with me in the back of her shop. She loves looking down her nose at me, so it's got to be killing her that she wants me. And now that I have intimate proof that her hot temper's got nothing on her hot body, I'm having trouble seeing the downside to exploring a little something on the side.

Everybody already thinks we're screwing, so why the hell not? I can keep the line drawn when it comes to Hollis, no problem. Inviting a fake, spoiled manipulator into your bed is one thing; letting her into your head—and your life—is another. I've got this.

Mama may assume something "unexpected" is sitting on the horizon when it comes to me and Hollis, but I know precisely how this will shake out. With each of us on our respective side of that wall, adding a few more orgasms to our spank banks. Back to business as usual.

That's why I'm game to go there with her—all the more after how hard she made me when she came like that. She is all fangs and claws until she comes undone, and it's a beautiful sight to see—and taste. I'm not sure how long I can wait to get inside her and feel all that velvet heat around me again. She can work her aggression out on me anytime she wants.

Especially now that I need the stress relief from all this shit with the brewery.

But Hollis hates that I've seen her come undone, so she's keeping her distance. For now. Not that she isn't still blowing up my phone, mind you.

My phone dings as if I telepathically reached through the taproom wall and nudged her.

HOLLIS:

> You know you need to come up with some sort of explanation for why you're doing all this extra stuff, don't you?

Oh, that's right. I almost let myself forget for a millisecond that she thinks I'm a moron.

ME:

> I got it covered.

Which I do, for the most part. I passed the gift card thing off as something I've been meaning to do for a long time. And the pub dog night—I refused to let Hollis call it a "sausage fest" on the flyers she printed up—is scheduled for tomorrow, which happens to be St. Patty's Day. Everyone agreed offering more substantial food on the biggest drinking day of the year was a smart idea. Of course, I let them assume we were doing it to lower our chances of too many drunk customers puking in our johns and passing out on our patio.

I'd almost forgotten about the holiday with everything that's been going on, and with any luck, we should raise a nice chunk of change from the drinks alone. We made a killing last year.

HOLLIS:

If you say so.

The woman trusts me even less than I trust Miller. She's an absolute control freak, which is just one more reason she's undatable.

HOLLIS:

What's everyone wearing tomorrow?

ME:

Clothes, I assume.

HOLLIS:

You should do stand-up. I mean, do you have themed shamrock shirts? Or at the very least, some green flannel?

I abandon our chat to serve a couple who just walked in. It's early afternoon on a Thursday, so it's just a skeleton crew. I'm cleaning draft lines, and Carter's lost in recipes, mash, and temperature readings, as usual. Cart's obsession with perfecting his art of brewing is the only reason I have any hope of pulling this thing off without him knowing. He trusts me with the books and the management, and I don't take that lightly.

Lucky for me, business has been great in general, and customers are loving the gift cards. The patio has also been filling up in the evenings now that the weather is mild enough for the propane heaters to keep it comfortable. And with March Madness starting, basketball fans are stopping by to catch the games on our taproom screens. We're by no means a sports bar, but just about everyone likes a beer with their basketball. And tomorrow will be our biggest day of the year.

Cart's been working for three months on a new session IPA to debut at our event, and I'm trying to convince him to open up a contest to let our customers pick the name. Hollis isn't the only one who can come up with ideas to sell beer.

He muttered something about the ignorant masses but didn't refuse outright. I've decided to wait him out until he realizes on his own that so long as the winning name has a sasquatch reference in it, it'll be as good as anything we came up with. I mean, this is the guy who wanted to name our signature ale "Big and Hairy."

I should get back to the draft lines, but I pick up the phone again instead.

ME:

> I thought you hated flannel.

She responds immediately, telling me she was waiting on my text.

HOLLIS:

> Hate is a strong word. I guess it's fine—if you're going for that mountain goat farmer vibe, that is.

That has me grinning as I picture her perched at that ridiculous pink counter, biting her lip and smiling at her own words.

It's been three days since I touched her, and I haven't had this many inconveniently timed boners since I was fourteen and the hot substitute took over our health class.

I decide to push my luck.

ME:

Are you done avoiding me?

HOLLIS:

Yeah, right. I happen to have a life that doesn't revolve around beer.

I'm crafting my smartass response when Carter rushes up to the bar looking like he's being chased by a disgruntled husband with a shotgun.

"Yo," I greet him, but he cuts me off.

"Get your shit. There's been an accident."

CHAPTER
SEVENTEEN
OFF THE DEEP END

CASH

BY THE TIME my tires squeal into the emergency room parking lot, Mama texts us that she's already there and Denny is on his way. But she doesn't include any update on Miller.

All I know is what Carter told me on the drive here—that Miller borrowed his car and got into an accident. The cops called Cart because his name was on the car registration. They said Miller was taken to the hospital by ambulance, but they didn't have any other news than that.

Mama's coming our way through the swinging doors to the treatment area when we walk into the ER waiting room.

"He's okay." She raises her palms and repeats herself. "He's okay."

The knot beneath my skull loosens at her words, and my brother and I release twin sighs. Mama looks more frazzled than I've seen her in ages, lines of tension clear around her mouth and eyes.

"He's just a little banged up," she continues as we all step aside for a couple EMTs. "Nobody else was hurt, thank the lord, but he ran a red light, it seems. He's grousing about the whole thing not being his fault, though, so we know there's no brain damage." She attempts a smile.

"Well, that's reassuring at least," Carter chimes in. "Fresh out of a car crash, and he's already shirking responsibility."

It's just like my baby brother to be so impatient he can't even wait for a traffic light to change. "He'll have to start owning up one of these days, so maybe today's the day." I can't count the number of jobs he's been fired from or commitments he's abandoned. And there's always some excuse—the boss is an asshole, someone changed the schedule, it's impossible, it's boring, my alarm didn't go off. It's why I didn't want to take him on at Blue Bigfoot, but I have to admit he hasn't messed it up yet.

Mama frowns at us. "Oh, leave him be. A little sympathy wouldn't be uncalled for right now. The boy does have a broken arm."

"Shit. He broke his arm? That means he won't be able to work St. Pat's Day." The words are out before I can censor myself.

"Are you honestly talking about the brewery when your brother could've been killed by some crazy person?"

"I thought you said this was his fault?" Carter's on it.

"Well, it might not be. How can we know for sure." She shrugs. "All right, let's go in and see him."

We follow her back through the doors and into a small room with a hospital bed surrounded by a bunch of equipment. It's a gut punch when I walk in and see the bandage on Miller's forehead and the abrasion along his jaw. But I cover it with a joke.

"Wow. I'm impressed they were able to fix you up around all that metal in your face."

"Haha. Ow! Damn, that hurt my lip." He examines an angry split in his lower lip with his fingers. His voice is hoarse, and it looks like he just went ten rounds with Manny Pacquiao. That sympathy Mama was talking about isn't hard to muster, but us Brooks kids have a natural talent for using humor and insults to push difficult emotions aside. Case in point, Cart's next comment.

"So, what is this? The second vehicle you've crashed in the last month?" His tone is light, so Mama doesn't smack him, but it does its job and riles Miller up. Another glimpse at the old Carter.

"Hey, my bike was a piece of shit, so that doesn't count." He points at Carter, the sleeve of his hospital gown gaping to reveal another long scratch along his bicep. "And there's something wrong with that car."

"Glad to see you're up to speed, little brother. The cops said it's totaled." Carter's tone isn't quite as light with the last part.

"I'm not talking about that—there was something wrong with it before you let me borrow it." Miller's hand goes back to his lip.

"Whatever you say, man. But it sounds more like there was something wrong with the driver, not the car. I should have told you to borrow Cash's car instead."

He's not wrong. My car is almost as bad as Miller's bike was. And the insurance money would have come in handy right about now—if I had more than liability, that is. Maybe I should update my policy and stage a crash for the insurance payout.

Nah, I'm not generally into fraud.

Mama fusses over Miller as we rib him a little more until Denny comes tearing into the room with Rosie on his heels. He's shaking, beads of sweat dotted across his forehead, and his eyes wild. Rosie's making hand signals from behind him that are impossible to interpret unless she is, indeed, trying to tell us she and Denny stopped to screw on the way here.

"Miller, oh god. What happened? Are you okay? What's wrong? What's broken? Have they checked for internal injuries?"

Oh, shit. Denny is goin' off the deep end.

"Darlin', I texted you he was fine," Mama reminds Denny in a soothing voice as she approaches and wraps an arm around his waist.

Well, I suppose we should have seen this coming. The only other time he's been to the hospital since our dad's death was when Mama had knee surgery a while back. We were all on edge to some degree, but the nurse had to give Denny his own bed because the guy was so close to passing out.

When our dad died—going into this same hospital for routine surgery and never coming out—we were all devastated, but Denny somehow took it worst of all. The rest of us eventually learned how to function while still grieving and keeping Dad in our hearts.

Denny, on the other hand? It fucked him up for years, so much so that he disappeared on us for almost four years, trying to forget he had any more family to lose. I did my best to intervene and coax him back, but it was Rosie who ultimately succeeded, and we're all indebted to her for it.

But it's unclear right now which brother I need to

worry about more, Miller or Denny. Even Miller picks up
on the vibe and lets Denny slobber all over him until a
nurse shoos us all out so she can take Miller to get his
arm set.

Mama's got her arm around Denny, whispering to him
as we walk back out to the waiting room. But the front
desk calls her over for some paperwork, so I take her
place.

Denny intercepts me, going for casual. But his voice is
jumpy. "Hey, man, how you doin'?"

I'm not buying it for a second. "You know he's gonna
be okay, right?" I drop a hand on his shoulder.

"Yeah, yeah, I know," he scoffs.

Rosie's biting her thumbnail as she watches Denny
from a nearby row of chairs. I wink at her, hoping she'll
stop worrying.

"You know Miller. He'll bounce right back." I give his
shoulder a playful shake. "How many scrapes has he got
himself into only to rebound the next day—even more of
an asshole than he was before?"

"Yeah." Denny ditches the bravado and looks over at
Rosie. I take my hand back and stand there like a third
wheel while they silently communicate through telepathy
or somethin'.

Denny eventually sighs and turns to me again. "Sorry
to freak out on you guys."

I give him a look meant to invite him to fuck right off.
"Nah, man. It's gonna be with all of us for the rest of our
lives. You're doing the best you can. You're doing fine." I
lean in to make my point. "And if you ever feel like you're
not, you know we've all got your back."

"Yeah. Thanks."

It's time to lighten things up. "And think of it this way: now we all have one more thing to give Miller shit about."

He smiles and I don't miss Rosie grinning from her chair. "That is quite the silver lining, isn't it?"

Mama decides to stay with Miller until they're ready to discharge him. He doesn't even have to spend the night, which is a good sign and a relief to everybody. No one in our family is fond of hospitals, and the longer we're in one, the itchier we get. I guess Denny's not alone.

Carter takes off in an Uber to deal with his car. Just what we need, another thing to spend money on. Hopefully, he has better insurance than me. And since Cart and I left Oscar on his own when we took off, I head back to Blue Bigfoot. Kelsie and Jodi should be showing up soon for the evening shift, so I'll send him home. He's earned it.

The crowd picks up around sunset, likely due to the perfect spring weather that had people out and about today. I'm feeling a touch of optimism about my money troubles when I sell almost a grand in gift cards. A bunch of regulars stop by, and only two of them pull out their gift cards to pay, despite the fact that at least a half dozen of them bought cards earlier this week.

I'm beginning to think Hollis is a genius.

Which reminds me I left her hanging earlier. When I pull up our text thread, I see she's been busy.

HOLLIS:

Sausage delivery at 9am tomorrow, so make sure somebody is there to sign.

The paper ran a free ad for your sausage fest. You're welcome.

Did you pick up the chips?

> Do you have a preference when it comes to tablecloths for the relish station?

> Your mom just texted me. Is Miller okay?!

> ???

> ???

It absolutely shouldn't surprise me that my mama has Hollis's number, yet it does. When will I learn not to underestimate her?

ME:

> He's fine. He'll live to whore another day.

My phone rings and I hit accept without even confirming it's her. She's becoming so predictable.

"Thank God. I was worried. Have you seen him? Does he need anything?"

"Hello, Ms. Hayes. How are you this evening?" For some reason, the kindergartner inside me is annoyed that it's my brother who finally got her to stop avoiding me.

"Better than your brother, it sounds like. Can I do anything?"

"While I'm sure he'd love his own personal nurse, I think my mom's got it covered. He's got a broken arm and some pretty good cuts, but nothing time won't heal."

"That's good, I guess." I can hear her yappy dogs in the background, so it sounds like she's at home. The idea that I'm talking to her outside our everyday universe has something close to satisfaction settling in my chest. That's new. "Your mom said he ran a red light?" Jesus, how many texts did Mama send her?

"I guess so. He totaled Carter's Nissan."

"Ouch." Her voice is muffled, and I wonder if she's

changing her clothes. There's no helping the road my imagination takes with that notion. But she and I are clearly not on the same page when she continues, "Oh, I'm bringing a friend tomorrow. She's a sausage expert."

"I'm not sure how to take that."

Hollis doesn't take the bait, instead hurrying on to talk about details we've already covered.

Contrary to my expectations when she first forced her help on me, Hollis has truly gone above and beyond for what was essentially a joke gone wrong. I should tell her at some point that I don't blame her.

I really should. And I will. Later.

But gratitude and concern over family and doing unnecessary favors sounds too much like real relationship stuff. And that's not us.

Hostility and sexual chemistry. That's all we share.

And whether she's ready or not, St. Pat's is tomorrow, and she'll have to tell me to my face that she doesn't want me as much as I want her.

I can't wait to see her try to convince herself it's true.

CHAPTER
EIGHTEEN
SEX EYES AND LIES

HOLLIS

"*THAT'S* the guy whose face you said could turn the straightest woman on earth into a lesbian?" Rylee points her bacon jam spoon in Cash's general direction. I don't look. My vibrator broke last night, and I took it as an omen, but hopefully I can avoid him by staying busy today.

It's two o'clock in the afternoon, and Rylee and I are setting up the "gourmet toppings bar" just inside the doors to the patio at Blue Bigfoot. She and Dean, along with Dean's older sister, Darcy, volunteered to help out tonight, but I'm pretty sure it was just so they could sample the product.

I didn't tell Cash, but I rearranged my clients so we only have baths this afternoon—that way Josh could take over for me. He has quite the talented hand for shampooing pups. I wanted to be free to make this sausage fest go off without a hitch so we can squeeze as much money out of it as possible.

The appraiser got back to me a couple days ago, and he can get me thirty-five hundred dollars for the earrings. I'm just waiting to find out how much Cash makes tonight before I go ahead and sell them.

"I was being hyperbolic," I tell Rylee, knowing she can see right through me.

"You were being a liar. Why are you fighting with… *that?*"

I finally follow her gaze across the room where Cash is hoisting a keg like it weighs nothing. The man must work out for hours before he comes in every day—there's no other explanation for all the firm muscle my hands encountered during our regrettable make-out sessions. I couldn't help my smile when I first walked in and saw him in a green flannel shirt. He's becoming an expert at worming his way past my saltiness. And that's a very dangerous sign.

"We're not fighting," I respond, shoving another pack of goat cheese into the cooler beneath the table. "At least not anymore. We've called a truce while I help him with a project."

"Is this project of the naked variety?"

"Gross." My frown is utterly unconvincing.

"Uh-huh, right." Rylee flips her long dark hair over her shoulder and bends to retrieve a chafing dish from the box we lugged in with us.

I told her I was helping out today because it's kind of a warehouse shops event—which is a stretch, but I had to come up with an excuse as to why I'd help Cash with anything. She knows how I feel about him. Well, sort of.

The taproom is starting to fill up with revelers in their green shirts and shamrock headwear, and the music and chatter make for a festive atmosphere. I chew on my lip as I try for the twentieth time to ignore the hundred-and-ninety-pound elephant in the room. But he's not making it easy. If I didn't know better, I'd say he's performing for my benefit, but his every motion is just innately sexy, I'm afraid.

Like when he effortlessly vaulted himself over the bar instead of walking to the opening at the other end. Or when he laughed at something Oscar said, exposing his Adam's apple and strong throat. Or when he bent over to wipe a table, giving me a perfect view of his butt.

I'm truly struggling here. He's right; I have been avoiding him. Spending time together is a big mistake. If I get comfortable being around him, I'm going to let my guard down—and nothing good can come from that. He may be playing nice for now, but Cash Brooks is only out for himself, and I'd do well to remember that.

Sure, he might deign to sleep with me a time or two; it's obvious there's an attraction between us. But I can hardly say goodbye to a dog that gets adopted from the shelter; imagine what bidding farewell to a man who gives me orgasms and flashes me that smile would do to me.

But I don't make stupid decisions. And opening my heart even a crack to someone as insensitive and self-righteous as him would be dumber than keeping a lion as a pet and then being surprised when it eats you. All Cash cares about is his bar, and he'd throw me under the bus without a second thought if it was good for his business.

He may draw the line at taking actual cash from me, but that's just because he's so bull-headed and proud. A tiny voice inside my head starts mumbling about pots and kettles, but I ignore it.

It's settled. No more making out with Cash, no more looking at his butt, no more letting him near my lady town, no more imagining him nudging my thighs apart with his nose, no more moaning his name when I make myself come, no more any of it!

It's purely business from here on out. I'll see him through this mess my family made and then it's back to ignoring him. I won't even bother pranking him anymore because that would require thinking about him—which I've just decreed I will no longer do.

"You okay?" Rylee asks, and I realize I've been staring into space with my hand fisting the green tablecloth I brought. "Did the tablecloth offend you?"

"Sorry, I was just thinking." I smile weakly. "Um, did we bring everything in, or is there stuff left in the car?" I could maybe use a few minutes alone.

She shifts her weight to one hip and narrows her eyes at me. "Okay, something is going on with you. I thought you were just acting weird because you can't stop thinking about banging the bartender, but it's more than that, isn't it?"

Crap. No wonder Cash can read me so well—I'm as transparent as a good pair of stripper heels!

When all I respond with is a panicked look, Rylee grabs my arm and pulls me with her in the direction of the bar. "There's plenty of time before this shindig kicks off. Let's get a beer and sit outside."

Of course she heads right to Cash instead of Oscar.

"Hi, I'm Rylee," she cheerily introduces herself to the man like he isn't the bane of my existence.

"Hey, Rylee. I'm Cash." His eyes pivot to me and turn way too sexy for daytime. "Hollis."

My returning smile is brittle as hell. I haven't been this

close to him since he had his hand between my legs telling me to come all over his fingers. Gah! A flush begins at my chest and rockets upward. Time to go!

Rylee rolls her eyes at me before addressing Cash again. "What do you recommend?"

They chat about beer while I think about abandoned puppies, and that time I accidentally walked in on Mom and Harry having sex. It does the trick. Kind of.

Rylee orders something called *Squatch Blossom*, and I ask for whatever is closest to Coors Light. Cash manages to look only mildly offended but does, in fact, come up with something that's light in color and transparent, so that's something. He tells me it's an American blonde ale called *Legendary Larry*.

"So, you must be the sausage expert," Cash says to Rylee.

She responds without hesitation, "I like to think of myself that way."

What is wrong with me? I can't let Cash think he's throwing me for a loop with his sex eyes.

"What, no green beer?" I frown pointedly at the boring amber liquid filling the glass Cash just passed to the guy next to us.

"This isn't Applebee's." He frowns right back.

"I work at the paper," Rylee interjects, openly grasping for any way to keep the fighting to a minimum.

"Oh, yeah?" He's being polite to Rylee just to make me look crazy, I'm certain.

I smile at my friend in solidarity. "She's the one who got us the free ad."

"Well, then, these beers are on me."

"It's cute that you think we were going to pay for

them." I turn my smile his way and add a little salt to it. This is more like it.

"I believe I already told you I don't want your money, *Ms. Hayes*."

There are so many ways I could take that statement, and he knows as much.

"Good. Because the only thing you'll get from me is hot sausage and onions, *princess*."

Thankfully Rylee steers me to the patio before things devolve into the kind of argument Cash likes to end by mauling me.

When we take a seat at a picnic bench, she doesn't waste any time.

"I can't believe you didn't tell me you're sleeping with him," she whisper-hisses at me.

"I'm not!" I shield my eyes from the sun and then scoot over so an umbrella blocks it.

"Then why did he look at you like he knows where all your hidden moles are because he's counted them with his tongue? I thought you were going to pass out up there. Well, either that or throat-punch him."

"Fine. We fooled around a little."

"And?"

"And nothing. We don't like each other—*at all*; we just have… chemistry." I try shrugging it off and take a sip of my beer. It's surprisingly tasty.

"That's an understatement if I've ever heard one."

"It's complicated," I say, tempted to roll my eyes at myself.

Rylee lifts her pint glass to her pink-glossed lips. "Spill it."

So I do. It's been killing me not having anyone besides Marco and Polo to share this Harry fiasco with, and although Rylee's not my only friend, she's the only one I've been keeping up with since I got so busy with the salon. It's due almost entirely to her being so good at keeping in touch. I've been juggling the salon and the shelter, and now this drama with Cash; it's a wonder I find time to sleep and walk my dogs.

When I'm done, Rylee stares into her now-empty glass, trying to let everything I shared sink in. "You honestly think Harry went that far?"

"I want to believe he didn't, but first, this is his princess we're talking about." I send her a pointed look that has her huffing in exasperation. "Second, Cash said they just passed an inspection a few weeks ago. Third, like I said, Harry thinks the little brother owns the brewery for some reason. He told me I was being naïve about predators and their manipulation tactics." This time I do roll my eyes. "As if the kid who just ran a red light and totaled his brother's car is the mastermind of a child sex ring."

Her hand slaps the table in solidarity, almost knocking her glass over. "Talk about naïve! Your sister has probably screwed half the football team."

"Lacrosse, but yeah. Probably." I chew my lip and watch a table of guys do a round of shots.

"And they still haven't called you? I mean, Hadley lying low, I believe, but your parents?"

"I don't know. The fight was pretty bad." I pull out my phone and scroll to my call history. "I did get a call from an overseas number, but there was no voice mail. And when I tried calling back, there was no answer." I shake my head. "See! I'm grasping at straws."

"No, you're just trying to have faith that Harry's good sense has overcome his insanely protective impulses."

"I wish. But he would have fixed this mess by now if

that were the case, wouldn't he? I'm going to kill Hadley."
I hit her number on impulse.

When her voice mail picks up, I take a deep breath and release it so I don't thoroughly lose my shit. "It's me. Again," I say through gritted teeth. Rylee nods at me from across the table. "Look, I know you're avoiding me, but this thing is bigger than you now. I think Harry is causing serious trouble for Miller's family. I know you said you came clean about what really happened, but I honestly don't know what to believe anymore. Do Mom and Harry know or not?!" My voice reaches a pitch I didn't know I could hit. "Will someone in this family please call me back?!" So much for not losing it.

Rylee wrestles the phone from my hand and hangs it up. "I think you made your point."

I glance around to see if I've attracted attention, but it's St. Patrick's Day at a brewery. Nobody is looking.

"So, if you haven't told Cash why you're helping him…"

"He thinks I used my 'connections' and summoned the health department to mess with him," I finish for her.

"You'd never do that!" She's offended on my behalf, and it makes me want to hug her. It also reminds me that I'm still angry with Cash for assuming that about me.

"I know, right? I'm a small business owner too."

"Exactly. And, besides, who does he think you are, Vito Corleone?"

I squint at her. "I have no idea who that is."

"*The Godfather*? Marlon Brando? '*I'll make him an offer he can't refuse,*'" she wheezes and gestures with her thumb and fingers together.

I shake my head, smiling at her ridiculous antics. "Never seen it."

She drops the old man act. "It was actually one of Dean's family's better movie night selections." She tilts her head and considers an invisible memory hanging out over my left shoulder. "Anyway, so you're not going to tell him about Harry?"

"What, and have him call the police or the FBI or something? Harry has his flaws and blind spots, but his intentions are kind of noble, if totally outdated and misguided. And complete overkill. Anyway, I'm still hoping I can make it go away with Cash none the wiser." Otherwise, not only could Harry be in real trouble, but Cash will lord it over me until the end of time that I'm the exact self-important, entitled, malicious witch he always assumed I was.

Rylee growls, and she looks like a wicked queen with her mane of dark hair and her sneer. "That little girl is going to get what's coming to her one day."

I sigh. "Promise?" We both smile but sober quickly. "She has a lot of growing up to do, but it's not all her fault. Mom and Harry have never made her take responsibility for anything. And who do you think taught her that money means you get to call the shots?"

"I can't believe you two turned out so different." She wrinkles her nose. "Well, you know what I mean."

Rylee knows some things about my childhood, but not everything. She knows Hadley is my half sister and that my mom and I didn't come from money. And she's quite familiar with my independent streak.

But I never talk about the rest—how I spent my childhood watching my beauty queen mother date loser after loser who'd promise her the world and then disappear when things got too real. How I'd make her tea and toast when she wouldn't get out of bed after her latest heartbreak. Or how pervy landlords would try to trade rent for a roll in the sack with her and then treat us like garbage when she turned them down. How we kept getting evicted and had to move to shittier and shittier apartments.

My mom did her best, though. And I know she wants better for me than she had. While she and Harry have a good relationship, I've wondered more than once if marrying Harry had more to do with security for me than love for him. Even through our moves and hard times, she always kept food in the refrigerator and bent over backward to keep me in the same school for some stability. We don't always see eye to eye, but I've never doubted her love—or her intentions.

Some things are just hard to forget. I've spent my life feeling like I have one foot in that roach-infested apartment and the other in Harry's palace. Never sure where I fit. That insecurity is why I wanted my own business, I think. My future is in my hands, not somebody else's. Because if somebody hands you your life, can't they just as easily take it away?

Oscar rolls a big grill onto the patio, the clattering sound catching our attention. The tipsy table of five nearby cheers. I guess that ad and all those flyers worked.

"Are you the grill master, Oscar?" I yell over to him.

"You know it!" He wields a big metal spatula like a sword, his gap-toothed smile growing wide.

"Looks like it's time to get to work." Rylee stands and grabs both our empty glasses. "Dean and Darcy should be here soon."

We return to the toppings table to start our shift. The crowd has grown in the time we've been outside, and I hope it's a sign of lots of sausage sales to come. When I glance over to the bar, Cash uses his secret radar to sense it, sending more sex eyes my way.

"Ready to raise money for your hottie?" Rylee wags her brows like a goofy cartoon character.

I exhale and do my best to keep my eyes off Cash. "As ready as I'm gonna be."

CHAPTER
NINETEEN
LARRY HAS LEFT THE BUILDING

CASH

MY EYE HAS BEEN on Hollis since she walked in the door in that tight green sweater and a snug pair of jeans. They hug her curves just right, tempting me to peel off every scrap of her clothing and set my mouth exploring—screw the crowd.

She's got me so geared up I've been running around this place like I'm hopped up on Adderall, using any excuse I can to exert some energy and distract my body from the snarky siren across the room.

I played it well when she and her friend came up to the bar for drinks—a good mix of antagonism and foreplay. Now she's out on the patio chatting with Rylee and distracting me from the work I should be doing to get this event going.

I head back to the office to get the extra point-of-sale device we're going to need to collect credit card and electronic payments for the food, and there's a surprise waiting for me.

My baby sister sits in my office chair, a horrified expression on her face and a headless German Shepherd on her lap. "Who hurt you?"

"Lynnie, hey!" I round the desk to sweep her up in a hug.

She reluctantly stands, letting the stuffed animal fall to the floor and allowing my hug. "There is something profoundly wrong with you, Cash Dallas Brooks."

"It was for a good cause, I promise, *Loretta* Lynn Brooks."

She shrugs my arms off. "You know I'm getting that legally changed the minute I graduate." Even as a baby, she refused to answer to her given name.

"Uh-huh." We both know she's full of shit. All of us kids were named after our parents' favorite music legends, and she'd never take that away from our mama, especially now with Dad gone.

"Did you see the invalid?" I ask her.

"Yeah." She winces, her dark eyebrows pulling together. She looks like our dad when she does that. "I told him girls like scars, so it cheered him up."

"The boy has already got more decoration on his face than a Christmas tree."

"Darn whippersnapper," she mocks me with a crotchety old-man impression. "I see you're still taking your dad responsibilities seriously."

"What is that supposed to mean?"

She gives me the look every teenager masters before their fourteenth birthday.

"Whatever," I grumble just as maturely as I open the drawer where the POS equipment is stored. "Don't you have classes today?"

Lynn is a freshman at App State up in Boone. She's

maybe the only one who's going to make a name for the Brooks family now that Carter's apparently abandoned his political ambitions. She's planning on majoring in Environmental Science and saving the world. And I hope she does.

"I drove down after. I've already been home—Mango's gone MIA again, so Mama's keeping one eye on Miller and the other one peeled for Mango." She perches her tiny rear end on the desk. "Did he really run a red light?"

"What's so surprising about that?" I set the slim tablet on the desk and go digging for the cord.

"I don't know." She shrugs. "Maybe he's just more careful when I'm in the car with him."

She doesn't need me to tell her we're nothing more than one giant cliché when it comes to her. One precocious teenage girl with four protective older brothers? The damn thing writes itself.

Everybody assumes Lynn is the sweet-tempered baby sister, but she's got more mischief in her than the rest of us. She spent her last two years of high school driving Mama and me to drink with all her late-night text chats and the boyfriends she accumulated. But she never lets them stick. Which is just as well because nobody's good enough for Lynn.

May I refer you to the aforementioned cliché?

And no kid is stupid enough to take on a girl with her gumption and four older brothers who've each been in a fistfight or two. In Miller's case, I doubt I can even count high enough.

"You gonna stick around for the festivities? We stock some organic hipster bottled soda, you know."

"Yeah, I think I'll pass. A bunch of drunk millennials giving me shitty advice and spilling beer on my shoes? No thanks." She wrinkles her nose and hops off the desk. "Besides, I told Mama I'd look for Mango if he doesn't show up before dark. They're doin' green Jell-O shots at the senior center tonight, so she's the DD."

Lynn heads for the door and it's only then I notice her hoodie has the words "Regulate Your Cock" with a drawing of a rooster on the back. "I'll catch you at home later." She waves over her shoulder. "And think about getting some therapy for whatever made you such a monster, okay?"

I kick the dog body aside with a scowl and shout after her, "I'm a *very young* millennial, you know!"

TWO HOURS LATER, I'm worried we're gonna run out of food. Some random guy who's helping Oscar at the grill has already come back to the cooler for a half dozen more packs of meat, and the real crowd hasn't even shown up yet.

But Hollis is in her element, smiling warmly at every customer as she hands over small plates piled high with whatever they ask for. It's the same smile she used the day I met her when my customers acted like lovesick idiots around her. My jaw ticks for some reason at the thought.

"Have you tried one of these?" Kelsie asks over a mouthful of food as she settles on a barstool across from me. She's holding her plate just under her chin and looking like a lost hiker who was rescued only seconds before resorting to cannibalism. She pauses her chewing when she sees my expression. "What? I'm on break."

I turn back to watch Hollis some more. A guy wearing a stupid leprechaun hat leans against the wall flirting with her. He'd better not knock that painting off the wall or I'm gonna kick his ass. That's a one-of-a-kind rendering of Bigfoot hiding behind a pine tree playing hide and seek.

There goes my jaw again.

"I've been meaning to ask you, where's Larry?" Kelsie asks around another mouthful, her purple hair sweeping her plate and picking up crumbs. I slide a napkin across the bar, but she ignores it.

My eyes flash to the empty spot on the other side of the register where the two-foot statue normally stands.

"Oh, uh, long story," I reply, not hiding an ounce of my discomfort.

Thankfully, a party of three steps up to the bar for beers, and Kelsie gets distracted making out with her pub dog again.

A few regulars have asked about Larry's whereabouts as well. I don't know what it is about him, but everybody loves that sasquatch. The regulars have even started rubbing his head for good luck when they pay their tabs.

My stomach makes a noise I don't like when I catch sight of Carter lugging kegs from the brewhouse to speed up the changeovers we'll be doing several times tonight. I look back at Larry's empty spot.

I repeat the same logic to myself that I've been using since last weekend. I had to grab that dishwasher before someone else did. I had no choice. It was a steal.

And the pawn shop will hold Larry for sixty days before they sell him, so that gives me plenty of time to get him back—with a shitload of interest, of course.

But I'm afraid I went too far this time, something my stomach apparently recognizes too.

The shit I'm keeping from Carter is just me cleaning up the mess I made—and covering for my own stupidity.

And, yeah, I could tell him. He's been showing more signs of the old Carter, and he can't be mad at me forever about being such a prick to the inspector.

But this? I can't.

Because Larry's not mine to sell. He belongs to our dad.

The artist was a friend of Dad's from childhood named Morton Frye, who gave him the carving years before he garnered a cult following for his cryptid art. One of his recent sculptures just sold for fifty thousand dollars in Charlotte, according to Mama. That's what gave me the idea to hock Larry in the first place.

But the value to our family is more about the memories than anything. The statue used to stand on the credenza in the den where Dad would gather us rugrats around to tell stories about Bigfoot—who he claimed to be on a first-name basis with. He had a special knack for spinning a yarn so captivating and hilarious, it became a Sunday tradition attracting the entire Carmichael family from next door as well as random friends from school. Dad had us all believing almost as much as Mama, though we pretended to be skeptics who were way too old for all that nonsense.

The day Blue Bigfoot opened, Mama walked through the doors with Larry in her hands and hefted him up onto the bar without a word. Then she kissed Cart and me and ordered a beer.

I'd never in a million years actually sell it, but letting someone hold on to it in exchange for five thousand bucks on the spot sounded reasonable to a desperate me. Until I walked in the next day to an empty spot next to the register and a sick feeling in my stomach.

I take a deep breath and serve another couple

customers. I'm worrying over nothing. Larry will be back where he belongs in a few weeks, and I'll just keep pretending he's being appraised for our insurance till then. What they don't know won't hurt them, and this isn't the first time I've employed that logic with my family.

Hell, they don't know how I pulled off half the shit I've done to keep us afloat, and this is no different. While I was working at Rabid full time, I pimped myself out as a handyman to some rich assholes by using a fake resume. It covered the new roof and the car insurance for three of us for a year.

A laugh catches my ear from across the room, and it's Hollis, her cheeks pink and her sweet lips spread in a joyful smile. The overhead lights reflect off the lenses of her glasses, so I can't see her eyes, but I know they're warm. The leprechaun douchebag is gone, and she's chatting with Rylee and the random dude from before, who must be Rylee's boyfriend from the way he just grabbed her ass.

I should be focusing on how well today is going. And on how much I owe Hollis for throwing herself into my problem. She may be a pain in the ass and rub me the wrong way, but what she's done is more than enough to atone for one stupid phone call.

Carter stalks up to the bar looking constipated. "Fine," he growls at me before turning and leaving the same way he came in.

I laugh and reach under the bar for the contest entry forms I printed earlier. Then I ring the last-call bell.

A taproom full of eyes turn my way.

"Who wants to win a hundred dollars?!"

The crowd cheers, lifting their beers high and toasting

each other without even knowing what I'm talking about yet.

I fuckin' love this place.

I feel Hollis's eyes on me, and yeah, there she is, arms crossed, head shaking at me—but her smile is even brighter than before.

CHAPTER
TWENTY
ALONE TOGETHER AND OTHER OXYMORONS

CASH

"DAMN, THAT'S A LOTTA GREEN," Miller says, leaning across the bar for a better look. But he forgets about his arm and hisses when he bumps it on the bar rail. "Ow. Shit."

He showed up around ten, saying Mama and Lynn were driving him nuts. When Carter asked him how he got here, he mumbled something about having to beg Lynnie for a ride. Now he's hanging out, hoping for a lift home.

We sold out of food before nine, and Hollis and her friends hung out on the patio for another hour after that. I only talked to her a handful of times tonight, mostly exchanging money and answering quick questions. But we kept up a near-constant awareness of one another, catching each other's eyes way too often for either of us to brush it off.

When she left, I was serving a throng of people who were laughing and shouting to be heard over the music and each other. She gave up trying to say anything and instead, brought her hand to her ear in the universal sign for "call me."

So, my plans don't include sharing a vehicle with my brothers tonight.

It was a regular family affair at Blue Bigfoot today, though. Denny came by with Rosie, looking a far sight better than the last time I saw him. Even more so when Miller showed up and started talking his usual shit. Rosie's brother, Luca, was filling in for Miller tonight, busing tables, flirting with women, and sampling a little too much of the product. He and Denny have been best friends since before they could talk—well, apart from the two weeks Luca froze him out when he found out Denny was banging his little sister.

Rosie ended up driving him and his car home, leaving Denny with us brothers.

"You in a sharing mood?" Miller eyes the money again and makes a pathetic attempt to garner sympathy by cradling his arm.

Unfortunately for him, Carter chooses that moment to walk by. "Every dime you earn from now until the end of time goes straight into my car fund, so don't even bother."

"I told you, it wasn't my fault!" He follows Carter to plead his case again.

"So…" Denny starts, pulling up a bar stool and using a tone I know way too well. "I finally met Hollis. She had a few interesting things to say about you." He's enjoying this way too much.

"Your point?" My eyes remain on the hundred-dollar stacks I'm making. Tonight is a record, for sure. I still haven't crunched all the numbers, though, so I'm holding off any celebrations.

"I've never had hate sex. Had just about every other kind, but never that one."

"You discuss your various kinds of sex with Rosie, and you'll get your chance, little brother," I warn him.

He coughs out a laugh and takes a swig of his beer. He and I share our mama's blue eyes, but his hair is the same dirty-blond as Miller's—only cleaner. He scratches his chin and pretends he's just makin' casual conversation.

I know he's expecting me to either confess to some feelings for Hollis or maybe confirm his hate-sex theory, but I'm not going there. I mean, he's not wrong—antagonizing each other does make it hotter—but what Hollis and I have going on is way more complicated than anything I'm telling him tonight. I don't even understand it myself.

"I guess I'll never know how hot it is," he laments with a dramatic sigh.

I shove the stacks of money into an envelope and start on the next round, but I look up to stop him from yammering on. "What about me says I'm the kind of bartender who has patience for this bullshit?"

This time, he practically wets himself laughing.

When he finally recovers, he takes another sip of beer and resumes his regular personality. "I'm not interested in any of that shit. What I've got is better."

I grin at the cash drawer. It's good seeing my brother happy. "So that's it, huh? You're done?"

"Stick a fork in me, brother." He spins on his stool and extends his arms, addressing the empty taproom, "I am done!"

Now I'm laughing. "When are you gonna pop the question?"

He spins himself back around. "Whoa, whoa, don't get ahead of yourself."

"Yeah, right. You already have the ring, don't you?"

"Who told you?!" He smacks the bar with an open palm.

"You just did. You fall for that every damn time."

"Have I told you to kiss my ass recently?" He grumbles for a little while, and I finish up securing the cash. "Yeah, well, I'm just waitin' for the right time. I don't want to freak her out—or Adrina, god forbid."

He's smart to be worried. Adrina wouldn't think twice about nut-punching him just for looking at her daughter wrong. "She is a little young—and so are you," I remind him. Rosie's all of twenty-two, and Denny is twenty-eight. But what the hell do I know? Maybe there's never a good or bad time.

"Yeah, but when you know, you know." He shrugs and drains the rest of his beer.

I look up from my envelopes with a frown. "I never understood that saying. 'When you know, you know.' It doesn't say a damn thing. It's an oxymoron, at least I think that's what they call it."

"Who are you calling a moron?" Miller glares at me as he grabs the stool next to Denny. We both ignore him.

"No, I think it's a paradox?" Denny muses. "Anyway, you'll get it someday."

"Are we leavin' or what?" Miller interjects.

I dig my car keys out of my pocket and toss them to him. "Those are for Carter, not you. He can drive you guys home."

Miller takes off to find Cart, and Denny stands as well, leaning forward as he does. "Maybe sooner than you think."

I shoot him a baffled look, and he jerks his chin to the

patio doors. Hollis is standing there getting ready to knock. When she sees we've spotted her, she smiles.

"See you later, man," Denny says as he heads for the hall. But I don't respond. I'm too busy making plans for the rest of my night—and the morning too.

I make a beeline for the doors and unlock one. A cold breeze rushes in, so I open it wider so she can step inside. "Isn't this a little late for you? I thought you got up with the roosters." Her showing up here means I don't have to hunt her down; it also means we're on exactly the same page.

"It's usually my dogs, but yeah. I just wanted to see how much we made tonight." She rubs her hands together and grins like she's five and it's Christmas morning.

It's impossible not to smile at her. A voice in the back of my brain warns me to keep to those boundaries I laid down for myself, but it's faint at best and easy to tune out. "I was just about to tally everything. Come on." I motion toward the bar, and she follows me over.

"It's so quiet in here." Hollis looks around the empty space. "Quite the contrast from earlier. I think I'll be hoarse in the morning from shouting to be heard all night."

She's right. The place is dead quiet. "Yeah. Everybody went home. It's just you and me." I make sure I'm looking at her when I say it because I know she's gonna blush, and I'm not missing it.

Yup. She's an open book.

A warm pink flush starts at the V-neck of her sweater and travels up until her cheeks are two roses. She's fidgeting with the sweater's hem but catches herself and struts the rest of the way like the queen of the warehouse shops.

I just watch her ass in those tight jeans and grin.

She gasps when she sees the envelopes of cash, and I tell her I still need to grab the credit card receipts and the electronic ones. I head back to the office while she totals the envelopes. By the time we've accounted for usual expenses, food costs, extra staff, and half a dozen other things, we're staring at four thousand dollars in profits.

"It was that contest!" Hollis exclaims, bouncing on the balls of her feet. "That was brilliant—you got them all to buy the beer so they could taste it before submitting their entries! You fully capitalized on a tipsy guy's valuation of immortalizing himself in the bro lexicon!"

I smile at her ridiculous enthusiasm and shake my head. "I have no idea what half of that means, but the winner was a woman, not a dude."

"Eh, women are vain too." She shrugs. "I left before the winner was announced. What's the beer name?"

The memory of Carter staring me down after the announcement has me grimacing. "*Sassy Q.*"

"Oh." Her expression sobers as she mulls that over. "*Sassy Q.* Hmm. It's kind of cute, right?" She can't hide her own pained expression.

"Just what we were looking for. Cute." I'd thought we were in the clear when I made a list of required sasquatch references they had to choose from. I was wrong.

Hollis waves off my revulsion. "Who cares? You made a mint on it!"

"Nah, it was your fancy gourmet hot dogs. We went through everything."

"I know!" Her eyes go wide. Her uninhibited joy is both charming and contagious. "We were pushing smoked venison with crushed potato chips and blue cheese by the end. Drunk people will eat anything. Rylee too."

We both laugh, but then she wrinkles her nose, her

mind moving in another direction. I just watch her because it's cute as hell. Finally, she asks, "Are we... getting along with each other?"

I nod my head yes but say, "Impossible."

She does the nose thing again. "We're being all... nice and happy." She frowns. "I think we even complimented each other."

I take a slow step toward her. "Well, there are one or two things I like about you, you know."

She starts to roll her eyes, but when she spots my intentions, she goes still, drawing that tempting lip between her teeth again.

Another step, and her lips part on a small gasp. "There's that smart mouth," I murmur.

One more step, and now I can see her pupils dilating behind her glasses, fighting for territory with the bourbon irises. "And the sound you make when I find that spot on your neck just below your ear."

Her pulse is visible at her neck now as I keep closing the space. "Your tight nipples that give you away." Like right now. She is pure temptation to me.

My voice drops to a whisper because we're so close I can feel her quickened breath on my throat. "And those soft thighs I want to trace with my tongue until you beg for me."

She lets out a whimper and meets me halfway as I lower my mouth to hers.

CHAPTER
TWENTY-ONE
GOD IS A WOMAN

HOLLIS

DEAR LORD BABY JESUS, I can't help myself. Those eyes, that voice, those words, that chest. It's too much to ask for a girl to resist.

I don't care if I regret it tomorrow or for the rest of my damn life; I'm having sex with Cash Brooks. Tonight.

My hands come up to graze his firm pecs as he takes control of the kiss. But this one is not as savage or rough as the other times we've kissed. He seems to be savoring this one, taking his sweet-ass time getting me worked up as his tongue does its sensual slide against mine. His hands take possession of my butt, squeezing me and pulling me into him. I can feel the hard press of his length against the denim of my jeans, and it's a struggle not to pull back so I can get a better look. From what I can feel right now, he's seriously packing.

I do a little more exploring of his chest and shoulders as he plays with me, letting his lips trail down my neck and then up to that damn spot that does, indeed, have my breath hitching in his ear. The scratch of his stubble on my sensitive skin spreads goose bumps across my shoulders and arms. My nerve endings fight for exposure to his touch, and my pulse quickens, the blood in my veins growing hot.

"You smell so good," Cash murmurs into my neck, making me smile. I'm not telling him I scrubbed the onion smell off my skin and washed my hair in my shop before I came over. He'll read way too much into it. I had no intention of things going here tonight. None at all. Nope. Not one bit.

Then he's kissing me again, and my head floats. I reach down to palm his arousal through his jeans, and when he groans and pushes into my hand, I can't help myself. I stroke over the fabric and then undo his belt buckle before unbuttoning his jeans. The zipper slides down, and he's in my hand, hot, hard, huge! My sex thrums and my clit throbs with every encouraging sound he makes as I squeeze him and let my thumb rub over the baby-smooth skin of his shaft and head.

But he pulls my pelvis into him again, and I lose hold as he spins us and kisses me, hard this time. The slow exploration portion of the evening appears to be over, because the edge of a solid surface bites into the small of my back, and then I'm boosted on top of it. Cash breaks the kiss, and I blink to get my bearings as my shoes disappear. My bare feet land on the cold floor, only for the millisecond it takes Cash to strip off my jeans and panties in one single motion. I yelp with each of the quick movements, marveling at his ability to retain coordination while being so turned on. I'm fumbling around like a drunk person in the dark, and he's coherent enough to perform brain surgery over here.

And there he goes again. His hands give my bare ass one bruising squeeze that's accompanied by an almost-pained groan from deep in his throat, and then my butt lands on the flat, cool surface again. I realize now it's the counter behind the bar, but all other awareness evaporates when Cash drops to his knees, pulls my hips forward and hooks my knees over his shoulders.

I throw my hands behind me so I don't crack my head on the bar, and Cash buries his face between my thighs. The first swipe of his hot tongue is a revelation. I moan so loud I can hear my own voice echo off the walls and ceiling. When he adds a finger and focuses his tongue on my clit, I nearly black out. His whiskers graze my mound as his finger slides through my wetness and delves in, sending my head back and my moans into the room again.

He sucks my clit while he expertly strokes me, and it's so good I can't even be embarrassed at the slick sounds of his fingers driving through my arousal. Especially when he goes deeper and crooks that finger right onto my G-spot. I come fast and hard, grasping at the counter for balance as my hips buck into his face, and I ride out my orgasm against his mouth. He runs his tongue gently over me until my quivering subsides.

"Fuck, you're hot," Cash growls before rising effortlessly to his feet again. He shrugs off his flannel shirt, cleaning up his face with a quick swipe of it before tossing it to the floor. "I'll be tasting you on my tongue for days." In just his gray T-shirt and unzipped jeans now, he comes in for another hard kiss, and our hot breaths mingle while I taste myself on his lips. Nobody has ever been so uninhibited and openly carnal with me.

Sure, I've had a few sexual partners, but it was never like this—never so open and raw. It was mostly lights-out, silent caressing, and then the deed itself. And rarely an orgasm that wasn't DIY.

But not with Cash. He's candid and unguarded here in this space. He doesn't play games or twist things to further some strategic plan. He's letting me into this part of him.

I have no illusions he'll invite me into any other part of himself or his life—not that I'd want an invitation anyway —but there's no hiding or holding back here. And our usual sarcasm and animosity have no place in this moment between us.

He releases my lips and pulls back a few inches. "I need to be inside you—feel you around me."

I can only nod because if I try to speak, it will come out as gibberish. Part of me reasons I should give him a blow job after what he just did between my thighs, but I realize there's no keeping score here—unlike in the rest of our relationship. He likes giving me orgasms, so that's what he's doing, no ulterior motives.

And, boy, oh boy, does he. He drops his jeans and boxers just as fast as he made my clothes disappear, and he produces a condom out of thin air.

I reach out for it, wanting to roll it on him myself so I can have him thick and hard in my hand again, but he pulls it out of reach. "Next time. If you touch me now, I'll go off."

A smile curves my lips, and the coiled sexual tension and pleasure is joined by a lightheartedness that feels natural between us.

"You like that idea, huh?" Cash asks while he rolls the condom over his thick shaft, and I get my first full view of him.

Holy mother of… I mean, I expected it from the earlier evidence, but seeing it now—jutting proudly from between his muscular thighs and out from the tuft of dark pubic hair—it wipes the smile right off my face.

He sees my expression and looks down at himself again. "Only you can get me this hard."

The spark of satisfaction hits again, but I don't know that I can smile this time. The walls of my sex contract, whether from the aftereffects of the orgasm he just gave me or the anticipation of his big cock sheathing itself inside, it's unclear. But nothing's been easy with Cash from the beginning, so why should this be any different?

Either he's unaware of his size or ignorant of my sudden soberness, but he doesn't say another word about it. He just reaches for the hem of my sweater and lifts it over my head. My bra is nothing but a memory after that, and he's got his hands on my thighs and his mouth on my breast. He gives my nipple a thorough going over with his tongue before pulling it between his teeth and tugging on it gently. My hips come off the counter at that, and then his cock is nudging my entrance.

"I love how you taste everywhere." He goes in for a swipe of my other nipple and presses a first inch into me before pulling back out again. "You're so tight, baby."

My taut nerves get a jolt when he uses the endearment. He's not thinking with the brain up top, that much is clear. But any thoughts I might have on his word choice disappear into thin air when he moves his hips again and fills me.

I make a sound that's somewhere between a moan and a shout, and I can feel his shaft flex inside me before he withdraws again and powers forward to bury his cock in me to the hilt. This time, when I open my mouth, nothing comes out at all.

He's stolen my breath and my voice. I'm fuller than

I've ever been, and I can feel my arousal drip down my sex to my ass crack while my inner muscles clench around him.

"Hollis," Cash groans.

His mouth is buried in my neck now, one hand gripping my hip and the other holding one of my thighs around his middle. My head rolls back and rests on the top of the bar, and I pull my arms up to support me for what I know is coming.

"Hollis," he says again before pulling out and thrusting his cock into me again.

The edge of the bar digs into my shoulder blades, but it's just one more sensation in the swirl of feelings assaulting my body.

I yelp when he shifts me precariously onto the edge of the counter, but his hands support my thighs as he spreads me wider. He straightens and watches with unabashed satisfaction as he thrusts into me again. And again.

"Cash," I whimper. I'm losing control of everything. My muscles, my voice, my breath. He's taking it all and building something powerful and vibrant and new inside my body.

I start to quiver around him, more of my arousal running down my crack as he keeps powering in and out, his grunts of exertion and pleasure filling the air.

"That's it, baby."

With my eyes squeezed shut, I can't see him, but I can tell his teeth are gritted over his words as he encourages me.

"Come around me. Let me feel it." He shifts his angle slightly, his cock sinking impossibly deeper as he continues his bruising rhythm.

I tip over the edge, crying out as my climax skyrockets.

I buck and gasp, my body entirely out of my control as I spasm around Cash. Exquisite torture and bliss meet in my core and radiate throughout my body, reaching the tips of my curled toes and the hairs on the back of my neck. Tears stream down my cheeks and into my hair as the orgasm goes on and on, Cash never letting up on his pace as he plunders me, strumming every raw nerve ending.

My hearing is muffled and I'm covered in perspiration, my hands useless from both slickness and weakness. The wood behind my shoulders bites at my bones as Cash's thrusts repeatedly drive me into it. I've never felt so unmoored yet fulfilled. Both feelings should alarm me, but there's nothing here but Cash's body and mine, sweat-slicked and writhing together.

Cash's rhythm gets impossibly demanding just before he climaxes. His shout of release echoes through the space and his strokes begin to slow until he finally stills inside me and drops his damp forehead to my breastbone. We're both panting, our chests rising and falling as our lungs claw for oxygen. I blink a few times at the light. My glasses are half-fogged and completely askew, but I'm too weak to do anything about it. Only when our breathing regains a more relaxed pace does Cash finally lift his head and look at me.

If I had a phone in my hand to snap a picture, it would go in an album titled, "Scientific Proof that God is a Woman." His skin is flushed, and his hair is damp and mussed, but his eyes are the purest blue pools of affection and bone-deep satisfaction. My stomach swoops in a way that's different from arousal, but I don't have time to examine it because it swoops again when one corner of his mouth lifts.

"Your glasses are crooked. I think I literally fucked them up."

I'm shocked I can manage even a weak smile in response.

Cash lifts his frame to pull out of me, securing the condom as he does. He quickly disposes of it, then lifts a hand to my face and gently straightens my glasses so they rest comfortably on the bridge of my nose. Then he does something that leaves me even more breathless than before.

He holds my eyes while he lowers himself and places the softest of kisses on my damp mound.

I let out a sound that's something between a whimper and a sigh as my brain tries to wrap itself around this entire experience. This isn't sex—at least not what I know of it. And it isn't the familiar vengeful neighbors, Cash and Hollis. This is something else, and I have no idea what it is.

But what I do know is that it's dangerous as hell.

CASH

HOLLIS IS SPLAYED out fully naked on the bench of the under bar.

It's my biggest fantasy come true.

Her whole body is pink and limp from our workout, and my dick starts getting more ideas at the sight of her soft curves and tight brown nipples. I can't believe just how hot and wet and tight she was.

We broke about a thousand health codes, but what better time to do it than when I'm already in the doghouse with the DOH? I'll leave the disinfecting for when I don't have a gorgeous naked blonde on my bar.

Hollis starts to shift, but I still her with a hand on her creamy thigh. "Stay there."

I hike my boxers and jeans back up my hips and turn to grab a fresh bar towel from the back bar. Then I run it under warm water at the hand sink before returning to Hollis. She's drawn her legs back together and shifted herself to pull her knees up. But she drops them apart when I raise my eyebrows at her. It's difficult as hell not to let that settle in my chest as some combination of satisfaction at her doing what I ask and gratification that she's putting her trust in me.

I run the cloth over her inner thighs first, cleaning them off before I move to her pussy. It's swollen and dark pink, her blood having rushed there with her arousal. I'm at half-staff now and on my way to a full salute inside my jeans when she flinches under me, the towel against her over-sensitized flesh too much too soon.

"Shhh." I put a hand to her belly, stroking the soft curve with my thumb. "I'll be gentle, I promise."

I'm as good as my word, and she watches me with her lip caught between her teeth. And just like that, I'm ready for another round. But she's clearly not there yet.

I'm not sure what time it is, but it's late as hell—or early, depending on how I choose to think about it. But if I stop to think about anything, this euphoric post-sex feeling I have will walk right out the door. Sex is always amazing—well, mostly—but this was next-level. Not only the chemistry between me and Hollis but her letting loose with me, like she opened a door into something I had no idea existed in my snarky, condescending neighbor. She was a different person with me.

And now I kind of feel like a different person with her.

She straightens and slides off the bench. "Can you, um, hand me my sweater?"

I pick it up from the floor, glad the mopping was done before I threw all our clothes on it. Hollis pulls on her panties and jeans, and I hand the sweater over. I have no idea where her bra ended up, but I'm of the mind that she should never wear one again with the way she looks in that sweater with her nipples prominent beneath the fabric.

She's getting skittish, and it's clear she's already in her head, unlike me. This isn't surprising given the well-known fact that a man's brain can either be in his skull or in his pants, but never both at the same time. Women are way more evolved.

I'd originally been thinking we'd go back to Hollis's place before things got out of control and we christened my bar, but I don't see that happening now. Looks like I'm sleeping on the shitty recliner Carter dragged into the brewhouse when he was babysitting some wort over New Year's.

Totally worth it.

"Hey." I grab her attention and she appears almost startled behind those glasses. Yeah, she's way in her head. "I know I should have said it before now, but I genuinely appreciate everything you've been doing to help me. Really, it's above and beyond for a stupid phone call I'm sure I deserved in the first place."

She bites her lip again and glances down at her feet before replying, "It's no big deal."

"Well, it is to me." I step into her space and lightly grip her upper arms. When she looks up at me, I bend to place a kiss on her lips. It's chaste in comparison to our earlier activities, but it still has me up for round two and Hollis looking drunk when I release her. I think we've created monsters of each other.

When she blinks herself back to reality, I know she's about to call it a night. Which is probably wise, though I wouldn't know because my brain doesn't even remember it has a skull to return to.

"I'd better go."

I don't stop her or touch her again as I let her retreat to the patio doors.

It's only then I realize we were screwing within view of anybody who might have been walking by. And I truly hope Hollis doesn't realize that, or she might in fact kill me this time.

"WHY ARE YOU SMILING?" Carter asks around the bite of apple he just took. I notice he's wearing a collared shirt I've never seen, which I take as an excellent sign that my brother is, in fact, returning to the land of the fully conscious.

"We had a great night last night." I make a note to do a better job of hiding my thoughts.

"I hope so. I just about busted my back hauling kegs last night. Do you know we're all out of *Swig Foot* and *Cryptid Chaos*? The new batch of *Cryptid* won't be ready for another two weeks."

"I know. That group of middle-aged women threw down. Left a great tip too, according to Jodi."

He swallows and frowns at me. "Maybe we have enough to give that lady another hundred to let us choose our own damn beer name, yeah?" It's gonna take years for him to let this one go.

But my urge to smile evaporates as well. "I mean, come on. *Sassy Q*? It's just…"

"Appalling," he finishes for me. "Luca had better do one hell of a job on the label if we're gonna move any of it with that name."

Luca's been drawing one thing or another since he could hold a pencil. Drove Adrina and Wes damn near crazy when he moved on to paint. They've still got some of his early work on the odd cabinet or wall. He does all our labels in exchange for free beer, and we're definitely getting the better end of the deal on that one.

"He'll work it out."

"You'd better hope so." He raises an eyebrow, trying to intimidate me by leaning in. Then he crunches the apple in my face and heads to the other end of the bar.

My phone dings with a text alert, and I hear Carter's do the same. We pull them out of our pockets simultaneously. It's our family text chat.

MAMA:

> Weather forecast for tomorrow is perfect, so we're doing a fire. Everyone there by 6pm sharp.

> Oh, Cash, I invited Hollis in case you didn't get around to it yet.

It takes my siblings all of three seconds to respond to that one with hearts and hahas. Jackasses.

ROSIE:

> Mamma's making homemade cannoli, guys, so leave room.

Of course Rosie's in our family chat.

Our dad's birthday is tomorrow, and like every year since his death, we all gather to tell stories, eat good food, and generally celebrate his life. Mama inviting Hollis is something I should have seen coming, but I didn't. I don't quite know how to react, but I'd better figure it out before I talk to Hollis again—which will be when she opens up shop for the day in just a few minutes. Not that I've been scoping the parking lot for her car or anything.

I'm lucky it's Carter here with me this morning instead of Miller or Denny, or I'd be on the hunt for the duct tape to shut somebody up. Carter goes on with business as usual—that's why we make good partners.

I still haven't worked out how to explain away the thousands of dollars in equipment that will hopefully be installed in another week and a half. I thought about making up some bullshit about coming into some money and wanting to invest in upgrades, but Carter's not stupid. The minute he sees not only the scale of the upgrades but the conspicuous similarities between my list and the "fake" inspector's, it'll be game over.

I applied for yet another credit card to cover the filtration system and some of the smaller crap, but cash is hard to come by, and I'm still a little short of what I expect to need at that auction.

When did my life get so out of control? I hate this feeling. I'm the one who reins things in and keeps them from going off the rails, and now I'm the damn engineer sleeping at the controls.

But I'm way past the point of blaming it all on Hollis.

Shit happens and you learn to either ignore it, fix it, or roll with it in any way that works. I'm pretty much an expert by now, so I'm looking forward to wrapping this up and getting back to business as usual.

The only problem is that doesn't include me fuckin' my neighbor. And I *really* enjoy fuckin' my neighbor.

HOLLIS

I WAKE up groggy at ten-fifteen with an aching body and a throbbing between my legs. It takes me a second to connect the dots, and then I'm rocketing upright in bed— no caffeine necessary. I fell asleep last night reliving my encounter with Cash, and I must have had some hot sex dreams if the state of my sheets is anything to go by.

My phone dings and I realize it was my text notifications that woke me. Thank god, or I might have slept till noon and been late to open the shop. I snatch the phone from my nightstand, ignoring the uptick in my heartbeat as I wonder if it's Cash.

It's not.

HADLEY:

> NGL your vm gets funnier each time we listen to it

> Does sober you remember m/d r on safari so no service?

Miller is dead to me btw

And I already apologized—duh

G2g to beach

Advil fy hangover kk

Safari? Hangover? What is she talking about?

ME:

Hey, you there?

While I wait for my sister to reply, I pad barefoot to the kitchen where Marco and Polo are passed out by their bowls. Marco's got his back legs splayed out and his tongue lolling to the side. I love these little weirdos.

We don't have a foster right now because I've been waiting for the boys to get comfortable before I bring another pet into the apartment, but it might be time.

"I'm so sorry, sweeties. You must be starving—and about to burst."

They spring to their feet and head for the door, little tails wagging madly. I throw on a light sweatshirt and some slip-on shoes and leash them up before heading outside.

Hadley hasn't replied, so I try calling, only to get her voice mail again. I was sure Mom and Harry said they were going to Lake Como, but that was weeks ago, and I'll admit I've frozen them out a little since they made it clear they weren't on board with my career change. A mental image of both of them in head-to-toe tan with big matching safari hats is way too odd to register.

I hang up without leaving a voice mail and look down to assess my state of being while the dogs sniff around on the grass across from my building.

I'm tender in lots of places, but nowhere more so than between my legs. Good god. He could warn a girl, you know. My belly does that swooping thing again, and I try to ignore it. I have no idea how to play this thing. I have no idea how *he's* going to play this thing.

Do we just resume sniping at each other? Is he going to start kissing me hello? Is there a repeat of last night on the horizon? Do I want there to be a repeat? Do we pretend this never happened? Was this all a huge mistake?

Of course it was a huge mistake, you imbecile! I knew that from the second I caught myself looking at his ass four months ago. But when he stepped closer last night and started whispering all those intimate things, it was impossible to walk away. And now I'm screwed. Literally and figuratively.

My phone dings again and I sigh with relief—not only because Hadley is finally communicating with me, but because thinking about other things means I can't think about the way Cash held my eyes when he bent to kiss my lady town. And now I'm sweating.

But, again, I'm wrong about who's texting me.

GINNY BROOKS:

> We're having a big party tomorrow at six, and we'd love it if you came. Bring a jacket.

This is followed by her address.

Well, that's not awkward at all. There is no way I'm going to Cash's mom's house—he'll think I'm stalking him!

And that's the last thing I need. What I *really* need is to get the power back in this relationship—friendship? Hateship? Partnership? Sinking ship? Whatever it is! That way, I'll know where I stand and what to expect.

Yes. I'll just pretend last night never happened, and as soon as Cash catches on, he will too. Perfect. Fabulous.

Time to get to work.

MY INGENIOUS PLAN works for the time it takes to drive to the warehouse shops and step from my car. Then I see him.

He's just inside the patio door to Blue Bigfoot, reaching for something up high and exposing a slice of skin at his abdomen that I immediately want to lick. I nearly lose the dogs' leashes when they make a run for the shop, and I end up stumbling after them like some fourteen-year-old who grew eight inches overnight and doesn't know how her legs work yet.

I'm not ready to see him—or talk to him—especially now that my resolve has gone directly down the drain without having the decency to even circle it for a few seconds before disappearing.

The dogs run right for the toy bin as soon as I unlock the door. Today is a light grooming day, and since the sun broke through the clouds and brought true spring temperatures, I'm wearing a cute little dress to boost my confidence. Not little by Hadley's standards—since I don't normally flash my underwear at strangers—but it's got cap sleeves and smocking on the top with a skirt that hits me just above the knees. And it's pink.

I'm running a sale on all my pet apparel today. My sidewalk chalkboard welcomes customers with "Your pet will look fetching in our custom apparel: 30% off today!"

I've posted some online ads and pinned a flyer to my sign by the dog park too. I carry some posh brands, so they're always good money-makers, even on sale.

When my bell rings a few minutes later, I look over with a smile, expecting to see a new customer, but it's Cash. And his face is a blank slate.

Crap. I'm not ready.

It takes everything I have to keep my smile looking casual and not manic like my insides. Why do I suddenly have no idea what to do with my hands? I grasp a pen from the countertop to keep myself from fidgeting.

"Morning," he says, strolling my way with his hands in his pockets. Hmm. Maybe I'm not the only one with this hand problem.

"Good morning… neighbor." There. I'm setting the right tone.

He tilts his head back a little, like he's farsighted and trying to read a menu that's too close. "Ah," is all he says before nodding his head. See, I knew he'd get on the same page.

I'm beginning to feel more confident and definitely not picturing him fisting his erection. So he saw me naked. Big deal. I was born naked.

"I trust you can handle the band on your own tonight." We booked one of the acts I found who'll perform for tips, and they're playing on the patio tonight. We're—I mean *he* —is hoping to make it a regular thing every Saturday.

He can get by without me from here on out. With the cash from yesterday and the gift cards bringing money in every day—and now the draw of a band plus anything else he can scrape together—he'll be fine. And if he's short, I'll sell the earrings and leave an envelope of cash in his office when he's not looking.

He's still watching me. I tell myself this isn't weird or awkward at all. Maybe I need to bring back the hostile vibe that worked so well for us before this mess started.

I open my mouth to say something snarky about his flannel shirt, but the blue brings out his eyes in a way that makes him look even more handsome than usual. Or the yeasty beer odor that sometimes follows him, but all I can smell is the clean soap scent from the other morning in my office. Or him still living with his mom, but now that I know more of their story, I think it's sweet. Or him being a grinch, but grinches don't make my heart skip two beats at once.

"I managed to survive just fine on my own till now," he says when I remain silent, my mouth like a goldfish sucking air. "*Princess*," he finishes.

The word and his tone do everything I wanted him to do—return to the before times and forget anything ever happened between us. Back to normal.

So why does it feel like I can't breathe?

I straighten my back and purse my lips, using every bit of willpower I own. "Glad to hear it. Now, if you'll excuse me, I have work to do." My tone is perfect, the words delivered with just the right mix of condescension and dismissal.

With that, I pivot on my heel and stride as regally as possible to the grooming area before I screw this up.

I can hear his boots on my tile, and I assume he's heading for the door. Until I hear his voice just a few feet behind me.

"*Jesus. What happened to you?*"

I spin around, not at all prepared for whatever strange fight he's picking, but his expression isn't hostile, it's... concerned.

Before I can protest, he holds me by the bicep and turns me around so my back faces him again. What is he doing?

"Hollis... did I... did I do that to you?" His voice is strangled, and I realize he's looking at my back where my dress reveals a large swath of skin.

His fingers gently slide my cap sleeves aside and pull down at the smocking in the back, and he sucks in a breath.

"It's nothing," I protest, remembering my shoulder blades banging into the solid edge of the bar last night. It's sore, yeah, but it hadn't even occurred to me to look in the mirror this morning to check for bruises.

"It's not nothing," he insists, replacing my dress to its previous state with the utmost care and then taking a small step back.

I try turning, but he doesn't let me until he's investigated the skin of my arms and the parts of my legs exposed by my dress. Then he lets me turn, but only so he can examine the front of me. Thankfully, he draws the line at lifting my dress over my head.

"Come on," he says in a voice that invites no arguments before taking my hand and pulling me gently toward my front door.

"Where are we going? I have a shop to run. My dogs are here!" I throw up my other arm, but he's single-minded in his intentions. "It's nothing, I promise."

He looks at me with his brows drawn and his lips a thin line. "It's not nothing. I hurt you. I didn't even have the decency to take you to a bed."

"Oh my god. Seriously?" My shop door closes behind us, and I try digging my heels in. Since he's treating me like some fragile glass figurine, he stops short of yanking me with him. I stare him down once he faces me.

"First of all, I was a willing and equal partner in what we did last night. Second, I bruise very easily, so you don't need to freak the hell out. And third, I have a business to run, and I'm expecting a very busy day. So, if you don't mind, I'm going back to work."

I pull my hand free and he lets me. He doesn't follow me back into the store where I immediately go to the bathroom mirror and attempt the impossible task of looking at my back. From the small glimpses I manage, I'll admit I kind of understand why he was alarmed. And, yeah, I'm sore, but the orgasms were totally worth it.

The bell on my door rings again, and I snatch a cardigan from a hook and throw it on before Cash can bring his doctor bag and speculum to check me over more thoroughly. But it's a cute couple dressed in matching T-shirts and hats browsing my sale instead.

"Hi," I greet them. They have a yellow lab with them, and it's clear they've been for a run. I look over at Marco and Polo, but they're dead asleep in their bed behind the counter. Some dogs are joggers, some dogs are nappers.

"Everything on that wall is thirty percent off, and I can do custom orders and personalization too."

The couple browses a bit more, and four more customers come and go in the next thirty minutes. By the time the door shuts behind them, I've sold two hundred fifty dollars in merchandise and booked a grooming appointment for a cocker spaniel named Ernie for next Friday.

With the store quiet again, I almost let myself be disappointed that Cash was so easy to get rid of earlier, but then I shriek as a shadowy figure emerges from my office. The dogs go nuts, barking up a storm and jumping at the gate that keeps them put.

"You scared the shit out of me!" I yell at Cash. "How did you get in here?"

"I came in when you were helping that couple with the lab. I've been waiting for everyone to leave."

I want to shove him and kiss him at the same time—which pretty much sums up our entire relationship.

"Wear a cowbell or something next time, will you?" My hand drops from my chest.

He ignores me and approaches, and that's when I notice a small container in his hand.

"Please don't tell me that's a promise ring. I don't think I can take you treating me like a virgin anymore."

He opens his palm, and it's a bottle of acetaminophen.

"Oh."

He's all business, his lips a grim line. "Two of these every four to six hours." He hooks a thumb over his shoulder. "Got two ice packs wrapped in a towel in your office. Twenty minutes on, every couple hours, then switch to heat tomorrow."

"Oh, okay. Got it." I take the bottle of painkillers from him, careful not to let our fingers touch. "Thanks."

It's kind of sweet, really, and Cash Brooks has never struck me as a sweet type of guy.

My awkward hands are back, but at least I have the bottle to occupy them. "I guess I'll, uh, see you around."

He doesn't smile or bid me farewell or move toward the door. Instead, he maintains his no-nonsense demeanor and walks around me so he's behind my counter. "Walk me through your POS. Is it a standard—"

"What are you doing?" I interrupt.

His brows pull together. "What does it look like I'm doing? I'm manning the sales floor while you ice your back."

"You're—" I stutter as I grasp for words that aren't just an echo of his crazy-pants statement. "Cash, it's only a bruise." I wasn't lying when I told him I bruise easily. I'm like a peach. So I tell him as much. "I'm a peach."

"Come again?" He tilts his head this time, and I can't help but think he looks like Polo when I hide a treat behind my back and his lack of object permanence awareness bites him in the ass. Except Cash is much hotter than my dog. "Shit, Hollis. Did I give you a concussion too?" He starts toward me, but I stop him with a hand in the air.

"No, you knucklehead. It's an expression. I bruise like a peach."

It's another few seconds before he takes me at my word and returns his attention to my computer and point-of-sale setup.

"So, what I'm saying is I'm fine to continue working." I shake the bottle of pills in my hand. "I'll take some of these and ice my back when I get home, okay?"

I walk to where he's standing, so he's forced to step back from my counter. We're close. So close I can see the flecks of navy in his blue eyes and the different shades of brown and black in his scruff.

He opens his mouth to protest, but I cut him off. "But thank you, Cash. Thank you for worrying about me." My words are genuine.

His eyes scan my face until his expression eventually settles, and the tension leaves his jaw. "I'm so sorry, Hollis. I won't ever hurt you again." He says it like an oath, and my darn belly swoops. So I'm not prepared when he dips his head and places the softest of kisses on my lips.

It takes another five minutes after he walks out the door for my breathing to return to normal.

CASH

I CHECK on Hollis twice more until I get swamped with the Saturday late afternoon crowd and then the evening rush with the band that plays only slightly better than Kelsie's. It's hard to focus with the sight of Hollis's upper back and shoulder blades covered in those angry red and purple marks swimming in my head.

I'm such an asshole. I was so anxious to get inside her. I treated her like some ragdoll and not the beautiful, living, breathing woman she is. There's a reason beds are the most popular place to screw.

Each time I go next door, Hollis is busy with customers or talking to the kid who works for her. And I don't think she would appreciate me chatting about her sex injuries in front of any of them.

Seeing how battered she was messed with my head, and I can't shake the restless feeling in my bones. I know she doesn't want me to take care of her, but I have to. It took everything I had not to drag her along with me this morning and set her up somewhere with a soft place to rest her head and an icepack on her back. But she loves being stubborn and contrary—especially with me.

That's why we've always been so good at fighting—we're too damn alike.

When seven o'clock rolls around, I ditch Kelsie at the bar and rush outside, knowing Hollis just closed up. But the salon is dark, and her car is nowhere to be seen. Maybe the band drove her so nuts she cut out early.

Or maybe she's avoiding me again.

It's not hard to figure out which.

I head back inside and go straight to the office while I text Hollis.

Me:

You okay? You left early.

I search through the loose papers on my desk to find the business card Rylee left me last night in case I wanted to do any advertising with the newspaper. As soon as I spot it, I snatch it up and text her cell.

ME:

> Hey, Rylee. This is Cash Brooks from last night. Do you happen to have Hollis's address?

I purposely leave out my reasons, and it must work because the dots start dancing on her end.

RYLEE:

> Hi there. Last night was fun. Thanks for the free beer.

ME:

> No problem. Thanks for the help.

I'm about to ask again when Hollis's contact info pops up in the thread.

RYLEE:

> Use it wisely, and don't tell her where you got it 😉

It's another three hours before the crowd starts to thin and I find my window to escape.

Kelsie jumps at the opportunity to close in my place. She's working a group of half-drunk single guys in the corner and seeing how high she can get her tip before turning them down with the news that she has a boyfriend. I think this month it's a ski instructor from Japan she met online.

I haul ass to my car and make a quick stop on my way to Hollis's place.

She lives in a complex in West Asheville with a park across the street and a half-full parking lot. When I find her building, I climb the stairs two at a time and knock on her apartment door.

I hear barking but nothing else, so I knock again after a minute. This activates more barking, then some mumbled words and the click of a dead bolt. The door opens only a crack. It's dark inside, but the light from the hallway illuminates Hollis's face. She has one eye scrunched closed, her hair is bunched in a knot on top of her head, and her glasses are nowhere to be seen.

"What is your face doing here? *I* live here," she says in a voice I hear all the time at the bar. Drunk girl. Then she smiles lazily and says, "Good morning," before closing the door in my face.

Her mixed message has me erring on the side of "like hell I'm leaving her alone injured and drunk with an unlocked door." She can cuss me out tomorrow. So I turn the knob and the door opens easily.

Two sets of paws attack me, jumping up on my jeans but not quite reaching my knees. When I switch on the light, it's no surprise to see Hollis's yappy little dogs, Marco and Polo, trying to climb me like there's a squirrel perched on my head. But Hollis is gone.

I walk past her kitchen and dining area, flipping another light on so I don't trip. Her apartment is neat and colorful, just like I knew it would be. There's a fluffy chair that reminds me of the one in her shop, and tons of pictures, paintings, and crafty décor. It doesn't take a genius to track her down in her bedroom.

The silhouette of her prone form shows her sprawled on her bed, and when I switch on her bedside lamp, I see she's lying on her face wearing tiny sleep shorts and a t-shirt with a chihuahua wearing a topcoat on the back. I can't help my grin.

"Hollis," I whisper. But I get nothing, so I stroke her bare arm and say her name again. This time she turns over partway, her hair covering her face.

"Hey, what are you doing here?" she asks like she didn't just see me two minutes ago. I brush her hair aside so I can see her face. She's squinting at me. "Did you bring cookies?"

I bite back a smile. "Hollis, you're drunk."

"No, I'm not."

Since that's what every drunk person I've ever spoken with has said, I move on. "Okay. Do you feel all right? How's your back?"

She sits up, looking very serious, the wide neck of her T-shirt sliding off one shoulder. "I can't catch my tail."

How much did she drink? I glance around for evidence to get an approximation, and I see a pill bottle on her nightstand. On inspection, I find it's prescription sleep medicine with her name and instructions to take one pill at bedtime as needed.

"How many of these did you take?" I ask in alarm.

"The doctor said one. Just one." She raises an index finger and brings it almost to my nose. "And in bed is where you eat it because it makes some people *crazy*." She whispers the last word while circling her ear in the universal sign for batshit loco.

"Ah. Then you should definitely stay in bed." I move to stand and she grabs my wrist.

"Where are you going with your face?"

"I'm getting ice. I'll be right back."

She lets me go and flops backward on the bed. "Ow. There's something wrong with my back."

I find the ice packs from this morning in her freezer and wrap one in a kitchen towel. One of her dogs is already asleep in a dog bed in the corner. The other one is chasing its tail.

When I return to the bedroom, Hollis is lying on her back mumbling to herself.

"Okay, peach, roll over." When she does as I ask, I know she's not in her right mind. I move her hair to the side and drape the ice pack gently across her upper back, just below that long ivory neck I took my time tasting last night. My dick starts stirring so I turn my thoughts to the least sexy thing I can think of.

I've always been a bit brusque and focused more on reaching the goal than the method I use to get there, but I never thought of myself as such an insensitive asshole.

"It's cold," Hollis mutters into her shoulder.

"Ice usually is." I put a hand on the pack to keep it from slipping.

The light from the lamp bathes her face, and I can see the freckles high on her cheeks that are usually hidden by her glasses. Her nose is slightly turned up at the end, and her long eyelashes brush her cheeks every time she blinks. She's downright gorgeous.

"Your mother wants me to stalk you," she says, this time more clearly. I have to still her with my hand when she tries rolling over to talk to me.

While I have no doubt my mama is capable of hatching such a ridiculous plan, I'm relatively sure she draws the line at restraining orders. Still…

"I guess you have to do what you see fit." She's not going to remember any of this in the morning, so I say more than is perhaps wise. "I can't think of anybody I'd rather have as a stalker."

This makes her smile. "I bet you say that to all the peaches."

"No, ma'am. You're the one and only."

Her drugged-out brain switches threads. "It's okay because I don't hate you anymore."

I stroke her hair, and she purrs like a lazy house cat. "I don't hate you either, peach. And I'm sorry I hurt you."

She lifts her head again and blinks at me. "Did you bring cookies?"

CHAPTER
TWENTY-FIVE
ONE TICKET TO ANCHORAGE, PLEASE

HOLLIS

THE SECOND I WAKE UP, I know something's amiss. My blanket is too heavy. And there's something hard pressing into my butt. My eyes pop open as realization dawns. There's a warm muscular arm draped over me. In my bed.

When I gasp, it moves, and I hear a familiar sound. But it's one I've only heard at the warehouse shops and definitely never in my apartment. It's a distinct Cash Brooks groan. That sound will live rent-free in my mind for decades to come.

The hard thing nestled against my butt moves as well, and I yelp, jumping out of bed and spinning around. "What are you doing here? When did you…? How did you…?" Cash rolls onto his back and stretches his arms over his head as he yawns widely. He's wearing a black t-shirt that almost matches his hair, the sheet covering the rest of him. I glance down and am relieved to see I'm wearing clothes. My back and my vagina also feel a lot better today.

"Morning," he says like this is a routine we practice every day. "Did you know you snore?"

"No, I don't." I bring a hand up to cover my mouth as I snatch my glasses from the nightstand and shove them on my face. I can't let Cash smell my morning breath. I can't let him even know I *have* morning breath.

"You do." He sits up, his hair a tumbled and incredibly sexy mess. "Trust me. It's cute though. Kind of like a tiny piglet." He grins and I look for something to throw at him.

What the hell happened last night? The last thing I remember is getting in bed and taking a sleeping pill so I could stop my mind from buzzing and get a good night's sleep. Those things can knock me a tiny bit sideways, but they can't be powerful enough for me to forget inviting Cash over to sleep in my bed!

I hurry to the bathroom and lock the door behind me so I can freak out in private. I pee, then scowl at my reflection, brush my teeth, and take a few deep breaths before opening the door again. The sight that greets me threatens to make me fall immediately in love with Cash Brooks.

He's on the floor in bare feet, a pair of jeans, and that black T-shirt, laughing at my dogs as they crawl all over him. My head drops back and I silently ask God why she's torturing me.

When he sees me, Cash gives Marco a scratch behind the ears and stands, casually resting his hands on his hips and making my womb literally tremble. This is not the time.

But before I can speak, Cash fills me in.

"You took off so fast from work, I came over to check on you when I got off. You were sky-high on sleep meds, and I didn't think it was a good idea to leave you alone with an unlocked door."

"So you slept in my bed?"

How do I not remember any of this?

Oh, crap. I mentally smack my forehead as I remember I skipped dinner last night! That must be why the pill hit me so hard.

"You asked me to." One corner of Cash's mouth lifts.

"I wasn't in my right mind," I protest, backing up a step.

"Oh, believe me, I know."

Oh, god, what did I say to him last night?

"That wasn't me!" I take another step back because he's doing that sexy slow walk thing that gets me in trouble every time. "That was some crazy version of me. You can't trust anything she says."

His eyes twinkle. The bastard is enjoying this way too much.

"So, you didn't mean it when you said mansplaining makes you want to stab people?"

I move to protest, then stop. "Well, yeah, that's true."

He advances with the sexy parade. "And…" He puts a finger to his chin like we're playing charades and he wants me to guess the word *thinking*. "You *don't* think oatmeal raisin cookies are underrated?"

"Duh, fruit *and* dessert? You can eat twice as many and not feel guilty at all." It's starting to sound like drugged-out me is kind of a legend.

Now he's getting too close, and my back is against the wall beside my bathroom door.

"But you definitely didn't mean it when you said kissing me makes your stomach do a 'swoopy' thing?" He even does the air quotes.

Crap.

"No comment."

He's so close now I can feel the warmth radiating off him. He lifts a finger and traces my jaw, brushing my bottom lip with the pad of his thumb. My breath hitches, and I know he hears it because his lips quirk just the tiniest bit. When his hand drops and he dips his head, I know it's no use lying to him. He can read me like a dirty romance book. I let my eyelids fall as I tip my head up to meet him halfway.

Then...

Nothing.

I open my eyes just in time to see him disappear into the bathroom, the door shutting behind him as he says, "I'll be out in a minute... *peach*."

My jaw drops as snippets from last night come rushing back. Oh no. No, no, no. I think I told him good orgasms make me temporarily deaf. I've never told anyone that.

There's nothing to do now but fake my own death and move to Alaska.

"OH, come on, it's a *little* funny." Cash smirks from the driver's seat of his car.

I ignore him like I've been trying to do since he faked me out outside my bathroom this morning. It turns out that I not only confessed some of my innermost thoughts to Cash last night, but I texted his mom to tell her how excited I was to come to her big party. She's texted me three times today to tell me how much she's looking forward to seeing me. Well, one text was to ask me if I have any food allergies, which I thought was quite considerate.

So, now I have to go to this party and look like a stalker following Cash around, as if I have nothing better to do. Never mind that Sunday is my day off, and I still had plenty of time to go to the shelter today.

If that isn't bad enough, Cash insisted on driving me himself since "the roads can be dicey up there," even though it's sunny and clear and I've been driving for twelve years now. I'd been hoping to just pop into the party for a few minutes and then split, so Cash driving me puts a damper on my plans. But when I protested again, he went on and on about his mother not raising an ill-mannered sociopath, and how she'd skin his hide if he didn't drive me. Like this is a date or something.

I ultimately gave in from sheer exhaustion, although I made it clear his mother did, indeed, raise an ill-mannered sociopath, and no amount of driving women around would alter that fact. He just grinned and gave me a heating pad he'd bought on his way over last night.

I grumbled a thank you and let him have this one—but only because I like Ginny.

And now the man is laughing at me again about what a nutcase I was last night.

"How many times do I have to tell you I was on drugs? People on drugs do all sorts of things that are uncharacteristic."

"Hey, I'm a bartender. I know all about inebriated people saying things they wouldn't otherwise say. Drunk people are more honest than sober people."

"Last time Rylee was drunk, she told me mole people live in the sewers. How's that for honesty?"

"I'd say… prove to me they don't." He steers his car

around a tight bend as we ascend the mountain road. "I just mean people are less guarded when they're not coherent enough to watch their every step."

I frown at him, knowing he has me pegged. What happened to my grand plan yesterday of going back to normal and pretending we don't have all this... this... whatever this is between us!?

I cross my arms and look out the window at the dense forest of evergreens. "Well, I do like cookies, so I'll give you that."

I hear him chuckle, but I keep my eyes on the scenery.

When we pull up to the house, there are no signs of a party in progress. Just two cars in the driveway and an abandoned basketball in the grass by the detached garage.

"Are we early?"

"Not exactly," Cash mutters as he takes off his seat belt and exits the car. I do the same, but I'm sure I'll regret it.

The house is narrow with two stories and wood planking that looks like the woodpeckers have been hard at work. A large garden plot is visible along one side of the house, and the forest comes almost right up to the back. Empty planters and garden ornaments litter one side of the front porch, and a bright yellow door holds a decorative sign saying, "Believe" with a big footprint under it.

Cash opens the door and stands aside for me to precede him.

"There you are!" Ginny appears out of nowhere with a bottle of lighter fluid in one hand and a stemless wine glass in the other. Both appear to be equally full. "I thought you two might have decided to ditch us."

Cash shakes his head and puts a hand to my lower back. A shiver shoots right up my spine at the contact. "Let's get Hollis a drink before she changes her mind."

Ginny tells us she'll only be a minute, and Cash steers me into the kitchen where a young woman with dark hair and long legs stands at the butcher-block counter talking to Miller. This has got to be Lynn, with her resemblance to her brothers. When she spots us, she rushes over. "You must be Hollis," she says, caramel eyes sparkling.

"May I hug you hello?" she asks, her voice oddly formal.

When I nod a hesitant yes, she gives me a quick squeeze, then turns to Miller. "See. You need to ask a woman if she minds being touched before you slobber all over her."

"That's stupid. It takes all the excitement out of it," he responds, tossing some peanuts in his mouth with his one good hand.

"It takes all the lawsuits out of it. Us women have had enough of you knuckle-dragging meatheads peeing on everything to mark it. We're people, not belongings."

Oh, I like her already.

"I thought you chicks liked romance. Nothing about handing a girl a contract to sign before making out is romantic."

"Actually, that kind of contract in all likelihood wouldn't stand up in court," she tells him.

"Hey, Hollis," Miller greets me with a wave. "Ignore my sister. She's on a rampage."

"You're just saying that because you know I'm right. And because you're trying to gaslight me." She smiles wide and crosses her arms.

"I can't take any more of this," Miller says, heading in the other direction toward what appears to be a living room. "I'll be outside where the beer is."

Cash shakes his head. "As you've no doubt concluded,

this is my bab… litt… full-grown woman sister, Lynn," he finishes with a stutter.

Lynn beams at him before shifting to me. "It's great to meet you, Hollis. I'll be sure to tell lots of stories about Cash as a teenager."

Cash goes after her, but she dodges him, retreating to the opposite side of a worn oak table with mismatched chairs. "You were too young to remember anything that far back."

I can't help but smile at all the back and forth between the siblings. It makes me wish I had a bunch of brothers and sisters to grow up with. I'll bet none of the Brooks kids are spoiled.

"Let me guess," Cash starts once Lynn follows in Miller's wake and we're alone again. "You're a… pinot grigio fan."

"Very good, Mr. Brooks." I cross my arms.

"It's the bartender in me. When someone asks for a light beer, they're usually a fan of sweet wines. *But* since you always have fruit behind your counter—and you're no pushover—pinot grigio it was." He opens the refrigerator and pulls out a fresh bottle of wine.

"Impressive." How does he know about my fruit stash? "But please don't open a new bottle for me." No way I'm getting drunk; I might say more things I don't want him to know.

He arches an eyebrow. "Believe me, this won't last long."

Once he hands me a glass identical to Ginny's, he takes me to a large side yard where a pile of logs and branches are arranged over a makeshift fire pit formed from cement blocks. Camp chairs make a circle around it, and a few people are standing around with drinks in their hands.

Most of them I recognize as Brooks family members, and there's Denny's girlfriend, Rosie, who I met on Friday. They make a pretty adorable couple.

I'm introduced to Rosie's older brother who's named Luca, and her parents, Adrina and Wes Carmichael, who live next door. They're complete opposites, Adrina talking our ears off and Wes just nodding along and sipping on his beer.

When Adrina goes to get a refill of her wine, Wes wanders off toward the firepit, leaving Cash and me alone in the growing darkness.

"So, where's everybody else?" I ask.

Cash looks around like he's taking attendance and replies, "This is it."

My eyebrows shoot for the sky. This is the *big* party Ginny invited me to? It's all family and people who've known each other their entire lives. Why in the world would Ginny—or Cash—want me here?

Cash is oblivious to my inner turmoil, but I can see Lynn and Ginny checking me out and not being very subtle about it.

Yeah, maybe I will get drunk after all.

CHAPTER
TWENTY-SIX
THE LOBSTER TRAP

CASH

I GO for casual so Hollis might believe I don't see anything strange about her coming to my family's get-together, but I know damn well it's crazy.

I've been thinking all day about why I didn't snatch her phone out of her hands the second I saw who she was texting last night. Maybe part of me wanted her to see where I come from. So much of what she knows about me is assumptions, not reality.

And vice versa, it turns out.

Everybody knows you lose your inhibitions and share too much when you're drunk or high. That's part of the fun. So Hollis can't be surprised she shared a little more than she would have otherwise. It's nothing to be embarrassed about—when it's not happening to you, that is.

The bit about orgasms making her deaf was fun, and I learned that she likes wearing glasses because it makes people take her more seriously, not because she can't wear contacts. But nothing was more revealing than when she looked at me, her forehead all creased, and told me her parents don't respect the life she's chosen, so there's nobody who's proud of her apart from herself.

She passed out soon after that and I stayed up for a while, staring at the ceiling and considering that maybe being Hollis Hayes isn't as easy as I thought it was.

Mama calls us all to fix a plate, and I watch Hollis experience the best chicken and waffles on earth. Everybody is digging in, our hands getting sticky and greasy, and, in Miller's case, his shirt wearing most of his. Lynn finally takes pity on him and cuts up his meal so he can eat it without wearing it—but not before Adrina takes a few snapshots to post on her Instagram. The drinks are pouring themselves, the fire is lit and keeping us warm, and I'm feeling more relaxed than I have in a long time.

So, of course that's when the true reason for the party is revealed, meaning I have to keep a close eye on Hollis to make sure she doesn't freak the fuck out.

"Who wants to start?" Mama asks.

"I'll start!" Adrina throws her hand in the air, and Mama nods.

"Okay," she begins, her Italian accent more pronounced now that she's a few glasses in. "Mine is about the time Wade brought home the Ferrari."

Denny busts out laughing, along with Lynn, Miller, and Luca. The rest of us groan.

But Adrina smiles and looks right at Hollis. "Since Hollis has never heard this one, I'll start at the beginning."

Everybody groans at that because it's a well-known fact that Adrina is the world's worst storyteller. Sure enough, she goes off on tangents and stops a dozen times to make sure every detail is accurate. But she eventually manages to tell the story of when my dad brought home a wreck of a car to restore, thinking it was a Ferrari. By the time he figured out he didn't know how to restore cars—which Carter and I could have told him from the start—he also discovered that the guy who'd given it to him had lied just to get the damn thing off his property. It was actually a Pontiac.

"That thing sat on the lawn for two years," Carter adds.

Mama chimes in as well. "The grass still won't grow there, you know."

We all smile or laugh and raise our glasses. Hollis follows suit.

"To Wade," Adrina says. Everyone responds with either "To Wade" or "To Dad," and we all take a drink—except me because I'm taking Hollis home after. Then Mama adds, "Happy birthday, sweetheart."

Hollis turns to me, just like I knew she would, but I keep my eyes on the fire. 'Cuz Mama and I both neglected to tell her this is a party in honor of my dad's birthday. The night is always a little sad and more happy, but most of all funny as hell because my dad was too. He lived more in his fifty years than most people could in twice that. He was famous for his humor and was always dipping his toe into one thing or another: brewing beer, rock climbing, Bigfoot hunting, bird calling. Some endeavors were more successful than others. Spear fishing? Not so much. Lock picking? Pretty damn good.

I know if I meet Hollis's eyes now, she's gonna lean over and tell me this should be a private celebration just for those who knew and loved Wade Brooks, and that she doesn't belong here. But I don't know how to explain to her that she's wrong and that Mama inviting her and me insisting on driving her means we want her here.

Before Hollis can throw something at me to get my attention, Mama speaks up. "I'm going next."

She scoots to the front of her chair like a kindergarten teacher at story time, the fire illuminating her face. "It was near our anniversary one year, and Wade was working long hours on some new delivery route. Lynn was all of four years old and sick as a dog with a stomach bug. So I reckon I made some offhand comment like, 'I guess that means no fancy dinner for our anniversary this year.' I was just making noise, but *somebody's* ears were burning."

All eyes turn to me, and I flip a few of the dickheads off.

"That's right, Cash picked up on it and lord knows what went through his head, but he got his mind set on fixing me and Wade that fancy dinner. So, the evening of our anniversary rolls around, and I get home from work to find Lynnie bawling her head off on the kitchen floor. Mind you, Cash is supposed to be babysitting her. So I pick her up and go looking for him.

"He's standing in the den crouching and swaying like a goalie guarding a net. And when I look down, there are two big old lobsters on the rug, snapping at Cash and scampering around. And one of them has Lynnie's giraffe lovey in its claw."

Everybody's smiling at Mama and me over the crackling fire, and Lynn is laughing with her hand clapped over her mouth.

"Lynnie starts screaming for her lovey, Cash is cursing up a blue streak at these lobsters, and I'm trying to figure out how these darn things appeared in my den!"

I remember that day. I was working bagging groceries, and the lady who ran the seafood counter told me lobster is a breeze to prepare. I'm sure once you get them in the pot, they are, but I never managed that part.

Mama continues with the story. "In bursts Wade through the back door, a pair of long metal grill tongs in each hand. He dives for the lobster holding the lovey, grabbing the body in one set of tongs and Lynn's lovey in the other. He rips the giraffe out of the lobster's claw and tosses it to Lynnie who starts clapping and jumping in my arms.

"But the other lobster's not stupid, so it uses the distraction to hide under the sofa. Cash is on his hands and knees looking under the furniture and Wade is yelling for him to back up so he doesn't lose an eye to this thing. But he's so busy yelling at Cash and waving the one lobster around that he doesn't watch his feet. The damn thing snaps at his foot from under the sofa, slicing right through the top of his Croc and gripping his toe like a chicken nugget."

"Of course he was wearing Crocs," Denny chimes in, and we all chuckle. Dad loved those ugly-ass things for some reason.

"He was so surprised he dropped the tongs with the first lobster," I add. I can still see the look on his face when that lobster grabbed his toe. He was trying so hard not to cuss in front of Lynn.

Mama laughs. "Yup. They were back to square one, but Wade's shouting for somebody to get the darn thing off his foot. Lynn's laughing her head off 'cuz she thinks Wade is playing. Cash races to the kitchen and brings back the big butcher knife which has Wade yelling even louder since he doesn't want to lose his toes.

"But Cash strides right over, hacks the claw off the lobster in one strike, and grabs the dropped tongs to secure it. Wade snatches up the other lobster and they both run into the kitchen and throw the beasts into the sink."

Everybody's laughing now because it's easy to picture my dad busting in the door with all the confidence in the world only for things to take a turn.

"Needless to say, once Cash told me what he'd been planning, I found it funny too," Mama says.

"Bruh, don't lobsters come with rubber bands or something around the claws?" Miller asks.

I can only shrug because I was a prize idiot back then. "Yeah, but I thought you were supposed to take them off before cooking 'em."

"How old were you?" Hollis asks, and since her voice sounds more amused than freaked out, I look over at her. She's trying to hold in laughter and doing a shitty job at it.

"I don't know—fourteen or fifteen, maybe."

"How could you afford lobsters at that age?"

I just shrug again. "I worked at the supermarket; they gave me a discount." I've been working since the day I legally could because money may not be able to buy everything, but it sure as hell can make everything easier. But sometimes—like now—it feels like I'm barely keeping my head above the water. I know Mama and Dad went through lean times and did their best not to let us kids catch on, but Cart and I always knew. So I did what I could to help keep the younger kids in the dark.

Mama speaks up again, looking at me with soft eyes. "I told him it was a very sweet gesture but to maybe make sure dinner is dead before he brings it in the house next time."

Everyone laughs at that, and we all raise another toast to Wade Brooks.

But I see Mama shift her eyes to Hollis, and I shake my

head at how she's managed to work this thing to further her grand plans.

"That was really sweet, Cash," Hollis says quietly, falling right into Mama's trap.

Mama chose that story because it was about me, not Dad. She invited Hollis here in the first place as part of her scheme to get Hollis to see the "real" Cash so she'll fall into my arms and Mama can move on to Carter.

"Well, I suppose I have my good days," I respond as I shake my head at Mama and she pretends not to see me.

HOLLIS

I'M NOT STUPID.

I know Ginny played me.

But I can't seem to summon up any reaction to it other than to laugh—and maybe shrug. Cash is obviously not who I thought he was at first, but I've known that for a while now. It doesn't change the fact that he's a danger to my heart—not one bit.

When I let myself admit the truth, I know the problem is we're too much alike. We're both independent, competitive, and always out to prove ourselves to the world. And we both hate—I mean HATE—when the other one doesn't give us the respect we think we deserve.

But that's starting to change, and it scares the bejesus out of me.

Ginny refills my glass two more times, and everyone but me shares at least one story about Wade Brooks. It makes me wish I knew him.

Although he undoubtedly would have driven me a bit

nuts if these stories are all true. Carter told one about Wade having a little paranoia when it came to banks, so he'd hide small quantities of money around the house and then forget where he put them.

I can only imagine what Harry would have to say about that.

According to the story, Ginny was preheating the oven one day and smelled something burning. And, sure enough, she'd burned forty dollars Wade had stashed in there. When they all sat down for dinner that night, Ginny served Wade the charred remains on his plate instead of dinner.

I can't remember a time when I've laughed so hard or felt so content. The Brooks family is crazy and loud and full of opinions and attitude, but there's so much love at the center of it all. It radiates from every story, every interaction, even from the insults and the bickering. It's beautiful, really.

I know I'm lucky to have the love of my family and every resource money can buy should I find myself in trouble. But sometimes I miss the early days when my mom and I would eat BLT sandwiches while cuddled up on the couch watching *Steel Magnolias* for the fourteenth time. We'd both bawl at the funeral scene, even though we promised each other we wouldn't this time. We never did that anymore after we moved in with Harry. Mom turned into a society wife, and she even started speaking differently.

But I'm acting exactly like the poor little rich girl Cash thinks I am. Thought I was? The lines are getting so blurred I'm not sure anymore.

The fire eventually dies down and people start grumbling about work in the morning. Lynn heads to bed so she can get up at the crack of dawn and make it back to Boone in time for her first class. I discover that Carter has been living in the attic since he came to town, and Miller lives here too. The only kid who's flown Ginny's nest is Denny, but it sounds like she wouldn't have it any other way. Hell, if my mom cooked like Ginny, I'd never move out either.

We say goodbye to everyone, and hugs are passed around freely, especially with Lynn in bed and not around to give the guys her two cents. Cash kisses Ginny's cheek and whispers something in her ear that has her eyes shining.

"It was so wonderful to have you here, Hollis. You're welcome anytime," she says as she hugs me goodbye. She's the kind of person who hugs with her whole body and soul, and I can feel the sincerity of her words in the embrace.

"Thank you so much. I had a great time."

Cash puts a hand to the small of my back again, and it gives me the same shivers, even though I'm dog-tired and a little tipsy.

The ride back to my place takes twenty minutes, and we pass the first few in silence. I'm replaying the entire day and evening in my head and trying to come up with some answers. Why would Ginny narrow her sights on *me* for her son when she doesn't even know me? And why would Cash be so willing to bring me there? And the worst question: what else did I reveal to Cash last night?

"I can hear you thinking from way over here."

I glance at Cash, but his eyes are on the road. "I'm surprised you're familiar with the concept," I say without thinking.

"So we're back to that, are we?" He's grinning.

"Did we ever stop?'

"Briefly." This time, he does look over, and his gaze is filled with meaning. I can feel myself blush at the memory of spreading myself out naked on his bar and acting like a porn star with all my moaning and shouting. The man is very good at what he does, that's all I can say in my defense.

"I like your family," I say, changing the subject as fast as humanly possible.

He lets me get away with it. "They're all right."

I laugh, because it's more than obvious that despite all his dismissive comments and cranky demeanor, Cash Brooks is both a family man and a mama's boy. And I'm finding all of it too damn attractive.

We fall silent again, and then apropos of nothing at all, Cash says, "When my dad died, I felt like it was my job to replace him—which is stupid because nobody could fill his shoes. He was wild, but never as much so as my mama. Somebody had to keep the train on the rails without him."

"That must have been a lot to carry," I respond quietly as I watch the passing lights illuminate his face and then plunge it back into darkness over and over. "From what I've witnessed, though, it looks like everybody is doing okay—great, in fact."

"That's because we're in the middle of *my* crisis right now. It'll be someone else's turn next."

"And you think it's your responsibility to what? Fight everyone's battles?"

"Somebody's got to. You'll understand next time my mama forgets to close the windows in wintertime or Miller gets arrested for indecent exposure." He goes for some levity, but his comment has my stomach sinking. I notice he's stopped blaming his current trouble on me and has taken all the responsibility on himself for some reason. I want to tell him it's *my* family messing things up this time, not his. But I can't yet. It would yield nothing with my parents MIA. It would only give him one more reason to think he was right about me all along.

"Why you and not Carter? Isn't he the oldest?"

"Yeah." I notice he only answers one question.

"Are you sure you don't *like* being the one who saves the day?" I'm poking the bear for sure this time, but I doubt anyone in his family *expects* him to fix everything.

"What is that supposed to mean?" The bear is testy now.

"Why haven't you told Carter about the inspector?"

His jaw is getting tight. "It's complicated."

"Doesn't sound very complicated to me."

And the bear has hit his breaking point. "You want to talk about me taking on things I don't need to? What about you? You come from a filthy rich family, and you're scrubbing dogs' asses when you could be eating bonbons by the pool."

"That's not—it's—"

"Complicated?" he finishes for me.

I open my mouth to bite back at him, but there's nothing to say. I've held back so much that, yeah, it's complicated. But, god, how I hate being judged for my family's money. And I hate even more having my chosen career belittled.

Cash pulls into the parking lot of my building, and I notice he doesn't park in a spot. That speaks volumes, so I undo my seatbelt and jump out of the car as fast as I can, slamming the door behind me. The side mirror falls to the asphalt with a telling *crunch*.

"You have got to be kidding me!" I glare at him through the window.

He responds with something I can't make out and then drives away. I stomp up the exterior stairs, cursing *him* for being a jerk and *me* for being stupid enough to think there might be something there.

I open my door, and the dogs run over, knowing my arrival means going outside. I leash them up and stomp back down the stairs, muttering to myself the entire time. Polo lifts his tiny leg to pee on every upright thing in sight and Marco catches the scent of something that's presumably rotting nearby.

Polo looks up at me with his big brown eyes, which I take as an invitation to share.

"Like I need him telling *me* about *my* life. He doesn't know the first thing about me. Everything is about him." I adopt a whiny voice that has Polo's ears perking. "Poor Cash, taking care of his entire family because, naturally, he's the only one who knows the right way to do *everything*." Marco joins us again, so I fill him in. "I'll bet they could all run circles around him if he let them."

"Who are you talking to?"

I shriek and spin around to see Cash standing there with one hand in his pocket and the other holding his cracked side mirror.

"What are you doing here?" My voice is accusatory, obviously.

He gives me a look that says I'm nuts. "I told you I was going to park the car."

"That's what you said?" Marco and Polo trot toward him, pulling on their leashes.

Cash steps closer so he can bend down to pet them. "What did you think I said?"

I blink at him. "'I'm a porcupine.'"

He grins. "Why would I say that?"

"I don't know. Maybe you were finally admitting how prickly you are."

He straightens and smirks at me. "I'm only prickly because you drive me crazy."

"Have you ever thought that it's your tolerance—or lack thereof—that's the problem, not me?"

"No."

I cough out an unamused laugh. "That's just like you. You can never be wrong, can you?"

"I've been wrong before. Once or twice."

"Oh yeah? Pick the wrong horse at a horse race? Bag the wrong girl and get crabs?"

"No, I thought you were a stuck-up, spoiled, rich girl with ice in your veins," he answers, casual as can be.

I start to rebut before his words register. "I..." That's all I have. Did he just...?

He steps closer, ignoring me when I put a finger in the air to stop him. "So imagine my surprise when I found out instead you're a warm, generous, hardworking, beautiful woman who lights up like the sun when I touch you."

"Stop with the sex parade." My finger hits his chest because, like a moron, I haven't backed up a single step.

"I have no idea what that means."

"I'm not falling for that again, Cash Brooks." Fool me once. He's not going to fake me out twice in one day. No matter how sweet his words are.

"Falling for what?" He's right up in my business now.

"You know exac—"

He cuts me off by sealing his lips to mine.

Either I'm the biggest sucker on the planet or Cash Brooks is turning out to be much more than I ever thought possible.

CHAPTER
TWENTY-EIGHT
BISCUITHEAD

CASH

IT TOOK me one point two seconds to admit to myself I was just being defensive in the car. Hollis is so good at getting under my skin that I snapped back with something I knew better than to use against her.

I keep thinking about what she shared last night in her drug-induced confession monologue. Even if she hadn't intended to, she opened up to me. So, I figured I owed her some opening up of my own. Looks like we both need practice in interpersonal conversation skills.

Her anger melted once I apologized and kissed her. So we went up to her apartment with the dogs, and for the second night in a row, I slept with Hollis in my arms.

She passed out almost immediately when her head hit the pillow, so I stretched myself out next to her doing some work schedules on my phone until sleep overtook me too.

Now I'm watching her make love to some bacon across the table from me at the Biscuithead near her apartment.

"Would you two like some privacy?"

She stills, her eyes popping open. She covers her mouth with her hand and says, "It's been so long since I've had real bacon."

"As opposed to...?"

She licks her lips, and that one gesture alone has my dick getting ideas. "I don't know. Turkey bacon? Microwaved bacon?"

"You need to come over to our house more often, then. We may as well have our own pig farm for how much bacon we go through," I tell her as I pick up my coffee. Black, just how it's meant to be.

The restaurant is loud and crowded as usual, with the scent of coffee and fresh-baked biscuits filling the air. But my attention is focused on the woman across the table.

"My mom was a beauty pageant contestant when she was younger, so she's always been a turkey bacon kind of girl."

"She doesn't know what she's been missing."

Hollis grins and turns her eyes lovingly to the strip of bacon in her hand. "No, she really doesn't."

I shake my head at her when she shoves it in her mouth and moans again. When she's done chewing, she says, "That chicken and waffles was so amazing, I'm thinking of asking your mom to adopt me. How are you not five hundred pounds?"

I shrug and set down my cup. "My job's a physical one, and I work out every morning before work." I glance down at our plates. "Well, most mornings. And not everything she makes is as sinful as last night. She's big on soups."

"My mom doesn't know how to cook, but she could teach you how to dance. Or play tennis."

"I think I'll pass."

She wipes her mouth with a napkin, and our waitress stops to refill our coffees. When she leaves, Hollis says, "Your dad sounds like he was a great guy."

"He was." My response is simple.

"You must miss him." Hollis's smile is sad, and I marvel again at how pretty she is.

"Every day," I answer, before tucking back into my bacon, egg, and cheese biscuit.

"I never knew my dad."

"No?" I ask over my mouthful.

She shakes her head and goes for the last bacon strip on her plate. "But my stepdad, Harry, has been a father to me since I was in middle school, so I'm lucky."

I swallow and ask, "You ever try to contact your biological father?"

"No. If you'd seen the guys my mom dated before Harry, you'd understand why. Apart from Harry, her taste in men is questionable at best."

That sounds ominous.

"My folks met in high school," I tell her. "They both came from the same dirt-poor town in Georgia. My dad was a bit of a delinquent, but they got married right out of high school when my mama was knocked up with Carter. Moved here and eventually saved enough money for a down payment on the house, and we've been there ever since."

"Did you ever think about moving anywhere else?"

I consider that. I'm not one of those die-hards who thinks Asheville is the best city on earth, but it's home, and it's where everybody I love is. "I lived in Greenville for a year and then Winston-Salem for a little while before my dad died and I came back home. What about you?"

She shrugs. "It's hard leaving the only place that's ever

been your home. Not that I have enough free time to even notice where I am. Sometimes I feel like I live at either the salon or the animal shelter."

"Let me guess. You were the type of kid who brought home any living thing you found outside." I could see her rescuing birds and groundhogs and using those big brown eyes to beg her mom to keep them.

"No. Before Harry, we moved around a lot and didn't have money to spend on pets. And if you saw Harry's house, you'd see why we don't have pets there."

I can only imagine. When I looked into the Hayes family, I had to stop after the article about her stepdad's art collection. He'd likely use Larry for kindling.

"So you never even had a cat or a hamster or anything?"

She shakes her head. That doesn't seem fair at all. Growing up, we had every kind of pet you can imagine at some point or another. Hell, Rosie and Luca had a pet raccoon for a while. I guess it wasn't technically a pet, but it liked to come in the dog door a couple times a week to scare the shit out of Adrina.

"Isn't it a rite of passage to walk into your bedroom one day and find your hamster dead in its cage?" I ask, sipping my coffee again and waiting on the caffeine to kick in.

"Ew. But no. I'm making up for it as an adult, though." She grins. "Speaking of, how did Ginny end up with Mango?"

I groan. "It's a long story having to do with a claimed sighting of Bigfoot. But basically, she found him injured on the side of the Blue Ridge Parkway."

"Why doesn't that surprise me?"

We chat a little more about growing up and about our

businesses, and I'm beginning to think Carter and I could have used her services when we were starting up. I never went to college, and Cart majored in political science. We've managed okay, learning as we go. But Hollis planned everything down to a T where her salon was concerned, and it sounds like she's closer to being in the black than we are, even with our head start.

When the waitress comes back to clear our plates, we both stand to go. I drop a few bucks on the table for a tip.

"I forgot we haven't paid yet," Hollis says, reaching into her purse.

"Yeah, we did." I gesture to the front counter. "When we ordered."

"Oh, crap. Let me give you some money."

I frown at her. "What for?"

"Breakfast, of course." I note she doesn't call me dummy or chowderhead or dipshit like she would have even a couple days ago. But she's out of her mind.

"You ain't payin' for breakfast." I turn to the door and she follows me outside.

"At least let me pay for mine."

"Why?" I ask over my shoulder.

"Because."

I bark out a laugh, and she catches up with me by our cars. We're both heading into work, but I insisted we stop for breakfast first. Between last night's dinner and today's breakfast, I'm gonna need an extra workout or two.

"Look," I tell her. "It may sound old-fashioned to you, but when I take a girl out, I pay."

"But…" she tries again, her brow crinkling over her glasses.

"But nothin'. I pay for dates. You can pay for, I don't know, takeout Chinese on the sofa or something."

She gestures back to the restaurant. "Are you implying this was a date?"

"Damn straight." I cup her ass and drop a kiss on her lips.

When I bring my head back up, she's looking dazed, so all she's got to say is, "Oh."

I know I'm wearing a shit-eating grin when I round the front of my car. "See you at work, peach!"

CHAPTER
TWENTY-NINE
THERE ARE NO ORGASMS IN SALES

HOLLIS

"WHAT ABOUT SMOKER'S PHLEGM?" I ask Cash, doing my best to sound serious as I nibble one of the cookies he bought me.

He pauses his hand's journey up my calf. "There's something seriously wrong with you."

I feign offense. "These are killer beer names and you know it." I break off a chunk of the monster cookie and feed it to him.

Somewhere between fighting in the car on Sunday and driving to work on Monday, our dynamic shifted, and we went from two people laughing *at* each other to two people laughing *with* each other. For the most part.

Now the only rivalry I'm engaged in is the one with myself. One side of me is basking in pre, mid, and post-coital bliss as well as Cash's surprisingly open admiration, and the other side insists we keep both hands on the wheel and one eye peeled for a crash down the road.

Tonight, Cash and I are lounging on my sofa half

watching a show about the Iditarod but mostly being lazy and throwing toys for the dogs.

He swallows before shaking his head and saying, "*Sassy Q* is sounding so much better after this conversation." Then he leans over to bite my thigh. I yelp and pull my leg back.

"There are only so many names out there with sasquatch references," I reason.

"You have no respect for beer—or Bigfoot. I'm not naming a beer 'Expired Last Week' or "Might Be Contagious.'"

His frown has me snickering, but this is essentially just payback for the time he changed the message on my sidewalk chalkboard from "We love doing pet parties! Inquire about our birthday package" to "We love doing it doggie style! Inquire about our orgy package." I can admit it's a little bit funny now—but just as juvenile as it was then. And I still don't regret my response, which was to hide opened cans of the smelliest cat food in existence in the bush outside Blue Bigfoot's door so customers were greeted by the lovely dead fish aroma.

I decide to stop torturing him. "I've never been a beer person, but that *Legendary Larry* is tasty, I must admit."

"I'm happy I converted you. It's my mission in life to convert one Coors Light drinker at a time."

I don't tell him I have a can in my fridge left over from a winter football game. "I keep forgetting to ask you what the deal is with Larry."

"Ah." He pulls my legs onto his lap. "Well, the original Larry is a carving my dad got from an old friend. If you haven't guessed, Bigfoot is popular at the Brooks house. When we were kids, my dad used to tell all sorts of crazy stories about Larry the sasquatch. Then when Cart and I opened the brewery, it was a no-brainer to honor him in a way. Bigfoot and the Blue Ridge Mountains became Blue Bigfoot Beer." He shrugs, and I smile at him because I love watching him when he talks about his dad. "We call the Larry on our logo Drunk Larry, as opposed to the statue which is simply Larry."

His smile falters a bit like he's just remembered something unpleasant, but he shakes it off after a second and resumes caressing my legs. It sends delicious tingles up my spine.

"I love it for you guys that you have so many great memories to keep with you."

"Yeah, I guess we're lucky in that way. We might not have had much money, but our childhood was fun as hell." He looks over with a sad smile. "I'm sorry you never knew your biological father."

"I'm not. Well, you know what I mean."

"You said before that your mom had shit taste in men." He sounds like he's treading lightly, but I don't mind sharing with him. Not anymore.

"I told you she was a beauty queen, right?" I ask and he nods. "Heads would turn when she walked into a room, and I swear she had a talent for picking the most handsome douchebag in the bunch. At one point, I genuinely thought ugly men were automatically good people because all the good-looking ones I'd met were complete wastes of space."

Cash brings a finger to his chin. "Your initial opinion of me is suddenly making a lot more sense."

I kick him and he laughs, grabbing my foot and tickling me until I almost pee my pants. "You are so full of yourself." I don't tell him that he's absolutely right and he's so handsome he makes my breath catch sometimes.

Marco tries jumping up to join the fun, but he's too short to make the leap onto the couch. Cash unknowingly elevates his sexy status by picking Marco up and holding him in front of his face. "Marco, don't grow up to be a douchebag, okay?" His tail wags so fast it's a blur. When Cash sets him back down, my dog takes off for who knows where, and Cash turns his attention to me. "Sorry, go ahead. Ugly dudes, good; handsome dudes, waste of space."

I nod, and it takes me a second to reengage my brain. "Yeah. But I learned the truth when I found out about the greasy mouth-breathers she had to educate on the meaning of the word no."

"Shit." He brushes his thumb over my knee.

"Yeah. She could hold her own, though." I smile wryly, one memory in particular surfacing. "We had this one landlord who was a real winner. He made sure my mom knew he had a key to our apartment, like a warning to play along or something. His wife found out he'd been perving around when he had to explain the broken nose he got when he used his key and my mom hit him in the face with a frying pan."

"Hard core." He looks impressed.

"We Mills girls could throw down with the best of them." I flex my bicep as proof, even though it barely changes shape. "That was our last name until she married my stepdad. The wife took Pervy McFryingPan back eventually, so we moved. Female landlords were few and far between, and we weren't exactly renting places in Biltmore Forest."

"It sounds like you've lived in a lot of places."

"Yeah, until my mom married Harry. He works in commercial real estate." I'm not about to tell Cash that

Harry spends more time on the golf course than he does the office. I don't want to think about Harry at all or I'll be tempted to spill my guts about this whole debacle. I shove those notions to the back of my mind.

The sled dogs on TV start barking, inviting Marco and Polo to do the same.

"Are you guys close?" Cash asks, muting the TV and consequently my dogs.

I groan at the question because the answer is so complicated—and it means I'll have Harry on the brain. "Kind of? We were closer when I was younger. That goes for my mom too. The teenage years were predictably rocky. And when I quit my job in sales to open Happy Tails, things froze over a bit."

"They don't approve." It's a statement, not a question.

"That's putting it lightly." I don't elaborate with some of the gems they've tossed my way like, "You're wasting your intellect," or "If you like dogs so much, become a veterinarian," or my favorite, "Are we supposed to tell our friends our daughter washes dogs for a living?"

"I'm sorry they make you feel like your business isn't worth your time. I've seen how hardworking and smart you are with the salon, and it sucks they don't recognize that."

"Yeah." My heart is lighter hearing those words from Cash. I marvel at this side of him I've uncovered, where paying me a compliment or being compassionate comes so naturally. As much as I hate to admit it, he's being much more open than I am, and it's a revelation.

"I guess I'm damn lucky my family loves beer so much —and that half of us never went to college." He goes for levity, and I smile in return. I can only imagine what Harry and my mom would think if they found out I was seeing a man who—gasp—doesn't have a college degree. My mom doesn't have one either, but she's dead set on Hadley and me living the kind of life she might have if she'd made different choices. I understand her wanting us to have the tools to succeed, but success doesn't look the same for everyone.

"Well," I respond. "I guess it's a good thing that I can stand on my own two feet without their approval. I'm proud of myself that I've done this on my own and cut myself off financially from them. The day I go begging them for money is the day I lose all respect for myself." My resolve to make Harry repay Cash is only hardened at the thought.

"Good for you. And, hey, maybe they'll come around one day."

"Maybe." I shrug. "But I'm not holding my breath."

Cash squeezes my thigh. "This is heavy conversation for midnight. What do you say we take these mutts outside and then find a way to entertain ourselves in the bedroom? I can show you just how much *I* approve of the things you do."

His words—and just his presence here in my apartment—make me feel lighter. I laugh and then let him feel me up a bit before we remember the dogs and take them out. After that, I do some of my best work with my tongue, and Cash makes it clear that I made the right decision setting up shop next door to him. There are no orgasms this mind-blowing in sales.

CHAPTER
THIRTY
BAKING TIME

CASH

"LET ME HAVE IT," I tell Hollis, and she moans again, riding me like she does in my dreams at night.

But I don't have to dream anymore because she's the real deal, and I'm finding it hard to think of any more reasons we shouldn't keep this thing going.

I have the best view in town, sitting in my office chair with a red-hot naked woman on top of me, her hands holding my shoulders while my fingers dig into the silky-soft skin of her hips. I lean in and flick my tongue over one delicious brown nipple as her tits bounce with her movements. The contact has her throwing her head back and moaning.

"Cash, oh god, I'm gonna come," she pants.

Her ass slaps my thighs every time she comes down to take my cock and I thrust up to meet her. She's so damn hot, tight, and sexy as fuck with her hair wild and not a stitch on apart from her glasses and the dainty gold necklace with her name on it that she always wears.

"That's right. Let go, baby."

She's moving faster now, and I can feel the beginning flutters of her orgasm, so I take a hand off her hip and give one of her nipples a pinch. It does the trick. Her pussy pulses around my cock, squeezing me hard and making me gasp for breath.

Hollis pants and whimpers as her climax rips through her. I use my hands to steady her and my hips to keep thrusting up into her. The combination of her hot pussy milking me and all her sexy sounds has that tingling radiating from the base of my spine. I know I'm gonna come any second, but I'm determined to let her ride out her orgasm as long as possible first.

"Oh god," she cries, her voice reaching a pitch I have yet to hear, and I try to think about anything but her gorgeous body on top of me. But it's no use. I come hard, pumping into her with abandon, each wave making my vision blur and my chest heave.

When we've both wrung every bit of pleasure out of our climaxes, Hollis slumps forward, her tits trying to suffocate me. You won't hear me complaining though. If I had to choose how to die, it would be right here with my cock buried in Hollis and her luscious breasts stealing my oxygen.

She's spent, panting into my ear, her bones turning to jelly, so I take advantage of the situation by reaching my hands around to squeeze her ass. I don't know that I've seen—or felt—one so perfect. In fact, I'm pretty sure at this point that I could identify Hollis's sweet ass in an all-ass line-up with my eyes blindfolded.

"I think *I* might have gone deaf this time," I say.

And right on cue, she sits up to glare at me. But it gives

me more of her to look at, so it's a win-win. I laugh and lean forward for another taste of her tight nipple.

Hollis swings her head around like she just remembered where we are. "Shit. How loud was I? I'll have to hand my business over to Josh and move if Oscar or one of your brothers heard us."

I could tell her everyone in Asheville knew what we were up to the second I locked the office door, but I enjoy her fucking me, and I don't want to give her any reason to stop. So I lie.

"It was your quietest yet. Seems I need to step up my game."

She brings her eyes back to me. "If you up your game any more, you'll send me into cardiac arrest. I'm not dying at twenty-eight."

"But what a way to go." I smile at her, and she leans in to kiss me.

By any of my previous standards, I'd want to punch myself in the face for acting as sappy and cheerful as I've been doing this past week. I've stayed at Hollis's apartment every night since Saturday, and we even started sharing rides to and from work. When Hollis closes shop for the day, she comes to hang out at Blue Bigfoot until closing or whenever I'm done. Then we head back to her place to screw each other's brains out like we're the last two humans on earth and are responsible for repopulating the whole planet.

We're still working on my money situation, but it doesn't dominate our time together like it did at the beginning. The auction is tomorrow, and I'm only short by a grand or so at this point after squeezing every dime out of anywhere I could think of. But, who knows, maybe I'll get the equipment for less than I budgeted. With the way things are going for me right now, I seem to be on a hot streak.

I help Hollis off my lap and take care of the condom while she cleans herself up. I have a habit of getting her entirely naked whenever we fool around, and this time is no different. So I sit back and enjoy the view as she puts her clothes back on. The way she wiggles her ass when she's pulling those panties up has me half hard again.

"Hey, turn around, peach."

She rolls her eyes but does as I ask. Her bruises have almost faded, with just a touch of green and yellow remaining, and she insists she can't feel them anymore. But I still get angry with myself when I think about them. I don't want anything bad touching Hollis. I want to protect her and make her feel cared for. And as much as I want them to fade completely, the bruises are a good reminder.

"Sometimes I think you just want to look at my ass, not my shoulders."

"Well, that goes without saying." I wink at her and she shakes her head at me. But she can't hide her pleasure and amusement. I never hold back telling her how sexy I find her, and it's only caused her to become more open and bolder with me.

"I gotta get back to work." She finishes fastening her bra and reaches for her top I tossed on my desk earlier. "I told Josh I was running out for a coffee thirty minutes ago."

"Believe me, he'd understand." Josh is a seventeen-year-old guy. He thinks about sex more often than he takes a breath. "You comin' over after?" It's likely to the point now where I don't have to ask anymore, but I like knowing I'm gonna see her.

She frowns. "I need to go to the shelter for a while. I

skipped Wednesday, and they said they could use a hand tonight prepping for an adoption event in the morning."

I smile as a memory from Wednesday plays in my mind. If I'm not mistaken, hot fudge was involved. And neither one of us missed the ice cream.

"Okay. I guess it wouldn't hurt for me to check in at home." I can catch a ride with Cart and Miller. Carter has a rental from his insurance company. It's a huge ancient Oldsmobile painted puke green, and it's one of life's greatest pleasures giving him constant shit about it. He tried to trade it for another one, but the guy at the insurance company has an excellent sense of humor.

"I can't imagine what your family must be thinking with you being gone all week," she says.

"I can tell you precisely what they're thinking. They're thinking we're screwing on every horizontal surface we can find and some of the vertical ones too."

Her jaw drops. "You're supposed to lie to me and tell me they think we're baking cookies or something!"

"Baking cookies?" I grin at her. "Really?"

"You know what I mean!"

I walk over and drop a kiss on her sweet lips. "You've got a post-it note in your hair."

"What?!" She turns around a few times, trying to figure out where it is, and she looks like one of her dogs chasing its tail.

Something occurs to me, and I start laughing. "That's what you meant!"

She pauses, batting at her hair. "What are you talking about?"

"The night you were doing your best imitation of Snoop Dogg, you said you couldn't catch your tail. I thought it was a hallucination, but you were just trying to get a look at your back."

She gives me the side eye. "Obviously."

"Get back to work, smartass." I smack her on her very smart ass and she jumps before glaring at me again. If I had my preference, I'd spend all day with one hand on her ass.

"See you tomorrow," she says, unlocking the door and swaying those hips to the taproom.

It doesn't occur to me until later that I've gotten so used to having her around, I never stopped to consider how much harder that will make it when she's gone for good.

CHAPTER
THIRTY-ONE

BAD LIAR

HOLLIS

"HEY!" Rylee walks through my shop's door, a big smile on her face. "Did you do that?" She's pointing in the direction of the brewery.

I set the Yorkshire terrier I just finished grooming on the floor while Josh sweeps up all the hair. "Did I do what? And what are you doing here?"

"Dean dragged me over because he heard the entire Arrows team is hanging out at your boyfriend's bar."

"He's not my—wait, what?" I close the half-door behind me, making sure Thor the Yorkie doesn't follow me out.

"So you didn't know? Damn, Cash must have connections."

Rylee trails behind as I rush out to the sidewalk where I can see through the patio doors. The place is packed. "Oh my god."

"I know. There are more people there than on St. Patrick's Day."

My heart is beating like a hummingbird's wings. They're going to make a killing today. I went ahead and sold the earrings earlier this week just for insurance, but it looks like he's not going to need it after all.

Rylee grins at me, arms crossed over her t-shirt that says *Synonym Rolls, just like grammar used to make.* "Look at you, all happy for him."

"Yeah, well." I can't help my smile as I watch a carload of women wearing Asheville Arrows gear filter into Blue Bigfoot.

"You've got it bad."

"Whatever." I'm not ready yet to fully trust this thing we have going, but it's getting harder not to fall for him.

"Seriously, I'm happy for you. He seems like a good guy."

"He is. He's nothing like I thought he was." I look for his familiar face through the crowd, but he must be behind the bar.

"Somebody can be right in front of your face, but it takes a while for you to realize they're the one for you."

I turn to Rylee to see her dopey smile. She's known Dean since they were kids, but it wasn't until last year that he made his move, and he went from her best friend's little brother to her hunk of burnin' love.

"I don't know that I'd go that far." That war inside me rages on.

"I'd better go keep an eye on Dean before he makes a fool of himself by offering to have Gunner Nix's babies," she says.

"By all means." I laugh and head back into my shop while Rylee goes to save her boyfriend from himself.

When I get back inside, I see that Cash has already left me two text messages about the Arrows team and the crowd. I can tell he's excited because he used an emoji, something he claims only Facebook moms do.

"I guess I'm heading out," Josh says, pulling on his backpack and moving for the door.

I stop him just before he opens it. "Hey, Josh, can I ask you a question?" He's an emotionally evolved teenage guy, so he should know. "Do guys your age use emojis when you're texting?"

He cringes, looking at me like I just asked him if he still wets the bed. "Who do you think I am, a Facebook mom? Later."

He walks out, leaving me to consider that it might be time to surround myself with more female energy. Hmm, maybe a female foster.

But all of this is just another attempt to distract myself from the very real issue at hand. The same one that had me telling Cash I'd see him tomorrow instead of planning something for after the shelter tonight.

My conscience won't stop pecking at me. It was one thing keeping Cash in the dark about Harry when we were playing frenemies, but it's another to keep something this big hidden from him now that we're dating for real. He's been an open book, which I haven't been in return. I'm my same old stubborn self, thinking I can handle it all on my own.

When I stop to examine my motivations, I can admit I don't want Cash to lump me in with the entitlement he despises. I also don't want Harry to get in trouble. He may be acting crazy, but he's my dad, and he's doing it because of a teenager's lies and his refusal to admit she's growing up.

There's also still that part of me holding out hope that I misunderstood and it's not Harry at all. Because I don't want to examine what it says about me that I won't take Harry's money on principle, but I'll protect him over a family who deserves it more than he does. Those are some pretty shitty principles. I've been telling myself that helping Cash until I can pin Harry down makes it okay, but does it really? In the end, I'm still lying to him while he's keeping nothing off the table.

I know Cash well enough by now to know that, whether I get Harry to fix things or not, Cash will never look at me the same if he finds out I knew from the start and didn't tell him. And that makes my heart ache and my stomach churn. It was so much easier when we were at each other's throats instead of each other's pants. And hearts.

I pick up my phone again and go to my missed calls. Nothing new. Hadley and my parents are supposed to get back in two days—the same day as the auction. And I need to decide if I'm going with Cash or heading down to the house to be there when they get home.

Hadley's texts responding to my calls over the past week have been unhelpful at best. When I asked her if she knew what might make Harry think Miller owns the brewery, she replied twelve hours later with, "Miller is a loser. Stop obsessing." So very informative.

But she's right about one thing. Obsessing doesn't solve anything, so I stash my phone and get back to work.

A half hour later, Rylee comes back to hang out with me while I give a Boston terrier named Pepper a bath. She gives me the rundown on which Asheville Arrows players are hot, which are douchebags, and which ones a girl could take home to her mom. She determines that Gunner Nix, Joey Martel, and Nathan Ryder are the only three to fit both the hot and mom categories. However, since

Nathan is gay, it won't do a girl much good to take him anywhere except the gym.

I don't follow baseball, so the names mean nothing to me, but Rylee is adorkably pleased with the thoroughness of her investigation. Rylee and Darcy were both on our high school's softball team, so I'll leave the Arrows players to them and stick with Pepper's bubble bath.

When I close up shop a couple hours later, my feet take me to Blue Bigfoot's door. The crowd is thinning out a bit, and I can see Kelsie busing tables while Cash and Oscar pour drinks at the bar. All of Cash's movements are practiced and smooth, and his smile is easy today. My belly dips at the thought of marching right in there and planting a hot kiss on his mouth and then luring him back to his office.

But if I go in to even say hi to Cash, I know I won't leave. And it's advice I should quite possibly remind my heart of as well—but I'm too distracted by how handsome he is and how it feels when he touches me or even looks at me with those intense blue eyes. Sigh.

I tear myself away and head to my car, telling myself the shelter animals need me more than I need Cash. In other words, I lie.

CASH

IT'S A GORGEOUS SUNDAY AFTERNOON, and we're headed down to Henderson County for the auction. With the profits from the Arrows crowd, I've got the money I need in my FUBAR fund. The radio is turned up, there's a beautiful blonde in my passenger seat, and I'm looking at the world through a new lens.

Nirvana's "Smells Like Teen Spirit" comes on, and Hollis starts singing along, so I join in too. It's Nirvana, after all.

"She saw the boar that's self-assured…" I sing in my, admittedly, awful voice.

I look over when I hear Hollis singing, "Cheese over-board and self-insured" instead. We both frown at each other and keep singing.

Again, I sing, "With the laptop, it sustains us," and Hollis, for some reason, sings, "When the light's out, it's a stained dress."

Now she's giving me the side eye. She sings, "Eat your

heart out lemon trainers," while I sing the actual lyrics which are, "Here we are now, Anastasia."

I get louder since I know the correct lyrics, but she gets louder too, presumably thinking she's in the right. My "Help the stupid and contagious," battles for dominance with her, "Dr. Stupid is contagious!"

She shouts her next lyric, "A Milano, I'm a dino!" while I fight her with the accurate, "I'm a liner in a bottle!" Then she goes with the ludicrous, "I'm a skater, Milo Beetle, yeah!" but my "I'm a Skittle, I'm a bleeder, hey!" is louder.

We continue in this vein until the song comes to an end, and she narrows her eyes at me. "You're ridiculous."

"*I'm* ridiculous? You have a nice voice, but you listen like you just had an orgasm."

She smacks my arm, but she can't hide her grin. I reach over to squeeze her thigh, and my hand creeps toward her heat like a mouse in a snowstorm.

"Watch your hand, Mr. Brooks. I don't want to end up in the ER."

I reluctantly put my hand back on the wheel.

The auction is being held in a big barn just off the road, and when we pull into the makeshift parking lot, there are more cars than I expected. But it's not only the brewery lots up for auction today, so I'm not worried.

Hollis usually volunteers at that shelter on Sundays—she says she has a snuggle quota she likes to reach each week or she gets symptoms of seasonal affective disorder. Which makes no sense. But the fact that she chose to come with me today instead says a lot about how far we've come.

"Oh, look at that carving." Hollis points to a huge bear carved out of dark wood. "Maybe I should get that for the shop," she jokes.

"If you want all the dogs peeing in your doorway, then yeah, definitely."

We walk around, and I show her the keg washer and the glycol chiller I'm bidding on, but we both play it real cool like we're trying to fake somebody out by acting uninterested. It's stupid, but it makes us both laugh.

I've laughed more with Hollis in these past couple weeks than I reckon I have in the past year. It may not be long until I find myself wrapped around her little finger. Surprisingly, the thought doesn't freak me out like it should. Being with her is easy, and the fact that she cares about my business and family too makes it so I don't feel like I'm taking my eye off the ball.

We check in and get our paddle with the number 19 on it, and I hand over my thousand-dollar deposit.

Once we step back outside again, I look down at Hollis and say something I can't seem to say often enough: "Hey, thanks for coming. And thanks for helping me with all of this in the first place. You certainly didn't have to, especially when I was being such an asshole about it."

She smiles, and it's the one I always feel in my chest. This time is no different. "I wasn't exactly friendly either. And while you may not agree, I did have to help. But you're welcome."

I steal a kiss before a bell rings and an announcement is made that the auction is starting.

Everybody files into the barn, and a guy in a dress shirt with no tie walks to the front where a small mic stand lies. He briefly explains the rules, and then he begins.

The first few items are from a farm, including a tractor that's parked outside and a bunch of attachments. Instead of watching the bidding, I take hold of Hollis's hand and trace her lifeline with the tip of my finger while I think about the things I want to do with her when this is over.

Denny and Luca are all set to help me with installation after hours this week, and we should have everything in order for when the inspector comes back on Thursday for a re-check.

It's another hour before the brewery lots get their turn. The glycol chiller is first. I researched this model, and it retails new for six thousand. I've budgeted thirty-five hundred to be on the safe side.

Bidding starts at a thousand, and there are three interested parties. Me, a big guy to my right wearing Carhartts and sporting a wicked handlebar mustache, and someone way in the back that I can't see without making a spectacle of myself. I don't want anyone to know how desperate I am.

We get up to two grand pretty quickly, and Hollis leans over and says, "Is it weird that I'm disappointed this auctioneer is speaking at a normal pace?" I grin at her, some of my anxiety settling.

Once we reach twenty-five hundred, Carhartts drops out, and it's just me and the guy in the back.

"Do I have twenty-seven fifty?" the auctioneer asks.

I raise my paddle.

"Three thousand?" Number 12 in the back raises his. Now I'm beginning to sweat.

"Thirty-two fifty?" My paddle goes up, and I hold my breath.

"Do I have thirty-five hundred?" The bastard outbids me again.

"Thirty-seven fifty?" My jaw locks as I do some quick thinking. For forty-five hundred, I could get a half-decent one new, but I'm out of time. I can afford this little bit extra unless it goes further. I raise my paddle.

The auctioneer acknowledges me and then asks the crowd, "Four thousand?" I close my eyes, and Hollis grabs my free hand to give it a squeeze.

"Going once."

I hold my breath.

"Going twice."

Come on.

"Sold to bidder nineteen for three thousand seven hundred fifty!"

My breath comes out in a whoosh and Hollis does a little victory wiggle by my side. That girl is cute as hell.

Another handful of brewery items come up next. They're ones I don't need, but I'm encouraged when Carhartts gets two of them at lowball prices. Thankfully, number 12 doesn't show any interest.

And next up is the keg washer. It's more than we need, but I couldn't find anything else I could afford that would get here in time. So I'm counting on my remaining thirty-two fifty to cover it. With any luck, I'll get it for a song and walk out of here with cash left over.

"Let's start the bidding at a thousand."

I play it cool, but the auctioneer points to the back of the barn, telling me 12 is bidding against me again. Dammit.

The auctioneer goes right to two grand, and I raise my paddle.

"Do I have twenty-five hundred?" he asks.

I'm starting to sweat again, but I need to stay positive.

Instead of just raising his paddle, however, the guy in back yells, "I bid four thousand."

Hollis gasps beside me, knowing I don't have the cash

to cover four grand, much less any higher. I rack my brain trying to figure out another way to get the equipment since I'm about to lose this one. Dammit. I should have known things were going too well.

"Do I have forty-five hundred?" the auctioneer asks. I stay still, my head beginning to pound from thinking too hard.

"Going once."

I curse myself. If only I hadn't shot my mouth off at that inspector.

"Going twice."

Maybe I'll donate plasma to afford the more expensive one I found online. Either way, I'm resigned and just waiting for the gavel to come down.

I hear Hollis fretting at my side, and then she rips the paddle out of my hand and thrusts it high in the air. "Five thousand!"

There are a couple gasps and more laughs in the crowd.

I turn to Hollis. "What are you doing? I don't have the money!" I whisper at her, not wanting to announce my financial status to a bunch of strangers.

The auctioneer doesn't know what's going on either. "Miss," he says, getting Hollis's attention. "Unless you've registered on the same ticket as this young man, you're forbidden from bidding."

"But I have the money!" she yells back, digging into her purse. She pulls out a stack of bills and waves it in the air before shoving it all at me. "And now *he* does!"

I just stare at her, but it seems good enough for the auctioneer because he continues.

"Going once."

Nobody moves.

"Going twice."

Number 12 stays silent.

"Sold to number nineteen and his generous friend for five thousand!"

Hollis grins at me, but I can only stand there like a statue. Where did she come up with a stack of cash that big? There must be four grand here. She must have asked her parents or sold something or raided her retirement account. Whatever its source, I can't take that money.

But I'm not about to argue with her in the middle of this auction, so I push the money into her purse and steer her out a side door and into the sunshine.

HOLLIS

"HOLLIS, I'm not taking your money." Cash stands across from me in some tall weeds near the barn. He's playing his pride card, and I can't let him.

"You have to," I insist, pulling the cash from my purse again.

"I don't know what you did to get that cash, but undo it, Hollis. This is *my* mess, not yours." His jaw is ticking, telling me he's warring inside.

"No, it's not." Oh, god, why did I let this go so far?

"Yes, it is!" he shouts and then takes a breath. When he's more in control, he puts his hands on my upper arms and holds them. "Baby, you don't owe me a thing. You've been so incredible, so selfless. You're…" He exhales through his nose, and I feel sick to my stomach. "You're all the things I wish I was."

Tears form, blurring him in my vision, and he brushes a thumb over my cheek. "I appreciate the sentiment behind it, I do. And I know you're just being your beautiful self and not patronizing me like I might have thought before I got to know you. But I can't take your money."

A tear rolls down my cheek because I know I can't let him think these wonderful things about me when I know the truth. And once I tell him, it will all be over. No more back and forth, no more mind-blowing kisses, no more cuddles in bed with the dogs, no more surprise cookie runs, no more of that smile, and certainly not one bit of respect for me.

But, of course, Cash doesn't understand the source of my tears.

"Tell me you didn't ask your parents—after all you've done to make it on your own. You can't clean up my mess by making one for yourself."

"You don't understand, Cash. It's *really* not your mess."

He shakes his head in barely controlled frustration.

I bite my lip and blink away the tears so I can look into his eyes one more time before they turn cold. "This whole thing, this entire ridiculous mess, is Harry's fault—and Hadley's."

He continues shaking his head. "No, it's not. That doesn't even make sense."

I open my mouth and let it all spill out. "Hadley told my parents the same story she told me about Miller, only they believed her instead of your brother. So Harry went after him and somehow dragged your whole family business into it. He wouldn't listen to reason when I told him Miller only started working there and has no—"

"Wait, hold on." His hands drop back down to his sides. "Are you being serious?"

I nod, tears beginning anew.

"I told him Miller doesn't own the brewery, but he said I was being manipulated."

"Fuck!" Cash's fingers drive through his hair. "Miller told your sister he owned Blue Bigfoot. Goddammit!"

As soon as I hear that, I know I've been kidding myself that Harry might not be involved. I finally know why he targeted the brewery. My heart sinks even deeper, but it hasn't quite hit the rock bottom that's coming.

I watch Cash as all the pieces start to fall into place. "So, you never called the health department on me?"

I shake my head.

"Then you insisted on helping me because…"

The moment it clicks, his back stiffens, and my stomach threatens to expel its contents.

"How long have you known about this, Hollis?"

I swallow past the lump in my throat and tell the truth. "Since the day after the inspection."

His hands are back in his hair, pulling at it now. "Since—how could you not tell me?!"

"I didn't know what you would do! And until you just told me about Miller lying to Hadley, I thought I might be wrong. Harry told me he'd make Miller pay the consequences for taking advantage of his baby girl," I rush on, my hands clammy and my head light. "But I thought… I thought I could get him to back down, make it go away. I thought I could handle it, and in the meantime, I'd help you the best I could."

His tone is frosty now. "And how'd that work out?"

My eyes drop to my feet. "They've been out of touch in Africa—on a safari, I think."

Cash laughs, and its sardonic tone has me taking a step back in preparation for his next words. "That sounds about right. Listen, why don't you go join them? I'm sure they'll have room for you in their luxury caravan or whatever."

"That's not fair." I hoped there would be a tiny part of him that would remember the me he's gotten to know. But I'm just his self-absorbed, annoying, entitled neighbor again.

"You know what's not fair, Hollis? Constantly having to dig my family out of one hole after another. Unlike some people, I don't have a rich family down in Biltmore Forest to be my safety net when things get too hard and I need a break. I live in the real world where we have real problems that are sometimes never solved at all."

His words are cruel, but he's right. Even the cash I'm holding in my hand came from my parents. The earrings really were a form of blood money after all. And all the effort, hard work, and sacrifices I made to start my business on my own don't matter in the end because I chose my family over him every time I had the opportunity to reveal the truth—even after I knew how much he meant to me.

"You're right. About all of it. And I'm sorry, Cash. I thought I was doing the best thing for everyone, but I wasn't. I was doing the best thing for me."

He doesn't respond. His body is coiled tight, eyes on his boots and hands on his hips.

"I know you have no reason to trust me anymore, but this cross you bear, Cash? I'm afraid you don't know just how much your family loves you and would do *anything* for you, the same way you do everything you do for them. They're so proud of you, and you're luckier than you know to have them in your corner."

He doesn't respond, so I step closer and force the stack of bills into his hand. "This is just a down payment on what we owe you. Go get your equipment."

I start for the barn, not sure where I'm going or how to get there.

"Hollis." Cash's voice is quiet, but I catch it and turn. "I drove you here. I'll drive you home." He still won't look at me.

I shake my head. "Thanks, but I've got a ride."

I walk to the other side of the barn where I pull out my phone, take a deep breath, and call Harry.

For the first time in two weeks, I don't get the buzzing of a failed call. Instead, Harry's big voice booms over the line. "Pumpkin! Hi!"

I smile through my tears at the voice of the only man who's ever loved me. "Hi, Harry. I know you just got back, but… do you think you could pick me up?"

HOLLIS

I HIDE out behind the barn when Cash goes back inside to pay, in hopes he'll think I'm safely tucked away in an Uber and he won't feel compelled to exercise his gallant mama's boy muscle. When he gets in his car and drives away twenty minutes later, I emerge so I can keep an eye out for Harry's BMW. The guy who kept bidding against Cash leaves as well—empty-handed, I might note—and I can't help but glare at the back of his head.

As soon as I open the passenger door and Harry gets a look at my face, he says, "Looks like we need coffee and pie." I don't argue.

We drive in silence, me trying not to cry, while Harry keeps an eye out for somewhere that supplies our elixir of choice. We end up at a small greasy spoon ten minutes down the road.

The waitress pours our coffee and I muster a half-smile for her benefit. Harry shakes out a packet of fake sugar and stirs it into his coffee with a spoon. I just hold mine between my hands, warming them up. Emotional turmoil apparently sucks all the blood to my head and chest, leaving my hands like icicles.

"So, you want to tell me what this is all about?" Harry finally asks. He's wearing a blue button-down and another pair of pressed slacks. A deep tan from his vacation colors his skin, and he looks better rested than usual.

I sigh, trying to prepare my words and fight the exhaustion setting in.

"I don't like seeing you so out of sorts, Pumpkin." His brow knits as he assesses me over his coffee cup.

The endearment reminds me of old times when Harry first came into my life. He and my mom had only been dating for a few weeks, but she was acting differently, so I knew it was serious. I'd just come home from a sleepover, and there he was, sitting on our itchy couch, smiling at me.

I'd never seen anybody whose clothes were so crisp and pristine. It was like they were made from a magical fiber that repelled wrinkles and those little fuzzballs that gather on cheap sweatshirts and pants. He smelled like something the ladies in the department store spray at you as you walk by, so I knew he must be rich.

My mom introduced us, beaming from ear to ear, so I took pains to be on my best behavior. Harry didn't know much about kids, that was clear when he asked me if I liked Sesame Street. But he had kind eyes, and I could tell how much he liked Mom.

By the time they got married and we moved in with him, I was ready to let him be my dad, and he seemed to genuinely love me, always calling me Pumpkin and asking about my day. Everything worked out like it was supposed to. Except he was never able to wrap his head around why I preferred to keep some aspects of the life before he and his money came to save the day.

I was always braced for questions like, "Why in the world would you want to go to public high school when we can send you to one of the best private schools in the state?"

Or, "Candace is the best tennis instructor in town, and she's opened up a spot just for you. Don't you want to learn so you can play at the country club with the other kids your age?"

Or, "Why aren't you applying to any of the out-of-state universities with more renowned business programs? I can send you anywhere you want."

Despite his intentions, it only served to make me feel like what I wanted for myself either didn't matter or was somehow less than the standards set by all the people around us. So I pushed back on the things I could, digging my heels in and insisting on clothes, friends, and activities that suited me, not whatever image he dreamed for me. My mom couldn't understand either, so I eventually learned to stop trying to please anyone but myself. But that didn't mean I didn't still crave the respect and pride of the people I loved.

Harry has always loved me, but he's never understood me.

"It hasn't been a great day," I tell him. "Or a great couple weeks, honestly."

"You could have come on safari with us if you didn't have to babysit that shop of yours."

I bristle at his dig. "I like working at my shop. It brings me a lot of satisfaction, and I love working with the dogs." But I wave a dismissive hand. "This isn't what I'm talking about." It's time to get down to business with him.

"Okay, then what's happening?"

The waitress returns to set two plates of apple pie in front of us, giving me another few seconds to arm myself. When she steps away, I get right to it.

"I've been helping my neighbor Cash at the brewery to raise money for upgrades to satisfy the health inspector." My tone does its own talking. "They're going to make it, by the way."

Harry unrolls his napkin and silverware and raises his fork. "Why do you feel like you owe any of them anything?"

I can only stare as he forks a bite of pie, shamelessly unbothered by his own actions. "Are you serious?"

"Yes, I'm serious," he replies over a mouthful of pie. "You're too easily swayed by sob stories and lost puppies. You let people take advantage of you. You always have."

I might crack my coffee cup with how hard I'm squeezing it. "I don't let people take advantage of me. And besides, I was trying to undo what *you* did. That's just basic human decency."

He wields his fork in the air again. "Look, I was within my rights as a parent to pursue some kind of consequences."

"That's like trying to justify burning down an apartment building because one tenant offended you."

It's like he doesn't hear me. "I honestly don't know what else you want from me, Hollis. I can't change my entire personality to be a bleeding heart like you. You're so smart and talented; you could do so much with your life."

Angry tears prick my eyes. "I'm doing exactly what I want with my life, Harry. Doesn't that count for anything?"

He sighs and finally sets the damn fork down. "I

suppose so. Look—" he begins, but I cut him off. It's time for me to do the talking.

"No, Harry. You need to straighten out Blue Bigfoot's reputation with the health department, and you need to pay Cash Brooks all the money he's had to work tooth and nail to raise." This will only end my way.

"Why—" he tries, but I don't let him.

"And you need to learn that you don't get to decide who's worthy and who's not. There are really wonderful, loving, generous, funny, kind-hearted people out there who make life so much richer just from knowing them." I push on through the tears and the giant lump in my throat. "And, yes, many of them work in bars and supermarkets and pet shelters and dog grooming shops. And they don't know how to play tennis or make money on the stock market or build a business empire. But they're just as worthy as you of the respect of their fellow human beings." I'm crying now, and Harry pushes his napkin across the table.

"Are you okay?" he asks inexplicably.

I swipe at my eyes with the napkin. "Do I look okay?"

"Does this have to do with a young man?"

I cough out a watery laugh and consider explaining to him that his question trivializes everything I just said. But, then again, he's not wrong.

"Hollis, I only ever want what's best for you. I always have. Maybe I do push too many of my opinions, but you're an intelligent, capable person, and I don't want to see you waste opportunities or let anyone walk all over you."

I sniffle and dab at my eyes again. "I can take care of myself, Harry. I think you're forgetting how stubborn I am."

This has a tiny grin forming on his lips. "True. I guess you do know how to stand on your own two feet after all this time." He shakes his head and watches me for a moment. "And if this young man who's got you crying is worth half his salt, he'll know what he has in you."

"I'm afraid it's not that simple."

"It never is," he says over the top of his cup.

I sigh and gather myself again. "Harry, I meant what I said about what you need to do for Blue Bigfoot. I'm not taking no for an answer."

He nods, and a little of the crack in my heart starts to close. "About that, didn't you get my voice mail?"

"What voice mail?"

He goes back to his pie. "The one I left when we got to Tanzania."

"No." I shake my head and think back. "I did get a missed call from an overseas number, but there was no voice mail."

He shakes his head as he chews and swallows. "The connection was terrible, but I left you a message to let you know I told the lawyer to drop the case and the investigation into that Miller kid. You were right, and your mom said so too. I guess I needed a couple days to get my head on straight. When I called Hadley for a talk, she admitted she made some of the story up, just like you said."

"Wait, what?" An electric pulse bursts in my head, sending a shooting pain throughout my skull.

"There's no case to pursue, like you said. Your mom wanted to ground Hadley again for lying, but it was her spring break, so..." He shrugs, his tone casual while my entire head is an active volcano.

"What do you mean? What about the inspector and Blue Bigfoot?"

He only shakes his head and forks another bite of pie. "It sounds like somebody needs a refresher on health codes. I guess it's a good thing we backed off; it seems like that family has enough to deal with on their own. And you shouldn't feel any obligation to help them with any of their proble—" He cuts himself off. "Unless, of course, that's what you want to do."

My jaw drops. "So... you didn't know anything about a health inspection at all until I just told you?"

His brow knits again. "Was I supposed to?"

Oh, god. "But what about Mr. Rhinehardt? You said you had connections when his restaurant was having trouble with the health department."

Again, how can he sit there casually stuffing his face with pie? "I do. I know a great outfit that supplies top-notch oysters to restaurants in Charlotte and Raleigh. I put him in touch with them."

What? "So, you never made his problem 'go away'?"

Harry almost chokes on his pie while he laughs. "What, like a mob boss? You've got one crazy imagination."

Good lord almighty.

CHAPTER THIRTY-FIVE

CASH

I DRIVE BACK to Asheville on autopilot, my mind playing back every encounter with Hollis since the day the inspector—the Hayes' family stooge, as it turns out— showed up on my doorstep. I was right from day one, and I never should have let Hollis convince me otherwise with all of her lying. My anger is spread pretty evenly across Hollis, Harry, Miller, and myself. But Hollis is the one that stings the most.

How could she protect her stepdad when she saw how this was all affecting me? She said she didn't know what I'd do? Did she think I'd go hunt him down with my BB gun from middle school? Damn straight, I would have confronted him—just like I plan to do when the asshole gets home from his safari vacation, whenever that may be.

I have no idea what to do about the inspector, but nothing I do is likely to change things anyway. Looks like Hadley wasn't lying about *everything*. Her dad's got more connections than a flight from Asheville to Antarctica. This is how the world works. A handful of people call the shots, and the rest of us just keep our heads down and move forward.

All I know for sure is I need to get back to town and clue Carter in. My auction winnings will be delivered in the morning, so it's time. There's no hiding new equipment in Carter's brewhouse domain without him noticing. Which reminds me I've got to get that dishwasher out of the she-devil's office ASAP.

I can't believe I thought my acting like an asshole to that sleazebag inspector was what got me into this! But I still blame myself for not listening to my gut when it told me to stay the hell away from Hollis Hayes and her toxic society set. To know now that I was right from the beginning, though, doesn't feel as good as I imagined it might.

And then there's Miller. His prioritizing pussy over everything else sparked this entire disaster. To think if he'd only told that little girl the truth, my brewery would be free and clear. Although, lord knows what Harry might have done to *him* instead. Fuck. It's probably best it played out like this. At least I've got our asses covered.

The worst part is that no matter the direction of my thoughts, I keep coming back to the same image of Hollis standing across from me, tears in her eyes, right before she dropped that bombshell. I'd do anything to freeze time there, and that fact alone has me calling myself every name in the book.

Because I let myself think we had something worth investing in, forgetting that the other shoe always—*always* —drops eventually.

By the time I pull into the driveway at home, a headache has settled behind my forehead and in the back of my skull. I'm giving serious consideration to parking my ass in a chair in the garage and drinking myself into a stupor. But ignoring shit doesn't make it go away.

Cart was nowhere to be found when I stopped at Blue Bigfoot, so I figured home was the best place to catch him before morning. Besides, I'm in such a mood, nobody at the taproom would want to be within ten yards of me tonight.

When I go inside, Mama's brown curls peek around the corner from the kitchen. "Hey, darlin'. What a nice surprise. I figured you'd be at Hollis's for the night."

"Nope," is all I say as I join her in the kitchen and head to the fridge for something to eat. She doesn't need to know I hope I never see Hollis's face again, much less sleep in the same bed as her.

"I'm glad to see you taking a little break from the brewery. You work too much." She nudges me out of the way and pulls a casserole dish out of the fridge. "Lemme heat up some chicken and rice for you."

"Thanks." What I want to do is take a sandwich up to my room and stew on my own, but she'll figure somebody died if I turn down a hot meal. So, instead, I take a seat at the table while she fixes a plate and puts it in the microwave.

"So, you never told me the other night how things went when Gunner paid a visit."

"Miller tell you about that? He was fangirling all over Joey Martel." I automatically smile at the memory of him getting tongue-tied when the new shortstop came up to order a beer.

"I might've done the same—that's one good-looking young man."

"Yeah, well, his looks don't interest me. His ability to

bring new customers in my door is the thing that really matters. I guess karma decided we needed a win."

Mama tucks a kitchen towel into her waistband like a makeshift apron. "I don't know how much karma had to do with it, but Lizzie sure did."

"That girl you work with? She sent them to Blue Bigfoot?" Damn, I owe her a thank you.

"Of course. I told her how great the place is and that y'all could use a little pick-me-up."

That has my Spidey senses tingling. "What do you mean?"

"You've been running around like a crazy person, conspiring with Hollis and rubbing your chin like you always do when you're thinking too hard."

My hand freezes where it was doing just what she said, and I drop it to the table.

"It's not my first day as your mama." The microwave chimes and she turns to retrieve my dinner.

How do I always forget how observant she is? Just because she acts like she doesn't have a care in the world, she still knows that's not the case for everyone.

I tuck into the chicken, rice, and green peas on my plate while Mama hums a Johnny Cash song and loads up the old dishwasher. That thing runs so loud we can't turn it on at night or nobody gets a wink of sleep.

I'm surprised I'm even hungry with my head aching and spinning with thoughts of Hollis, each one bringing on a new wave of pain behind my eyes.

Miller's working—he insists his broken arm doesn't get in the way, and I'm letting him. And Cart is who the hell knows where, so it looks like it'll be a quiet night at least.

Mango trots into the kitchen, a plastic sandwich bag in his mouth. When Mama sees him, she tuts at him. "I've been looking for you all over. Where in the world do you keep sneakin' off to?"

She bends to take the bag from him so he doesn't eat it and make himself sick. But she stills as she takes a closer look at it.

"What is it? Miller's weed?" I ask around my last bite.

"No," she replies distractedly. "It's… money."

I swallow and look down at Mango. He's lying flat out like his day was too downright exhausting to continue. "Nice to see he's finally pulling his weight. It's about time that pile of fur got a job."

Mama ignores me. "No, it's real money." She opens the seal to take a closer look. "And a lot of it."

"No way." I stand up to join her in front of the dish-washer, and she hands me the bag.

The bag itself is filmy, but the money inside is fresh and crisp. I pull it out and start counting. "There's five grand in here. Where the hell did he get this?"

We both look down at the mongrel as if he might explain himself.

"Do you think he dug it up in the woods or something?"

"I don't know," Mama says, picking up the empty bag. "The bag's got no dirt on it, it's just worn."

"Well, nobody in this house is hiding any cash, that's for damn sure." Miller is incapable of saving anything. I'm pretty sure his first paycheck from the brewery went directly to either his piercer or the guy he buys stolen ciga-rettes and weed from. And Carter? No way would he leave cash lying around when it could be earning even a penny in interest at the bank.

Mama suddenly throws her head back and starts laughing like a maniacal cartoon character.

"What's so funny?"

"It's Wade. It's got to be." She's about to pee herself. "Right before he passed, he was saving up for another pickup."

The F-150 he was driving at the time was a genuine piece of shit, so that actually makes sense. If he'd only used a bank, that money would have come in handy for the funeral, not to mention all the other crap I scrambled to cover.

"And you didn't even look for it after?"

"Oh, I did. I just never found it. Figured maybe I baked it into a pie and we ate it." She bends down to pet Mango. "You are such a good boy."

"Well, mystery solved, I guess." I hand the money back to her, but she pushes my hand away.

"Oh, no. You keep it."

"It ain't mine." I try again, but she puts her hands behind her back this time. What is it with women shoving money at me today? My head resumes its pounding, so I push away any thoughts of Hollis and refocus my energy on the present.

Mama keeps shaking her head. "Well, it ain't mine either. And you need it more than I do."

"No, I don't. Buy yourself a new dishwasher or pay Miller's hospital bill." I haven't let myself think too hard about that one yet, but I know it'll show up in the mail eventually.

Her eyes fill with affection. "I'd rather you use it to get Larry back from the pawnshop."

Oh Shit. I'm a dead man.

She knows she has my number when I don't respond. I can't lie to her, but I'm embarrassed as hell she knows what I did.

"Mitch called me as soon as you walked out his door."

I run a hand through my hair. How is she not livid with me? "Who's Mitch?"

"Mitchell Reyes from the pawnshop on Broadway."

"How do you even know him?" I stare at her.

"He takes my yoga class at the senior center. And we sometimes walk Mango together. I'm trying to convince him he needs a pet. He's a big fan of Morton Frye, you know."

Mama truly does know every person in this town.

She brings a hand up to my cheek. "We'll keep this between you and me. I won't tell anyone Larry was in hock and you won't tell anyone they missed out on free cash." She laughs and turns back to the dishes. "Now, are you gonna tell me what's really been going on, or do I have to conduct an investigation of my own?"

The pain in my head spikes and Hollis's teary expression surfaces again, despite my efforts to banish it. Mama stands at the sink and hums like a woman with way too many ideas.

I guess I owe her the truth now, but she's not gonna take Hollis's betrayal well. Not one bit.

CASH

"DO YOU HAVE ANY *LIGHT* BEERS?" the customer across the bar from me asks as he unzips his jacket to reveal a crisp button-down with tiny mushrooms on it. I'll never understand fashion.

"No. We've got a blonde ale that's the closest you're gonna get."

"Do you know how many calories it has?"

What is this guy even doing here? There are a million bars in this town where he can get whatever the hell his heart desires. But, since I can ballpark it, I throw out a number that has him wrinkling his nose and looking back up at our board with today's available selections.

"I'll give you a minute and be right back," I tell him, hoping he gives up and leaves. I'm not in a position to turn down business, but my fuse is short today.

It's Monday midday, and Carter never came home last night. Mama and I talked for a while before I begged off and went to bed with a couple acetaminophen tablets. She took it better than I thought she would, generally just letting me talk and doing a lot of nodding and tutting. Every time I said Hollis's name, the dinner in my stomach swirled.

First thing this morning, I went and got Larry out of hock with Dad's money and paid the interest with some of Hollis's leftover blood money. I honestly don't even know if I could take the rest if Hollis gets it from Harry. It feels dirty as hell. But seeing Larry look out over the taproom again settles my soul a little.

The equipment from the auction was delivered earlier, and I'm getting impatient for Carter to show so I can get this over with. Miller's been able to find creative ways to get his job done with one arm in a cast, so he's unloading the dishwasher down the bar from me. Ever since he broke his arm, he's been wearing a belt; it's hard pulling your pants up every thirty seconds with one hand. It might be time for me to admit he's a better employee than I expected, but I'm not all that fond of humble pie, as you might have guessed.

Giving voice to my failures doesn't mesh well with the role I've chosen in this family and in the world in general. I tend to fix problems, not make them.

When I come back to the customer a minute later, he orders a water.

I'm muttering to myself, and Miller gives me a look I try to ignore. It doesn't work.

"You okay?"

"Fine. Why the sudden concern?" Is he trying to butter me up for time off?

"You kind of look like shit—I mean, more so than usual."

Kelsie chooses that moment to walk by and toss in her

two cents. "I agree. You look like you just surfaced from a three-day bender at a shady poker tournament in Shia LaBeouf's windowless basement."

Miller and I both stare at her. "That's awful specific," Miller says. "Speaking from personal experience, are we?"

"Maybe." Her grin is terrifying. "Hey, Carter just came in the back—I know you were waiting on him." She gives me a knowing look telling me she's seen the new shit in the brewhouse.

Well, I guess it's time.

I toss my bar towel down by Larry and review the main facts in my head. I don't want to drag this thing out, so I'll just lay it all out and tell him it's all under control. Piece of cake.

My phone dings in my pocket, and I grab it out of habit. It's probably Mama reminding all of us about some obscure holiday in honor of skunks. But it's not. It's Hollis —or more accurately, "Peach" as I've nicknamed her in my phone. I'll be changing that today. In fact, I'll be deleting her contact altogether.

I go to shove my phone back in my pocket when the first few words catch my attention.

PEACH:

Harry is home and I was wrong.

I tap the notification to read the rest.

He had nothing to do with your inspector. Looks like you're on your own. Have a nice life.

Wait. What the hell?

I flash back to our conversation outside the barn. She said her stepdad was dead set on consequences for Miller, and since Miller told the sister he owned the brewery, it all fit. She said so herself.

Now she's going with, "Oops, my bad?"

Why would she tell me that—why would she think that in the first place—if it wasn't true? Why would she put us both through that? Why would she fuck up what we had?

Or maybe… she's lying again.

ME:

> That's awfully convenient for you. How do I know you're not lying again?

PEACH:

> I guess you don't. I just thought you might want to know before you got yourself into more trouble. Goodbye, Cash.

I take a detour to the office to try making sense of this new information before talking to Carter. I read Hollis's texts a few more times and stare at the wall for several minutes as the implications settle in.

Lying about this makes even less sense than the original lying! And between the snark in her first text and the more sober finality of the second, I think she's being straight with me. She may have played me to save Harry's skin, but she doesn't want my business to fail or for me to get in any deeper shit than I already am.

So, if Hollis wasn't the anonymous caller, and if Harry didn't pay the guy off to target us, then that means…

"Fuck." I drop my head back.

"More like 'what the fuck?'" Carter says from the doorway.

I swivel to see him standing there in a clean shirt and

pants with his hair combed, if I'm not mistaken. He almost looks like the Carter from the old days.

"Sorry. I was just thinking," I say, still trying to process all of it. Looks like I'm the only asshole accountable for the inspection report. Aw, shit. And I even took Hollis's money!

"So was I. You want to know what I was thinking about?"

I turn my focus to Carter. I'm in no position to try to stop him, so I don't.

He takes a step into the office. "I was thinking how odd it was that a fancy keg washer and an upgraded glycol chiller found their way into our brewhouse. And then I was thinking it must be a mistake because my business partner would never blow over ten-k on shit we don't need—and certainly not without talking to me first."

I have to say, he's not half as angry as I'd imagined, especially with his resemblance to the Carter I know.

Everything I'd prepared to say no longer fits, and there's no reason to make excuses or joke around to stall the inevitable. So I say the only thing there is to say.

"Cart, I fucked up."

Ten minutes later, we're sitting across from each other at a corner table, drinking a couple beers while Miller promotes himself to head bartender and tries bossing Kelsie around. She puts him in a headlock until he cries uncle.

"On the bright side, that keg washer will save a lot of elbow grease," Carter says. He's taking this extremely well. I didn't tell him Hollis or her family's role in this because, as it turns out, they never played one. It was all me and my big fuckin' mouth.

"Like I said, I'll figure out a way to earn some side

money to put back in the coffers. We really did have a great couple weeks." The best two weeks since we opened the joint.

He takes a sip of his *Hop Squatch*, a tasty, bitter double IPA. "I was a skeptic, but I just figured you and Hollis were engaging in a new phase of your odd-as-hell relationship. I'll never argue with profits, though."

"Yeah, well, that odd-as-hell relationship is no longer, I can tell you that." I scratch at the coaster under my beer.

"Why? I kind of enjoyed you two together."

"Long story." One that I now realize I play the lead villain in.

Carter sits back in his chair, sipping on his beer while I try pinpointing exactly when things between me and Hollis became unsalvageable. Even if Harry didn't do anything, she thought he did, and she didn't trust me enough to tell me.

"I still don't get why you didn't just tell me," Carter says, and I wonder for a second if I've been thinking out loud. Until he continues with, "We're partners, right?"

"I know. We are."

"And?"

"I thought I could handle it on my own." As soon as the words are out, I can hear Hollis saying the exact same ones outside that barn when I asked her the same question. Shit. We may just be the same person.

"Why do you always do that?" He lifts his chin toward me.

"Do what?" Drink beer?

"Take on the world without giving anybody else a turn. Nobody expects you to."

I really don't want to talk about this, but I can't exactly

get up and leave with how understanding he's being. "Have you met our family?"

He looks offended. "Have you met me?"

I know he's referring to the extra shit he and I did as the oldest kids growing up—and to the lawyer we never could have afforded after Dad died. But if he's going there, I will too. "Actually, I'm not sure I have."

"What does that mean?" He straightens and crosses his arms on the table.

"You know exactly what that means. You ain't been the same since you appeared here out of nowhere with zero explanation."

His jaw tenses. "That's my private shit. I've had a tremendous amount on my mind."

"Join the club."

"This is different. This is one hundred percent my business and doesn't concern you or anyone else in the family." He exhales through his nose and then shakes his head.

We're both silent for another minute before his posture relaxes again. "And I'm working on it."

"Yeah, well." I suppose he's within his rights.

"Excellent retort." His lips twitch.

"Good god, you are turning back into the real Carter. 'Excellent retort, old chap.'"

"Fuck you."

I grin at him and take a big sip of my beer. "Now you're speaking my language."

He raises his eyes to the ceiling and exhales. "You genuinely felt compelled to ask that inspector about fornicating with livestock, did you?"

I keep my mouth shut.

But he's not done with me quite yet. "Hey—no more

keeping secrets from your business partner." The tone is quiet, but I know he's serious.

"I know. I won't." Shit. I suppose this means I have one more thing to tell him. "So… funny story." I brace myself. "You know Larry?"

HOLLIS

LIONEL BITCHY, the toy poodle I'm grooming, pulls his paw from my hand for the third time.

"You need to let me trim your toenails, little boy," I tell him, taking hold of his paw again and making quick work of his nails.

It's been two days since my fight with Cash and the eye-opening conversation with Harry. When we finished, he drove me to my apartment where I cried myself to sleep with Marco and Polo on either side of me. There truly is nobody more sympathetic than a dog.

As if reading my thoughts, Lionel leans forward to lick my nose when I hold his ears to check if the trim is even. "Aw, thank you, sweetheart."

I did something yesterday that I haven't done since I opened Happy Tails. I called in sick. To myself, since I'm the boss, but also to Josh to ask if he could cover the two baths scheduled in the late afternoon. Then I snuggled with the dogs before heading over to the shelter. Like I said, dogs are experts at this stuff.

Devon, the manager of the shelter and mother of four girls—bless her—didn't bat an eyelash at me showing up on a weekday at noon, and I didn't stop to chat like I normally would. The face staring back at me in the mirror that morning wasn't one I wanted too many people seeing.

I used my key card to enter the kennels, and the familiar cacophony of barks, howls, and yips commenced. Whenever people come in, they always comment on the smell, but it's to the point where I don't even notice anymore.

I made my way down the center, stopping to chat with a few of my canine friends on my way to the kennel at the very end on the left. Betty, a skinny pittie mix, raised mournful brown eyes from the spot where she rested with her chin on her front paws. She's a sad girl, and so am I.

And now, she's my new foster pup. She's asleep in the bed behind the counter where my boys usually nap, although I left them at home to entertain themselves today. Betty is bigger than both Marco and Polo put together, but she only watches so far and doesn't join in playing. But I'll get her feeling more comfortable and happy eventually.

My bell chimes and I shout, "I'll be with you in just a minute! Feel free to look around!"

When I get no response, I glance over. Cash is standing by my counter looking... well, I imagine as uncomfortable as I look right about now. I was pretty sure we'd avoid each other from now until the end of time, especially with our last text exchange.

When I sent him that text yesterday, my emotions were all over the place. I was mad at myself that I'd screwed this up so royally. I didn't tell Cash my suspicions when I should have, I let myself believe things about Harry that weren't true, and I opened up my stupid heart when I knew better than to let someone in. It's only supposed to matter what *I* think of myself and my choices, but now even *I* don't approve!

And I'm mad at Cash too because, apart from making me have feelings for him, he apparently doesn't know how to keep up with health codes! And, honestly, that's like business 101.

Lionel Bitchy barks, and I shush him as I set my shears down.

"I didn't mean to interrupt you," Cash says, his tone flat and holding none of its usual mischief or even grumpiness. "I just wanted to return this." He raises a white envelope before setting it on my countertop. "I'm fifteen hundred short. I spent it before I got your text, but I'll get it to you as soon as I can."

Of course his visit is about the money; his pride would have to hang itself by the neck from the industrial ceiling if he didn't settle up. I should have predicted it. "There's no need," I reply, but I might as well be talking to a wall.

"I pay my debts," is his only—and predictable—response before he turns to leave.

But right before he reaches the door, I panic and jump off my stool. I have no idea what I intend to say or do. I just saw him walking out my door and couldn't imagine this being the last time he'd be so near. I may be mad at him, myself, and the world, but I can't just erase my feelings overnight.

But there's no point, so I sit down again before he notices, and I bring Lionel Bitchy in for a hug. He allows it.

There's no chime of my bell, so I know Cash is still there. Hell, I can feel him from all the way over here.

"Thank you for your help, Hollis. I couldn't have saved the brewery without you."

I start to tear up again, so I bury my face in Lionel's coat. "No problem." I hate that I can't control my emotions. I predicted from the start that letting myself get attached to him would end badly. Why didn't I follow my own advice?

The man is apparently feeling chatty because he still doesn't leave. "It's for the best this way. We never trusted each other."

I finally turn, but he's looking at his shoes. "It was me. I didn't trust you," I croak. I can admit that because it's absolutely true. I constantly questioned his motives, his actions, his abilities, his driving skills, his taste, everything. I never even told him how handsome he is. Or how generous. And funny. And kind-hearted.

When he looks up at me this time, his eyes look dull and lifeless. "I was just as guilty. More."

I gather he's talking about not believing me when I denied everything in the beginning. It did burn to have him think I'd deliberately sabotage his business, but that was… before.

"No," I insist. He became so open with his compliments, his praise, his gratitude, even his apologies. I was the one who held back. "It was me."

He shakes his head and scuffs his boot on the tile.

It's just like him to insist he's right about even this!

"You want to know why the inspector threw the book at us? The real reason?" he asks.

I don't tell him my thoughts on it. I'm sure he knows what his bar smells like.

Cash continues without my response. "I was so damn cocky and sure of myself that he was a fake, that I treated him like he was a joke. I mocked him, I insulted him, I was an egomaniacal douchebag. I am the exact person you always accused me of being."

I inhale, absorbing his words.

With that, he walks out the door, the bell's chime like a death knoll. Well, maybe that's a little dramatic, but it's been an emotional few days, okay?

CHAPTER
THIRTY-EIGHT
PENMANSHIP

HOLLIS

I SPEND the next hour trying to hate Cash and telling myself that I was right about him from the start. His arrogance, his rudeness, his self-righteousness all got him into this mess with no help from me! And to think I spent so much time racked with guilt and helping him fix his problems. It's easier to be mad at him than to miss him, so I'm creating a nice little rage spiral to drown in while I do inventory this evening. But I'm having a hard time erasing his defeated look from earlier, despite the fact that I now know he was keeping something from me too.

So, of course, that's when my mother chooses to drop by.

"What are you doing on the floor?"

I look up from where I'm counting bags of dog treats to see Mom in a white sheath dress that shows off her amazing tan.

"Wow. You look great. Nice vacation?" I'll admit Harry and I didn't get around to discussing their trip.

But she ignores my question entirely, her smile dropping when she gets a good look at my face. I forgot I probably look like a celebrity mug shot. "You've been crying." Her voice is all concern and sympathy, so when she pulls me up by my hands and hugs me, I let her. Then, like the disaster I am this week, I cry into her dry-clean-only dress. It's a guess, but a safe one.

"Oh, Hollis, sweetheart." Her voice is a stream of soothing words whispered in my ear while she strokes my back and rocks us side to side.

I'm embarrassed that I'm losing my ever-loving shit in my place of business. What if someone walks in? This isn't the image I like to project to my customers.

But sometimes a girl just needs a good cry and a hug from her mom.

When I've exhausted my tears, she lets me pull back and then digs a pristine white embroidered handkerchief from her purse. I take it and clean myself up the best I can.

"Is this a man's fault?" She gestures to my face and I can only shrug.

"Sort of. A little. Yeah." The tears start to well again.

"You tell that bastard your mom is going to—"

"Please," I cut her off. "I beg you. No more retribution schemes. I'll be okay."

When she sees I'm serious, she lets it go. "Let's go for a little walk," she suggests, and I nod, figuring my face would frighten any customers away for the next fifteen minutes anyway.

I get Betty leashed up and lock the door behind us before leading my mom down a walkway that circles the shops and offers a nice view of the French Broad River. I love springtime in Asheville, and I promise myself right then I'll make more time to stop and enjoy it. See? I'm already feeling better.

My mom doesn't say a word about Betty.

"Harry told me what happened."

So much for feeling better.

"What exactly did he tell you?"

"Well, I'm only summarizing, mind you, but he said that you thought he played mob boss and hired someone to mess with Miller Brooks's family, that your heart is the size of the sun, and that we need to stop trying to make you into something you're not."

"Wow." I blink a few times. "That's… a lot." I can't believe he told her all that from our conversation. Usually, he only hears every third thing I say and disagrees with half of it. But the part about my heart? That's Mom, not Harry. But it feels good anyway.

"We had a long talk, and it had me thinking about you and me." We sidestep a couple taking a selfie with the river in the background, and Betty follows right along. "You know, I try to treat you and Hadley the same because that's what you're supposed to do as a parent. But you're not the same."

I brace myself for where this might be going, but I'm surprised by her answer.

"I know we spoil your sister, and we probably shouldn't. But going without for most of your life and then not having to anymore makes you want to give your daughters all the best things. Make their lives easier than yours was. You know what I mean?"

"I understand that, Mom. I know it all comes from a good place."

She stops, so Betty and I do too. "But when somebody doesn't want the thing you're offering, it's not a reflection on you, and it's not them being ungrateful; it's just them having their own taste and preferences. I think I understand that a little better now."

I nod in agreement, teenage me wishing she'd had this lightbulb moment a bit sooner. But I would have found a way to ruin it. Teenage me could be a real pain in the ass.

It's not like her to initiate difficult conversations, particularly ones where apologies are involved, so my chest swells a little, and I pull her into a quick hug.

"So, just to be clear, are you saying you want those earrings back?"

She laughs into my hair. "Goodness, no. You keep them. They're your *signature color*." She adds a thick southern accent to the words. They're taken right from *Steel Magnolias* when Julia Roberts's character proclaims pink to be her *signature color*. I'm sure that memory is why it's my favorite too.

Not wanting to spoil the moment, I decide to tell her another time that I sold them. Or, who knows, maybe I'll buy them back with the money from Cash.

We separate, and since we're in a sharing mood, I ask her something I've wondered for years. "Mom, if I hadn't been around, would you have married Harry?"

"You mean, did I marry him for his money?" Her grin is playful, so I know I haven't offended her.

"Well, I wasn't going to put it that way. More like, did you marry him so I would have a better life?" She knows I love Harry, and I'm not suggesting he's worth nothing but his money. We're all imperfect humans, and at the end of the day, we love each other.

She tucks her long hair behind her ear and I can tell she's thinking back because her smile is soft. "Yeah, partly.

You'll understand better when you're a mother. But I also married him because he's Harry."

I smile. There are a lot of great memories with him at the center.

"Do you know the first compliment he ever paid me was about my handwriting? 'Bianca, you have such beautiful penmanship.'" She does a perfect impression, making me laugh out loud. Her smile goes soft again. "He didn't tell me I was a knockout or had nice legs or a beautiful smile or eyes he wanted to swim in." She makes a gagging gesture. "He admired my penmanship, of all things."

"The man does love you to pieces."

"And I love him right back. And that's what I want for you." She taps my nose.

"You want a man who admires my penmanship? Because that's never going to happen. I still don't know how to write in cursive," I tease.

"No, smartypants, I want you to find a man who sees the beautiful person inside and wants nothing more than to make you happy."

I nod, but I need to say something more to her.

"Mom, my job makes me happy. I love my shop. I love the dogs. I feel fulfilled in a way I never did in itchy suits and high heels, attending meeting after meeting. This is what I want for myself, and I refuse to feel bad about it."

She nods. "I know. And I'm sorry I haven't been very supportive. I promise that's going to change. If you're happy, that's all that really matters."

The damn tears threaten again, but I hold them back. "Thank you. It means a lot."

We turn around to head back to the shop, and she loops her arm in mine. Betty walks calmly beside us like the good girl she is. "Oh, by the way," Mom says. "You should expect a call from Mrs. Faulkenberry. She has a wretched little chihuahua that smells awful. I told her about your shop and she said she'd make an appointment. She asked if you do nail painting, which I found confusing, so I told her to ask you."

I laugh. "I think it's something only dog moms understand."

"So you actually paint the dog's toenails?"

"Yeah, it's a thing. I'll show you." We walk back to the shop arm in arm, another little bit of my childhood weaving itself into the present.

CHAPTER
THIRTY-NINE
SECRETS

CASH

IT'S THURSDAY MORNING, and we've all busted our asses to get the new equipment installed and scrub down the brewhouse, taproom, johns, and every other inch of the place till they shine. I was shocked by how much pink and purple glitter kept showing up. That stuff will still be here years from now to remind me not to make the same mistakes.

I haven't seen Hollis since I stopped by the shop to drop the money off the other day. Her eyes were swollen, undeniable evidence she'd been crying. It took all I had not to push through that swinging door and pull her to my chest. But she's better off without me. Hollis had good reason to keep her secret from me. I, on the other hand, kept mine just because I didn't want to look bad. Pride. It'll fuck you every time.

It took me longer than I care to admit to figure out why she didn't tell me what she suspected about her stepdad, and then I felt like the idiot she used to call me all the time.

Despite Harry not always supporting her life choices, she loves him. And besides not wanting to believe he was capable of such a devious move, she felt duty-bound to protect him. They're family. Just like mine. Reverse the situation, and I would have done the exact same thing— even if it was Miller. You protect the ones you love. That's it.

And it doesn't mean she didn't care about me like I accused her of. She employed the same logic I did with Cart: What they don't know won't hurt them, and I can handle it all on my own. That has nothing to do with her feelings for me or my feelings for Cart. It's what we do. Because Hollis and I are the same in almost every way— right down to the annoying younger sibling who drives us nuts.

Except I'm the asshole who shot his mouth off at the health inspector. And if I'd fessed up to that from day one, she would have had less reason to blame Harry and no reason to help my sorry ass.

The inspector is due sometime today, and I'm ready to grovel if necessary to make up for my behavior the last time. All that matters is the business and the family. That's all that ever matters, and I promise myself to remember that next time my pride tries getting the better of me.

"You look like you're gonna puke," Miller says, helpful as ever.

Everybody here at Blue Bigfoot knows the basics of what went down, but a few details were left out—like Larry. Carter decided it wouldn't do any good to share that part, largely because I'd managed to get Larry back. Cart also didn't spill *everything* I said to the inspector, but I did admit to the general tone of it and accept responsibility. I also apologized for jeopardizing everyone's jobs. The look on Miller's face when I apologized told me I'll never hear the end of this.

"I just wanna get this over with," I tell him through my clenched jaw. "I have a killer headache that won't go away."

"Oh, I got this." He rests his elbows on the bar between us. "That's a tension headache."

"Thanks, genius."

He ignores my sarcasm and holds up his hand. "You want to pinch the skin between your thumb and forefinger." He demonstrates with his opposite hand. "Hold it for ten seconds, or just massage for a minute." He drops his hands again. "Or you can push the tip of your index finger into the muscle right under the base of your skull." Again, he demonstrates.

I'm desperate enough to fall for whatever this might be, so I try the finger thing. The pressure eases almost immediately. "Hey, that actually works. Thanks."

He nods, a goofy-ass grin on his face. "The student has become the master." He turns to the hall. "Weed works too, FYI."

"Places, everybody! It's go time!" Kelsie shouts.

When I look to the door, I see the guy heading our way from the parking lot. Everyone hurries to their designated spots we assigned earlier, and we all look like clowns while we pretend to act naturally. Kelsie is wiping down already immaculate tables with a clean towel and disinfectant, Carter is standing guard by the brewhouse door, Miller is pretending to run the new dishwasher, and Oscar is... I shake my head because Oscar is whistling and polishing the cooler for some reason. He must be nervous.

I head to the door to unlock it and hold it open as the guy walks in. He's in his fifties with thinning brown hair and wire-rimmed glasses, and he's wearing the same tan jacket and white shirt as last time. His expression is blank, which I count as a win because I was expecting hostile.

"Good morning, sir," I greet him, setting an entirely different tone than last time.

He doesn't respond, but he and his clipboard come in and he immediately walks toward the bar. Oscar's humming gets louder, and I try signaling for him to shut up, but his eyes are glued to the cooler.

It's time for my official apology. "I'd like to apologize for my behavior last time you were here. I was under the false impression that someone sent you here as a prank and that you weren't, in fact, from the Department of Health and Human Services. I'm so sorry for the things I said… especially about your wife."

Miller's eyes flash at me from the dishwasher. He's biting his lip ring so he doesn't laugh, and I signal for him to cut the shit and get back to his fake dishwashing operation.

The inspector has either become deaf since his last visit, or he's ignoring me. All I can do now is follow him around the place and keep my mouth shut.

Instead of going behind the bar to inspect every detail like last time, he walks around it, glancing only briefly at the dishwasher, the hand sink, and the cooler. Then he moves on, hardly stopping to take more than a cursory glance at everything. When we go into the brewhouse, he spends even less time there before heading back to the taproom. He writes nothing on his pad and doesn't even open the bathroom doors.

Carter follows us out to the taproom, and I'm exchanging nervous glances with everyone while the guy finally scribbles something on his clipboard. He tears off the top sheet and hands it to me, his expression more bored than anything as he turns and walks wordlessly out the door.

I look down at the sheet, zeroing in on the word PASSED and exhaling. "Thank god."

Kelsie wolf whistles, Oscar collapses against the cooler, and Miller vaults the bar to give Kelsie a high five while I smile back at them.

"Was that weird for anyone else?" I ask, glancing over at Carter. "I mean, he didn't check half the stuff we did, not that I'm complaining."

But Carter is busy watching the guy until he gets in his car, maybe thinking this whole visit was too good to be true. Then, for some reason, my brother strides through the front door and stands on the sidewalk, hands on his hips, watching the guy drive away.

I shake my head at his antics. I'm taking this as a win and not questioning it.

When Cart comes back in, he's wearing an intense frown, his eyebrows pulled together like they've been super-glued to each other.

"What did he say when he came the first time?"

I eye him, wondering if he's fucking with me. "Hey, man, it's over."

He only stares, so I answer his question. "You know how they operate. He gave himself free run of the place and flashed his badge when I walked up. You were there for most of the rest."

Carter gives a quick shake of his head. "But why did he come when we'd just had our inspection the month before?"

"Oh, I see what you mean." I recount what happened. "When I went to the DOH, they checked the record and said he got an anonymous tip. Which is weird, now that I think about it, because he's a regional supervisor or something. He doesn't work in Buncombe County." What is he trying to get at?

That frown isn't budging. "And you don't have any idea who might have called?" He glances around at all of us. "We didn't piss someone off earlier that week or something?"

"Why are you looking at me?" Miller throws his hands up.

I answer for all of us. "No. Like I said, I assumed it was Hollis at the time."

He takes the paper from my hand, looking for something. "You remember what day that was?"

Now I'm frowning almost as intensely. "Sure. It was the tenth. One week before St. Pat's. What the hell is going on, Cart?"

He reads the new report, his eyebrows slowly releasing while I wait until he finally looks up at us. He shakes his head and musters a smile, but it's fake as hell. "Nothing. Just my imagination getting away from me." He claps me on the shoulder and says, "Great job, everybody. Thanks!"

Kelsie rounds the bar and starts pouring beers, and Miller follows to help himself to one. Oscar turns on some music and starts doing the robot. It's not good.

Cart nods and I watch him until he disappears down the hall.

So much for not keeping secrets from your partner.

HOLLIS

IT TAKES two days to get over my mad and settle only into sad, no matter how I tried holding onto it. I miss him. I miss us.

Today is the day the inspector comes back, and I've been a nervous wreck all morning, not that I have any real stake in the results anymore. I nearly cut myself again as I was grooming a Bichon and startled when my front bell rang. It turned out to be the mail carrier.

I may need to call Blue Bigfoot later and ask Oscar how it went just so I can sleep tonight. But the normal everyday noises are bleeding through our shared wall, so either the inspector hasn't come yet or they passed. I'm clearly hoping for the latter.

Just to torture myself, I keep scrolling to the picture I took of Cash on St. Patrick's Day when he wasn't looking. He's smiling at a customer, and even in the quick snapshot I can see the bright blue of his eyes and the warmth of his smile.

He was never the unfeeling caveman I originally thought, and I hate him distilling his personality down to egomaniacal asshole. Because he's not. He's generous and funny and always, *always*, putting other people first—even when they don't need him to.

He put me first.

The way he wanted to take care of me, his guilt over those stupid bruises, paying me compliments, giving me the bigger dessert, letting me pick the show we watched, wanting to drive me and pay for dates. He was telling me with every action and every word that I meant something to him. That he was making room for me in his universe of people he's devoted to.

And maybe, just maybe, if I had told him how I really felt about him, it would have made all the difference.

I think even Marco and Polo miss him. Polo stood by the apartment door last night after I got home and didn't budge for another half hour. I told him it was just me from here on out, which he responded to with a burp.

Betty is now to the point where she'll let Marco and Polo snuggle against her to nap without hiding under my bed, and she destroyed a plush caterpillar toy, which I consider progress. We don't know anything about her past, but I'm determined to make sure her future is whatever she dreams of.

I sweep the floor and tie up my trash bags to take out back before unpacking some boxes that arrived earlier. It's impossible not to set aside an adorable pink sweater for Betty and matching blue plaid ones for the boys. I entirely ignore the fact that they bear some tiny resemblance to the flannel shirt that brings out the blue in Cash's eyes.

When I'm done, I carry the trash bags out back to the

dumpster, but I stop short when the familiar gray hunk of steel is nowhere to be seen.

In its place is the most adorable—as much as a dumpster can be adorable—pink dumpster with a lively assortment of happy, goofy dogs painted all over it. The bags fall from my hands, and I stare at it for a good minute before bursting out laughing at the mental image of Cash not only arranging this, but using it for his manly man brewery.

The heaviness in my chest that I've been carrying around this week begins to lighten. I run back inside to grab my phone before returning to snap a picture—oh, and throw away my trash. Then I quickly type up a text message and attach a picture before pressing send.

It's time to let Cash Brooks know what I really think about him.

CASH

CART SNUCK BACK into Blue Bigfoot yesterday afternoon without bothering to explain his odd behavior earlier in the day. But we were slammed for a Thursday, so I couldn't pin him down before he disappeared again for the night. In fact, ever since half the Asheville Arrows team stopped by last week, business has been on a steady incline. A couple of the players even popped in again on Tuesday for a pint. We've also had people asking when our next pub dog night will be.

The fact that my mama and Hollis's interference saved my ass is not lost on me. Those two didn't even bother waiting for my permission, much less for me to ask. They just jumped in and did what had to be done. The same with the crew around here as soon as they found out about my fuck-up. It made me sit down and take a better look at myself and admit that Hollis had a point when she suggested I *like* being the one to charge into the burning building—even when there are plenty of other people who'd be happy to lend a hand.

Everybody pitched in to fix my mess, and it all turned out fine in the end. In fact, we had so much help that I was able to work on a special side project with Luca's help.

Some people might argue a dumpster ain't romantic or sexy in the least, but I wasn't going for that this time. I was trying to think of a way to let Hollis know I see her without putting her on the spot or expecting a response. And that stupid dumpster fit the bill. It was our first fight, so I thought it only appropriate to give it to her. She deserves it. And a whole lot more. And just knowing it will make her smile is good enough for me.

"I sold another three gift cards already, man," Oscar tells me as we pass each other in the hall. Looks like it's time to place another order.

I head behind the bar and serve up a few pints. The patio is almost hot today, so it's filling up with people desperate for sunshine. My current plan is to keep myself as busy as possible for the foreseeable future until I don't feel it in my chest when I see Hollis's car or catch a glimpse of her through her shop window. In other words, I'm gonna be busy as hell.

The phone rings and I snatch it up while I wait on a guy to swipe his card on the POS tablet. "Blue Bigfoot Beer."

"Is this Cash?" a voice on the other end asks.

"Speaking." I print out the customer's receipt and hand it over. He steps to the side and rubs Larry's head a couple times before heading for the door. I grin into the phone.

The woman on the line says, "This is Laura Seeburg from the Asheville Post. I was hoping to get a quote from you about your nomination if you have a minute."

"Nice try, Rosie or Lynn or whoever this is. Get a hobby." I hang up the phone and check how full the dishwasher is. I didn't want to admit it at first, but this thing is so much faster than our old one, and it fits more trays too.

Kelsie rounds the bar and pulls a half dozen glasses, and I help her fill an order from the patio. The *Squatch Blossom* starts spitting, so I head back to switch out the keg.

"Yo, Cash!" Miller yells. "Line one for you."

Dammit. I abandon the keg and swing back up to the bar to grab the phone, but Miller's on line two already, so I head for the office phone. "Cash Brooks."

"Hello? I think we were cut off before." It's the same lady. "Or you thought I was someone else?"

Shit. "Oh, hey, sorry about that. I thought somebody was… never mind." I have a fleeting thought that maybe it's Hollis who's behind this, but I let that go immediately. "How can I help you?"

"That's quite all right. As I was saying, I'm calling from the Asheville Post and I'd like to get a quote from you about your nomination."

"What nomination?"

"Well, oh. The one for Asheville's most eligible bachelor."

"I'm sorry, what?" I glance to the office door looking for Miller or Kelsie or someone to be standing there laughing their ass off, but all I hear are the usual noises filtering down the hall from the taproom.

She repeats herself, which tells me nothing.

"Sorry. Is there a link you can send me or something?"

"I apologize. I thought you knew about it. That's strange." I hear papers rustling in the background and then she asks for my email address. I swear, if one of these asshats is trying to set me up with a woman, I might need to fire them.

I tell the woman I'll get back to her and hang up before clicking my inbox on the laptop. A new message pops up and when I click the enclosed link, it takes me to a short news article that confuses the hell out of me. There's a photo of me behind the bar that I don't recognize and a headline reading,

"Local Brewery Owner Nominated for Asheville's Most Eligible Bachelor"

What the hell is this?

When I see the byline, *Rylee McAvoy*, I get a strange burning in my gut and start reading.

Local brewery owner Cash Brooks of Blue Bigfoot Beer is the first, and only, contestant to be nominated for Asheville's Most Eligible Bachelor 2023. Yes, you read that correctly; there are no other contestants. Nor is there an official contest. That, however, did nothing to stop his neighbor Hollis Hayes of Happy Tails Salon from nominating him.

When asked what makes Mr. Brooks such a catch, Hayes replied, "Cash is a terrific person all around. He works harder than anyone I know. He's generous, thoughtful, kind, hilarious. He's a great listener and would do just about anything for the people he cares about. And he's obviously dead sexy, as you can see from his picture."

While Mr. Brooks does sound like a good bet from her description, we asked Ms. Hayes why she doesn't scoop the man up herself instead of recommending him to all the good people of Asheville. "He needs someone who trusts him in all the ways that matter in a relationship, so he can give that same trust in return. I'm afraid I haven't been very good at that to this point. But I know I can. If he'll let me."

It sounds like this story just got more interesting. If you'd

like to see what happens with this eligible bachelor and his lovely
neighbor, head down to Blue Bigfoot Beer today at 4:30 pm. It's
located in the warehouse shops in the River Arts District.

I squint at my screen and read it again, sure I'm
missing something. But, no, it's just as strange the second
time around.

When I pick up my phone, I see that it's 4:29 and I
freeze in my chair.

Just then, Miller's voice calls out, "Yo, Cash, we need
you at the bar!"

My heartbeat picks up speed as a bead of sweat drips
down my spine. What the hell is wrong with me? And
what the hell is going on? Is Hollis here? Is this a joke?

But there's only one way to find out, so I haul ass out to
the taproom and almost skid to a stop just inside.
Everyone in the place—customers, staff, and a bunch of
people falling under neither category—stand crowded
along the walls, leaving a wide empty space in front of
my bar.

And on top of my bar is Hollis. She's standing on the
wood bar top in sneakers, a pink dress, and those sexy
glasses, her cheeks almost as pink as her dress, and a smile
directed right at me. She's so beautiful, she almost takes
my breath away, and if that makes me a giant sap, then
that's what I am.

I take a step closer, shoving my hands in my pockets
and feeling everyone's eyes on me. "Hey. What…" I start.

But before I can get another word out, Hollis turns so
her back faces the room and she starts tipping backward
like a tree falling to the forest floor, her body stiff as a
board. I don't even think, I just run, tearing my hands
from my pockets as I race to break her fall. I make it just in
time to catch her in my arms, my heart racing like I ran up

a hundred flights of stairs and my nerves a shattered mess.

"Are you crazy!?" I pant.

But she just smiles up at me, calm as can be, not a drop of sweat or a racing pulse in sight. Everybody in the place starts cheering. But the only voice I want to hear is hers.

"I knew you'd catch me." Her smile turns softer. "I know you'll always catch me."

As her words sink into my thick skull, I lean down and do what I've been wanting to do for days. I kiss Hollis Hayes's sweet lips. The cheering gets louder, but I don't care about anything apart from her lips on mine and her soft body in my arms.

When we come up for breath, Oscar's standing there looking worse for wear than I likely do. "Woman, you could warn a guy, you know." He swipes his damp brow with a bar towel. "I was about to slide in and break your fall with my belly!" He looks at both of us and shakes his head. "You two are messed up." He continues muttering to himself as he walks away. Hollis laughs.

"You think he's right?" she asks as I set her on her feet.

I hook my arms around her waist and pull her in. "I'd say yeah. Luckily, we're both the same kind of messed up, so that makes us perfect for each other."

She grins, drawing me in with those soft lips and sparkling brown eyes. "Then I guess it's time to officially call a truce. What do you say, neighbor?"

My only answer is to lean in and kiss her one more time.

EPILOGUE

HOLLIS

"WE TALKED ABOUT THIS. STRIP."

Cash drops his chin to hide his laugh.

"Tit for tat." I point from my naked boob to his mostly clothed form. I'm truly perplexed at how he manages to do this every time we get even remotely intimate. One minute, I'm standing there minding my own business and then he starts doing the sexy slow walk my way. Before I know it, I'm not wearing a stitch of clothing and he's still got four layers on. It's like a magic trick using his hypnotic eyes and clever hands.

But not this time. I may be shirtless and braless, but this thing is going no further until he gets naked.

"Which part of me is tat in this scenario?" he asks through his smartass smile.

I point to the noticeable bulge in his pants.

"I thought that was the full monty?"

"You'll be getting *no* monty at this rate." I pretend to

reach for my T-shirt, and that has him finally moving his ass.

"Okay, okay. So impatient." Cash shrugs off his shirt with a beleaguered sigh and then does that unconsciously sexy man move of reaching behind his head to grab his T-shirt with one hand and pull it off. Where do they learn to do that? Panty-Dropper Academy for Hunks? I'll bet he was a 4.0 student.

He makes quick work of his jeans and boxers, leaving him perfectly bare for my eyes to feast. Damn, he's pretty. I might never get used to this view.

I don't get much time, though, because he's got me pinned to the bed in the next nanosecond.

"Much better." My hands reach around to skim over the muscles of his back while he nibbles on my neck, making me shiver.

When I try moving for a feel of his butt, he shifts his mouth down to my breasts, pulling out of reach. Oh well, we've got plenty of time.

I'll admit I was a little reluctant when he started removing my clothes in his childhood bedroom, but Ginny is next door, so there's nobody to interrupt us. Adrina's brother and his wife from Greensboro are visiting, so she's having a cookout. Cash and I volunteered to grab some cans of Blue Bigfoot beer from Ginny's fridge and bring them over.

We got a little sidetracked.

My legs wrap around his middle as he circles one nipple with his tongue and pinches the other between a thumb and finger. My hips come right off the bed, apparently making him rethink things because he shifts back up so I can feel every inch of his hardness against my sex through the thin material of my leggings. He thrusts forward, making us both groan at the sensation while our lips find each other's and I get the sensual slide of his tongue against mine. Everything south of my neck clenches at the riot of sensations.

When Cash rolls his hips again, I can't help myself. I reach between us to take his rock-hard length in my hand, and he thrusts into it, groaning into my mouth again. The feel of the velvety skin covering the hard steel of his erection has me slowly stroking him and letting my thumb slide across the head.

"Peach, if you keep doin' that, this'll be over before we start." He grins against my lips. And since I've got zero complaints about what he's doing to my body, I release him and slide my hands around to his back instead. God, he's so warm and solid.

Without warning, Cash rolls us over, so I'm on top and straddling him. "Sit up a sec. I want to see you."

When I do, his eyes roam over my face, neck, and breasts, and just that look has my womb contracting. "Damn, you're gorgeous," he says, making my chest and cheeks start to heat. How is it that this man can take complete control over my body?

"Right back atcha," I say with a naughty smile as I let my eyes travel over his muscular chest and shoulders.

He plays with my breasts and nipples for another minute while I close my eyes and grind into him. It's time to get the rest of my clothes off. I don't know how long I can stand this without having him inside me, thick and hot. The way he fills me and strokes all my nerve endings to life is unlike anything I've experienced before. It's a kind of torturous pleasure that I'm now addicted to.

Cash is clearly of the same mind because he slides a hand into the front of my leggings, stroking a finger through my folds and finding my clit with his thumb. "I love how wet you get for me."

I shamelessly grind into his hand as he watches me, his eyes burning with need and intention. But just as I move to the side to strip off my leggings and underwear, a loud succession of knocks hits the bedroom door.

I panic and lose my balance, kicking my legs for purchase before my head hits the wall. Cash falls to the floor with a loud *thump* and I realize I just kicked him off the bed. Oops. We both scramble for our clothes, Cash pulling his jeans up while I fasten my bra and pull my shirt over my head.

"Yo!" comes a voice from the hall, followed by more pounding.

When Cash swings open the door, Miller stands there poised to bang on it again.

"What took you so long, man?"

Cash's response is immediate. "We were baking cookies."

I beam at him, and Miller finally notices me, a knowing grin forming. "Oh, hey, Hollis, I didn't know you were here."

"What's up?" Cash goes for casual, but we're both solidly busted, so I don't know why he bothers.

"Put a pin in your 'baking' plans. Adrina's asking for beer."

Since the mood is kind of ruined and Miller doesn't appear to be in any hurry to leave us be, we finish straightening ourselves and head next door again, a couple six packs in hand.

The Carmichael house is… interesting. I get brief

glimpses as we pass through it to the back porch, but every room is cluttered, although clean, and there's an alarming amount of both taxidermy and florals. If pressed to describe the style, I'd have to say cozy hunting lodge meets Midcentury American Grandma. But the whole family is welcoming and warm, so I'm choosing not to be unnerved by the tableau in the window of two dead squirrels dressed as Sherlock Holmes and Watson.

"Cash, what's this I heard about a contest for the hottest young man in town?" Adrina asks as she carries a bowl of greens from the kitchen, with her sister-in-law, Marisol, following behind.

All eyes flash to Cash, where he sits next to me on a wooden bench. My grin is enormous and a little evil. Let's just say some of the local single ladies took the thing a little too seriously.

"It's nothing, I promise," Cash says, shooting threatening looks at Denny, Luca, and Miller. It does no good.

"This one girl came into Blue Bigfoot in an actual wedding dress," Miller shares. "Cash had to hide in the office until we got her to leave."

"I had work to do," Cash responds with a frown before taking a long drink of his beer. I give him a consolation hug and a kiss on the cheek.

Ginny watches us from across the patio, smiling like the cat that caught the canary. She may pretend to be flighty, but that woman can work a scheme like nobody's business. Lucky for me, she likes me. And it goes without saying it's impossible not to adore that woman right back.

When Adrina looks around for more explanation, Rosie fills her in. "It was super sweet, Mamma. Hollis got her reporter friend to write a story about all the things she loves about Cash. The contest bit was just part of the story; it wasn't real."

Adrina turns to me with a dreamy smile. "Oh, that is so sweet, *cara*. You two are good together. You'll make beautiful babies."

Cash and I both choke on our drinks at that, and Rosie saves us by distracting her mom with a question about the side dishes.

It's only been a week since my epic trust fall, but things are so good between Cash and me that it feels like we've been together for ages. We haven't spent a night apart since, and while we're both a little sleep deprived, it's one hundred percent worth it.

Marco and Polo are over the moon that Cash is back in our lives, as am I, of course. Betty surprised the heck out of me by latching onto Cash from the first minute she met him. Her tail starts wagging whenever she hears his voice, and the lovefest has become so mutual that she won't be my foster much longer. Cash wants to adopt her and make her an official Brooks. It's so damn sweet, it makes me tear up sometimes.

Harry and my mom have been as good as their word and are making a real effort to embrace me and my choices. Mom has sent two more of her dog-owning friends my way, and Harry even complimented me on my choice of property for the shop. He's also made himself familiar with the booming dog industry, and who knows, maybe he'll dip his toe in himself one day. We've all been talking more often too, so with any luck, the freeze will be completely thawed soon.

Hadley and I had a long talk when I stopped to visit the other evening, and she's the same confident, impulsive girl I know. She's looking at colleges and is leaning toward somewhere out of state, but not for reasons Harry might have hoped. She said Mom and Harry are starting to crack down on her "super hard" and she wants to escape their reach by moving away. I think it's a great idea. Either she'll thrive on her own, or the big bad world will kick her ass—it's a valuable experience whichever way it goes. And we'll be here for her no matter what if she needs us.

"Does anybody know if Carter's coming?" Ginny asks as she takes a plate of burgers over to Wes and Adrina's brother, Stefano, at the grill. "I left him a message, but I haven't heard back."

I look at Cash to see him shaking his head. He told me all about Carter coming back to town and acting differently, and I know it's weighing on him that his brother is being closed-lipped. But if I've learned anything about the Brooks family, they lead with love, so it's only a matter of time before things fix themselves—either that or Cash will assign himself captain of the campaign to get Carter sharing his troubles.

"He told me to get a ride tomorrow to work 'cuz he won't be around," Miller volunteers.

Before Cash can go down whatever spiral might be starting in his head, I lean over and whisper in his ear, "Do you think later tonight you can do that thing that makes me almost pass out?"

It does the trick and has him squeezing my thigh and thinking about us being alone. And since being alone with him is my favorite place to be these days, I'm looking forward to it just as much.

"This playlist is painful," Luca says, prompting Adrina to start lecturing him about the merits of golden oldies.

"I vote for country," Ginny suggests, but Luca switches

to a 90s station and everybody gets sidetracked snacking on the brownies Rosie brings out from the kitchen.

When "Smells Like Teen Spirit" by Nirvana comes on, Cash and I both narrow our eyes at each other and start singing along. That man might be the worst singer I've ever met, and he doesn't even know the lyrics. I raise my voice to drown him out, and he does the same. It takes a minute for us to realize everybody is staring at us.

"What the hell are you guys singing?" Denny asks from his chair next to our bench.

"Nirvana," Cash answers, the added *duh* silent. "Well, I am. I don't know what she's singing."

I give him the side eye. "Cash doesn't know the lyrics."

"You're both idiots." Denny types into his phone for a couple seconds and hands it over to us. The lyrics to "Smells Like Teen Spirit" are on the screen.

Cash and I lean in to examine the text. "Oooh," we say simultaneously.

"Yeah, these lyrics make a lot more sense." Cash hands the phone back, and the radio switches to a Goo Goo Dolls song.

"I can't believe you thought Kurt Cobain was singing about a wild boar and some girl named Anastasia." I scoff at him playfully.

"Me? You're the one who sang about cheese and insurance," he counters, turning to face me.

"That makes a lot more sense than a giant pig—or a laptop!"

We continue arguing, and everyone eventually ignores us when Stefano announces the burgers are ready.

Being together hasn't altered our personalities, so Cash and I still like to argue with each other. Especially because it often leads to mind-blowingly hot sex. But the one thing that has changed about how we fight is that now we both know that at the end of the day, we're on the same side. We're each other's biggest fans, and what could be better than that?

~THE END~

NEXT IS CARTER'S STORY, *Smooth Hoperator*. What is he up to with all this sneaking around? And who is he doing it with? You'll find the answers in *Smooth Hoperator*!

EXCITING UPDATES, **freebies, new releases, swag, and more when you sign up for Sylvie's newsletter: http://bit.ly/sylvie-nl**

WE HOPE you enjoyed *Ale's Fair in Love and War*. The best way to support an indie author is to leave a review and tell your friends! Thanks so much!

HAVE you read **Denny and Rosie**'s story? Get a *FREE* ebook of *Full-On Clinger* at sylviestewartauthor.com

You can also find **Rylee and Dean**'s story in *Booby Trapped*, as well as **Lizzie and Gunner**'s story in *Nuts About You*.

· · ·

IF YOU'RE interested in signed paperbacks or merch (stickers, pins, bookmarks, pens, bags…) hop over to Sylvie's website: sylviestewartauthor.com

WANT TO HANG OUT? Join Sylvie's Facebook Group, **Sylvie's Spot for the Sexy, Sassy, and Smartassy!**

FULL-ON CLINGER

PREQUEL TO THE LOVE ON TAP SERIES

Back in high school, the only thing I was more desperate to ditch than my virginity was my clinging crusher, Rosina Carmichael.

That was then. This is now.
Rosie is back, and those long legs and sassy mouth have me cursing myself for wasting so much time. I want a do-over, and I've got two days on a rafting trip to convince her I'm worth a shot.
Rosie can snarl at me and push me away all she wants, but I'm not letting her out of my sight—or my arms.

Who's the clinger now?

Read Denny and Rosie's story in *Full-On Clinger (FREE ebook for a limited time at sylviestewartauthor.com)*

THE FIX

CAROLINA CONNECTIONS,
BOOK 1

"Hilarious, super sexy, and swoon-worthy..." - 5-star review

Single mom Laney's house needs some attention—just like her love life. But falling for the hot handyman is one thing that's NOT on her fix-it list.

When I asked for the fairytale, I forgot to specify which part. Now I'm stuck in the early chapters with no happily-ever-after in sight and a to-do list longer than Cinderella's. When my freeloading brother finally gets off my couch and gets a job, things are looking up--until his hot new boss decides my house is a death trap and designates himself as my own personal handyman.

Nate Murphy may be good at fixing things, but he has heartbreak written all over him. And as a single mom, my heart isn't the only one on the line. But keeping my distance is getting harder the more he invites himself over and flashes those damn dimples my way. Is it time to take a chance and let Nate in? Or should I close the book on this chapter and get on with my life?

Where's my fairy godmother when I need her the most?

Get *The Fix* and start the hilariously addictive Carolina Connections series now!

If you like hot chemistry, hilarious banter, over-the-top friends, funny kids, and family you love but don't always like, then The Fix *is your next weekend read! It's part of a series but can be read as a standalone. No cheating.*

FREE ebook for a limited time at sylviestewartauthor.com!
Also available in audiobook

EXCERPT FROM THE NERD NEXT DOOR

CAROLINA KISSES, BOOK 1

New town, new job, new neighbor… new crush.

I've got a serious problem and it goes by the name of Ted Jones. Even his name is nerdy! Combine that with his glasses, lean runner's frame, crazy smarts, and superhero addiction and he's got my lady engine revving hard.

What can I say? I've got a thing for hot nerds.

But our shy glances and awkward exchanges in the elevator aren't going to cut it. This nerd is mine; he just doesn't know it yet.

Grab your copy now and start the sexy, laugh-out-loud Carolina Kisses Series today!

CHAPTER ONE

HALEY

… Pulling up to our building in a dark blue late-model Mazda is the object of my… fascination? Obsession? Slightly stalkerish tendencies? The car settles in a spot by the curb, the driver's side door opening shortly after. And out steps Ted Jones.

My Ted Jones.

Well, he would be if I had my way about it.

Tilting my head to the side, I admire him for a moment or two while Tank sniffs a dandelion. Now, here's a man who knows how to rock an elbow patch. *Oooh, yeah*. I don't know what it is about Ted Jones' particular brand of nerdiness, but it is friggin' hot. I've done a little, let's call it… investigating and discovered he teaches in the liberal arts school at NCUW, so I know he's whip smart. He also wears the sexiest black-framed glasses over brilliant blue eyes, has little to no affection for his razor, and exercises a habit of smoothing his hair down to fight a stubborn cowlick. It never obeys, much to my delight, making him sport a constant just-rolled-out-of-bed look.

In contrast to that, he is always dressed neatly, often in a traditional tweed jacket with elbow patches which he pairs with jeans that do amazing things for his ass. Something about that combination of tweed, leather, and denim sets off an odd Pavlovian response in my uterus. I can't explain it. To top that all off, he's a runner, and I've seen the muscles of his thighs and calves bunching as he powers through his evening runs, leaving him coated in sweat and me with plenty to think about when my head hits the pillow.

It's safe to say I'm gone over Ted Jones.

The only problem is we've never actually had a single conversation.

To be fair, we *have* spoken to one another—on several occasions, in fact. But you couldn't exactly call these interactions conversations. As I recall, my first word to him was, "Hi." To which I got zero reply.

It was the afternoon I moved into my apartment, the unseasonably cool temperatures making my fingers ache from cold. I'd just returned a borrowed cart to maintenance and was trying to remember which walkway would take me to my building when I got my first glimpse of my future boyfriend (positive thinking is always recommended). Although, to be honest, it was the teenage girl speaking to him who first caught my attention and caused me to do a double take.

The two stood on the sidewalk while the brisk early-spring temperatures caused us all to tighten our coats around us. When I first saw the girl, I could have sworn a bag of cotton candy rested on her head—the classic dual pack with sugary clouds of half pink and half blue. But, no, it was just her hair, so my attention quickly shifted to take in the man beside her.

He wore a dark wool coat, and I could see the puffs of his breath on the air as he laughed at something the girl showed him. It was a magazine of some sort, called *The Weatherman*, although I'd never heard of it. Both the girl and man were seemingly enthralled, and neither one noticed me as my insides turned to mush. His laughter skipped toward me on the breeze and made my stomach flip—and this was before I'd ever even seen him in his tweed, denim, and leather trifecta of hotness.

The two spoke animatedly, the girl gesturing with wide sweeps of her arms as her cotton-candy hair swished around her ears. He flipped some pages until he found what he was looking for and they both buried their noses —and every other sense, it seemed—into the magazine. I felt oddly left out, even though I'd never laid eyes on either of these people before in my life. After a few moments, I stole one last look and retreated down the cement walkway to what I was almost certain was my building.

So it was no surprise that I all but gasped when I found myself on the elevator of my apartment building not two hours later with the very same man—sans teenage girl this time. I mean, what were the chances of him living in the same building as me in such a huge complex? It was clearly a sign, as was the uptick in my heart rate as I got my first close-up view of him. I drew in a breath and uttered my very first word.

"Hi." Yes, I am available to teach flirting lessons should anyone need my brilliant advice.

He didn't even glance my way. Here I was in an enclosed space with this delicious guy who immediately pushed all my buttons—making *me* want to push the emergency button on the elevator and make out with him in a really dirty way—and he wouldn't even acknowledge me.

I've never been great with guys, but I do okay. Certainly well enough to spark up a casual conversation in an elevator. When he left me hanging, I felt a sharp pang that this guy who was friendly to *Weatherman* girls and was my type in every way was actually kind of a rude jerk. That was, until I noticed he was wearing a pair of those wireless earbuds. This discovery brought some relief, but I still stood awkwardly until we reached the third floor where I got off.

Refusing to concede defeat, I waited until the elevator was about to close behind me and turned to give him my best smile and a friendly wave. Unfortunately, I missed the small fact that he had stepped out after me. Which meant when I whipped myself around, my forehead made audible contact with his very defined cheekbone, causing us both to stagger back.

"I'm so sorry!" I put one hand to my head and one out toward him, as if my hand held a magical power that dulled the pain from blunt-force trauma.

He held his cheek and blinked a few times, his jaw working as if to test the level of injury. Then he pulled out an earbud and shook his head, his gaze dropping to the floor.

His voice was a deep, quiet rumble when he spoke. "No problem."

Then he snatched a set of keys from his pocket like he thought I might attack again and made quick work of the lock to apartment 3-C. The apartment right next to my 3-B. Ack!

"Happens all the time," he mumbled before disappearing behind his door. I continued to stand in the hallway, unsure of what had just happened and wondering if I should run to the store for some frozen peas or something. But I got the distinct feeling that would just make things more awkward.

Little did I know, awkward would be our go-to vibe for all subsequent encounters.

Like the time my grocery bag split, sending a bottle of wine, a huge roll of chocolate-chip cookie dough, and a box of panty liners tumbling out at his feet. Instead of just picking them up like a normal person, I, for some unknown reason, felt compelled to share that I was

PMSing. I believe my exact words were, "Gotta love that time of the month."

You know, because those are the exact words that will make your crush confess his undying love for you. *Oh, Haley, there's nothing I find sexier than the mental image of you stuffing your panties with cotton personal products before binge drinking and shoving raw cookie dough in your face. Come to daddy!*

Yeah. That's pretty much how things have gone since.

But not today! Today, I'm going to have a real live conversation with Ted Jones if it kills me—which is a distinct possibility at this point.

I straighten my back and then glance down at my clothes. The old t-shirt and capri leggings can't be helped. I take a quick sniff in the general direction of my armpits and resolve to just keep my arms glued to my sides during the course of our scintillating discussion. Hell, he's a runner. Maybe he's into girls who work up a sweat.

I stride forward, pulling Tank along as I watch Ted stop at the communal mailboxes on a grassy patch of lawn. He stands with his back to me, his legs shoulder width apart and covered in the familiar denim.

I can do this. I'll be confident and charming and not even a little bit weird—I'm sure of it. That is, until I actually reach the mailboxes and catch Ted's scent. Lordy, he smells like pencil shavings and leather. I want to bite my fist and then lick his neck. Instead, I pretend to search for my mailbox key which I know to be sitting in a dish on my entry table at this very moment.

Ted doesn't turn his head or acknowledge me in any way, instead closing his mailbox and removing his key before sifting through the stack of white envelopes and coupon fliers.

It's now or never. I take a deep breath and turn to him, one hand on my hip and the other gripping the leash as Tank circles our feet. "Beautiful evening, huh?"

Dammit! *The weather? Seriously?* I'm a walking cliché, but it's too late, so I widen my smile. Ted turns to me and, upon taking in my overly enthusiastic smile, takes a step back.

Right into the pile of shit my dog just dropped behind him.

Find out what happens next in *The Nerd Next Door*
Also available in audiobook

ALSO BY SYLVIE STEWART

Smooth Hoperator (*Love on Tap,* Book 2 - Coming Summer 2023)

The Fix (*Carolina Connections,* Book 1)
The Spark (*Carolina Connections,* Book 2)
The Lucky One (*Carolina Connections,* Book 3)
The Game (*Carolina Connections,* Book 4)
The Way You Are (*Carolina Connections,* Book 5)
The Runaround (*Carolina Connections,* Book 6)

The Nerd Next Door (*Carolina Kisses,* Book 1)
New Jerk in Town (*Carolina Kisses,* Book 2)
The Last Good Liar (*Carolina Kisses,* Book 3)

Between a Rock and a Royal (*Kings of Carolina,* #1)
Blue Bloods and Backroads (*Kings of Carolina,* #2)
Stealing Kisses With a King (*Kings of Carolina,* #3)

ACKNOWLEDGMENTS

This book and series have been a LONG time coming, and I'm so thrilled to finally bring them to life.

These past few years have been rough, and I can't thank my family, friends, and book world buddies enough for sticking with me, sharing their compassion and patience, and helping me power through. This series would still be living only in my head without all of you.

Big thank yous also to my kick-ass editor, Ellie, from My Brother's Editor; Krista and Tina from Mountains Wanted for saving me with the last-minute proofread; my lovely assistant, Annette, for keeping me from panicking; and all you fabulous readers!

I'd also like to thank the hard-working bloggers, reviewers, PR folks, and social media bad-asses who love and support all of us indie authors! We see you, and we appreciate you!

More thanks to Carrie (and Ryan) at Full Pint Beer in Warrendale, PA for answering questions and offering inspiration for Blue Bigfoot Beer and the sausage fest. The elk sausage really is to die for, and it's available every day!

I also need to thank one special reader, Brandy Devier, for making the ugliest book cover cookie imaginable and, therefore, earning the privilege of naming the characters Hollis, Hadley, and Harrison Hayes. Excellent job, my friend. You are silly and wonderful, and I adore you.

ABOUT THE AUTHOR

USA Today bestselling author Sylvie Stewart loves dad jokes, hot HEAs, country music, and baby skunks—preferably all at the same time. Most of her steamy contemporary romances and romantic comedies take place in North Carolina, a.k.a. the best state ever, and she's a sucker for hugs from her kids and a good laugh with her hot-nerd hubby. She also cusses like a sailor and can't bring herself to feel bad about it. If you love smart Southern gals, hot blue-collar guys, and snort-laughing with characters who feel like your best friends, Sylvie's your gal.

- facebook.com/SylvieStewartAuthor
- twitter.com/sylvie_stewart_
- instagram.com/sylvie.stewart.romance
- bookbub.com/authors/sylvie-stewart
- tiktok.com/@authorsylviestewart
- pinterest.com/sylviestewartauthor

Made in United States
North Haven, CT
31 March 2023